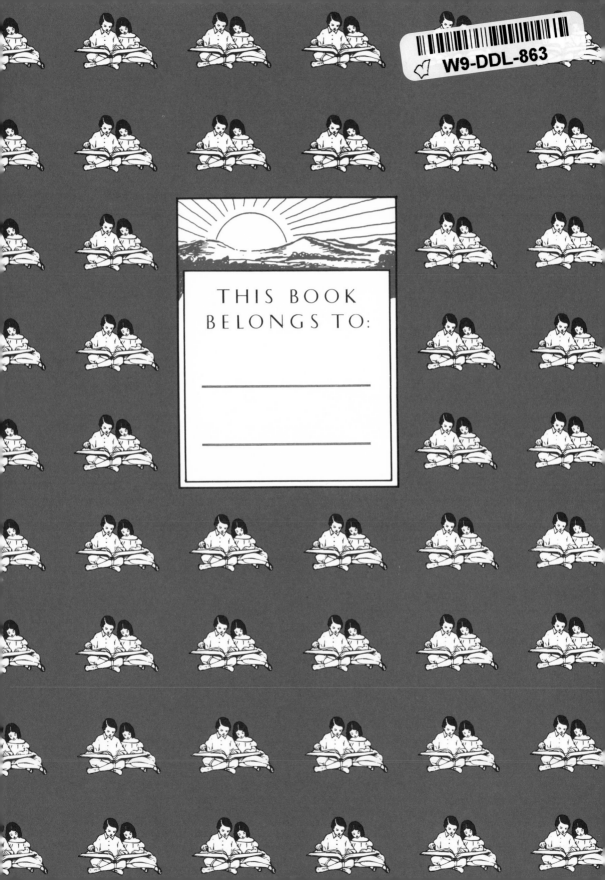

W9-DDL-863

THIS BOOK
BELONGS TO:

_____

_____

GREAT
DOG STORIES

CHILDREN'S CLASSICS

This unique series of Children's Classics™ features accessible and highly readable texts paired with the work of talented and brilliant illustrators of bygone days to create fine editions for today's parents and children to rediscover and treasure. Besides being a handsome addition to any home library, this series features genuine bonded-leather spines stamped in gold, full-color illustrations, and high-quality acid-free paper that will enable these books to be passed from one generation to the next.

Adventures of Huckleberry Finn
The Adventures of Tom Sawyer
Aesop's Fables
Alice's Adventures in Wonderland
Andersen's Fairy Tales
Anne of Avonlea
Anne of Green Gables
At the Back of the North Wind
Black Beauty
The Call of the Wild
A Child's Book of Country Stories
A Child's Book of Stories
A Child's Book of Stories from
   Many Lands
A Child's Christmas
A Christmas Carol and Other
   Christmas Stories
Cinderella and Other Classic
   Italian Fairy Tales
The Complete Mother Goose
Great Dog Stories
Grimm's Fairy Tales
Hans Brinker *or* The Silver Skates
Heidi

The Hound of the Baskervilles
The Jungle Book
Just So Stories
Kidnapped
King Arthur and His Knights
A Little Child's Book of Stories
Little Men
The Little Princess
Little Women
Peter Pan
Rebecca of Sunnybrook Farm
Robin Hood
Robinson Crusoe
The Secret Garden
The Sleeping Beauty and Other
   Classic French Fairy Tales
The Swiss Family Robinson
Tales from Shakespeare
Through the Looking Glass and
   What Alice Found There
Treasure Island
A Very Little Child's Book of
   Stories
The Wind in the Willows

GREAT DOG STORIES

by
ALBERT PAYSON TERHUNE

Illustrated by
Marguerite Kirmse

CHILDREN'S CLASSICS
New York • Avenel

Foreword and preface copyright © 1993 Outlet Book Company, Inc.
The Heart of a Dog copyright © 1924, copyright renewed 1951 by Alice
Terhune. *My Friend the Dog* copyright © 1926,
copyright © renewed 1954 by Alice Terhune.

This 1993 edition is published by Children's Classics, a division of
dilithium Press, Ltd., distributed by Outlet Book Company, Inc.,
a Random House Company,
40 Engelhard Avenue, Avenel, New Jersey 07001,
by arrangement with Albert Payson Terhune, Inc.

DILITHIUM is a registered trademark and
CHILDREN'S CLASSICS is a trademark of dilithium Press, Ltd.

Random House
New York • Toronto • London • Sydney • Auckland

Printed and bound in the United States of America

Library of Congress Cataloging-in-Publication Data

Terhune, Albert Payson, 1872–1942.
Great dog stories / by Albert Payson Terhune ; illustrated by
Marguerite Kirmse.
p.   cm.
Summary: A collection of dog stories by Albert Payson Terhune.
ISBN 0-517-09337-5
1. Dogs—Juvenile fiction.   2. Children's stories, American.
[1. Dogs—Fiction.   2. Short stories.]   I. Kirmse, Marguerite,
1885–? ill.   II. Title.
PZ10.3.T273Gt   1993
[Fic]—dc20   93-17369
                                                           CIP
                                                            AC

8 7 6 5 4 3 2

Publisher's Note: The stories and illustrations in this collection were
selected from two previously published collections, *The Heart of a Dog*
and *My Friend the Dog*, and have been edited for today's young readers.

Cover design by Bill Akunevicz Jr.

CONTENTS

Fox! 1

The Coming of Lad 33

"Youth Will Be Served!" 51

Lochinvar Bobby 65

"One Minute Longer" 99

Runaway 111

The Feud 131

The Destroyer from Nowhere 151

Foster Brothers 171

Collie! 187

PREFACE TO THIS ILLUSTRATED EDITION

ALBERT PAYSON TERHUNE was the master of classic dog and animal stories that were well loved by generations past and are most welcome today for their strong sense of adventure, drama, and wit. Terhune was, above all, passionately on the side of these loyal, strong, devoted, and intelligent creatures. Anyone who cares for the rights of animals today will see that he was an early advocate, far ahead of his time.

Terhune's favorites, of course, were the collies, which he bred at his famous home, Sunnybank, in Pompton Lakes, New Jersey. But he knew, cared about, and wrote about many breeds of dogs and many kinds of animals.

Collies, though, are the stars of these stories, and they, as well as other animals, have been portrayed here in beautiful color paintings and black-and-white drawings by Marguerite Kirmse, an illustrator of the early twentieth century.

It is a special pleasure and honor for Children's Classics to reprint these splendid stories and fine illustrations for a new generation of readers.

CLAIRE BOOSS
Series Editor

1993

LIST OF COLOR ILLUSTRATIONS

Opposite Page

Into the middle of the warm bar of radiance Laddie
   stepped—and stood 50

"The pup's a wonder, but the old dog is still the best
   of the lot" 51

The police dog halted, growling far down in his
   throat 82

He was red-gold and white of coat—a big, slender
   youngster 83

At once his ears went up, their tulip tips enlivening his
   whole expression 146

A huge raccoon had thrust forth his comedy mask of a
   face 147

A yellow-tawny thunderbolt launched itself from the
   rocks above 178

Ursus came slowly down to earth again, hindquarters
   first 179

FOREWORD

It has often been said that a dog is man's best friend. While this maxim is certainly a cliché, you would, if you were to think about it, come to the conclusion that it holds a lot of truth. For what comes to mind, first of all, when you ponder what it means to have, or to be, a best friend? A best friend is a pal, a companion, someone with whom to share adventure, with whom you can have a good time or a heart-to-heart talk. A best friend is someone you really care about, someone for whom you'd do anything and, most important, who feels exactly the same way about you.

Dogs offer their human companions all this and more. (Have you ever had an adoring puppy that sticks to you like glue, that you couldn't shake no matter how many times you told it, "Go home"?)

They can be the most undying and loyal friends of all. Dogs are fiercely protective toward their human friends, have been known to rescue them from danger even at great risk to themselves, and indeed have sometimes given their own lives to save those of their owners. In our culture, dogs are the very symbol of security, companionship, home, and hearth.

However, as domesticated as they may be, dogs boast a wild and fearful ancestry. They are directly descended from wolves, and their lupine heredity is evident not only in physical characteristics (sharp teeth; pointed ears and snouts; keen senses of sight, hearing, and smell) but also in their fierce nature when threatened or under attack. A dog's howl is eerie and wolflike, its snarl can be terrifying, its speed of attack and fighting skills as instinctive and uncheckable as those of the most untamed animals.

Dogs live hard. It is said that every year of a dog's life is equivalent to seven human years. They grow fast and mature quickly, and, if they are well cared for, can keep a human company for as long as fifteen years—a long time for a friendship.

All the domesticated and wild characteristics that can appear in a canine personality come into play in the dog stories collected in this volume. The man who wrote them, Albert Payson Terhune, knew dogs well and loved them more than any other four-footed creature. Terhune wrote almost exclusively about collies, and his stories and novels are filled with boundless admiration for what he considered their sterling qualities. His collies are *always* heroes and very often are portrayed as far more noble creatures than the people who own them.

When he wrote about dogs, Terhune was writing about purity of motive, hearts full of trust, nobility of spirit. All the dogs in these stories are magnificent—whether they are purebred, only part collie, the pick of the litter, or runt. Even if they don't start out that way, Terhune's dogs grow into the beauty and nobility with which nature endowed them.

These dogs are loyal to their masters, willing to give even those humans who mistreat them the benefit of the doubt. When faced with trouble they always rise to the occasion, defending their owners, leading them away from danger, summoning help when they themselves can't effect rescue.

Terhune obviously was fascinated by the evolutionary history of his beloved dogs. He made it a point to include in almost every story an episode in which the canine hero suddenly reverts to its ancestral, wolf-like behavior and appearance while engaged in mortal combat with a wolf's natural enemy such as a bobcat, raccoon, rampaging buck—or even another dog. In one unusual tale—"Collie!"—he tells of a lonely fugitive who raises a wolf cub from birth to be his pet dog, thereby reversing the natural order of evolution.

Terhune was clearly of the opinion that it is no small thing to be a dog owner—it is a responsible role, not to be taken lightly. Indeed, in a number of these stories, a young boy, and sometimes a young girl, is charged with the care and training of a puppy or even a full-grown dog as a test of maturity. For overcoming many trials and tribulations, the reward is, of course, being allowed to keep the dog, a sure sign that the young person finally has reached responsible adulthood. And to be deemed a worthy master of a dog is perhaps the highest honor in Terhune's world.

As you make your way through these stories, you'll find yourself moved, amused, even amazed by what you read. You'll learn a lot along the way—about dogs, wolves, evolution; about nature, history, farming; about raising, training, and showing collies. You'll learn a lot about people, too.

And don't be surprised to find yourself looking at your canine companions with new interest and respect. Who knows—if you don't already have a dog, you may find yourself planning to make the acquaintance of a new, four-legged best friend.

NAOMI KLEINBERG

New York, New York
1993

Fox!

When the Stippled Silver Kennel, Inc., went into the wholesale raising of silver foxes for a world market, its two partners brought to the enterprise a comfortable working capital and an uncomfortable ignorance of the brain reactions of a fox.

They had visited the National Exhibition of silver foxes. They had spent days at successful fox farms, studying every detail of management and memorizing the rigid diet charts. They had committed to memory every fact and hint in Bulletin No. 1151 of the United States Department of Agriculture—issued for the help of novice breeders of silver foxes.

They had mastered each and every available scrap of exact information concerning the physical welfare of captive silver foxes. But, for lack of half a lifetime's close application to the theme, their knowledge of fox mentality and fox nature was nil.

Now one may raise chickens or hogs or even cattle, without taking

1

greatly into account the inner workings of such animals' brains. But no man yet has made a success of raising foxes or their fifth cousin, the collie, without spending more time in studying out the mental than the physical beast.

On the kitchen wall of the Stippled Silver Kennel, Inc., was the printed dietary guidelines for silver foxes. On the one library shelf of the kennel was all the available literature on silver fox breeding, from government pamphlets to a three-volume monograph. In the four-acre space within the kennel enclosure were thirty model runways, twenty by twenty feet each equipped with a model shelter house and ten of them further fitted out with model brood nests.

In twenty-four of these thirty model runways lived twenty-four model silver foxes, one to each yard at this autumn season—twenty-four silver foxes, pedigreed and registered—foxes whose lump value was something more than $7,400. Thanks to the balanced rations and meticulous care lavished on them, all twenty-four were in the pink of form.

All twenty-four seemed as nearly contented as can a wild thing which no longer has the zest of gambling with death for its daily food and which is stared at with indecent closeness and frequency by dread humans.

But the partners of the Stippled Silver Kennel, Inc., failed to take note, among other things, of the uncanny genius certain foxes possess for sapping and mining; or that some foxes are almost as deft at climbing as is a cinnamon bear. True, the average silver fox is neither a gifted burrower nor climber. But neither are such talents rare.

For example, King Whitefoot II, in Number 8 run, could have given a mole useful hints in underground burrowing. Lady Pitchdark, the temperamental young vixen in Number 17 run, might have qualified as the fly of the fox family. Because neither of these costly specimens spent their time in sporadic demonstration of their arts, in the view of humans, those same humans did not suspect the accomplishments.

Then came an ice-bright moonlit night in late November—a night to stir every quadruped's blood to tingling life and to set humans to crouching over fireplaces. Ten minutes after Rance and Ethan Venner, the kennel partners, finished their perfunctory evening rounds of the yards, King Whitefoot II was blithely at work.

Foxes and other burrowing beasts seek instinctively the corners or the edges of yards, when striving to dig a way out. Any student of their ways will tell you that. Therefore, as in most fox-kennels, the corners and inner edges of the Stippled Silver yards were fringed with a half-yard of mesh wire, laid flat on the ground.

Whitefoot chose a spot six inches on the near edge of a border wire and began his tunnel. He did not waste strength by digging deep. He channelled a shallow tube, directly under the flat-laid wire. Indeed, the wire itself formed the top of his tunnel. The frost was not yet deep enough or hard enough to impede his work. Nor, luckily for him, did he have to circumnavigate any big underground rock.

In forty-two minutes from the time he began to dig, his pointed black nose and his wide-cheeked, stippled black face was emerging into the open, a few inches outside his yard.

Wriggling out of his tunnel, he shook himself daintily to rid his shimmering silver-flecked black coat of such dirt as clung to it. Then he glanced about him. From the nearby wire runs, twenty-three pairs of slitted topaz eyes flamed avidly at him. Twenty-three ebony bodies crouched motionless, the moon glinting bright on their silver stipples and snowy tailtips.

The eyes of his world were on the fugitive. The nerves of his world were taut and vibrant with thrill at his escape. But they were sportsmen in their own way, these twenty-three prisoners who looked on while their more skilled fellow won his way to liberty. Not a whine, not so much as a deep-drawn breath gave token of the excitement that was theirs. No yelping bark brought the partners out to investigate. These captives could help their comrade only by silence. And they gave him silence to a suffocating degree.

With their round phosphorous eyes they followed his every move. But twenty-two of the twenty-three avoided so much as a single motion whose sound might attract human ears. Crouching, aquiver, turning their heads ever so little and in unison to watch his progress, the twenty-two watched Whitefoot make for the high wire boundary fence which encircled the four-acre kennel enclosure—the fence beyond whose southern meshes lay the frost-spangled meadow.

Beyond the meadow reared the naked black woods, sloping stiffly upward to the mountain whose sides they draped—the mountain which was the outpost of the wilderness hinterland to southward of this farm valley.

But, as Whitefoot set to work at the absurdly simple exploit of digging under this outer fence—a fence not extending underground and with no flat width of wire before it—the twenty-third prisoner could stand the emotional strain no longer. Young and with nerves less steady than her companion's, little Lady Pitchdark marred the perfect symphony of noiselessness.

She did not bark or even yelp. But she went into action.

By natural genius she was a climber. Up the side of her ten-foot run wire she whizzed; her long-clawed feet scarcely seeming to seek toehold in the ladder of meshes they touched. Like a cat, she sped upward.

To provide against such an unlikely effort at jail breaking, the four wire walls of the run sloped slightly inward. At their summit, all around, was a flat breadth of wire that hung out for eight inches over the run; projecting inside the walls. As a rule such deterrents were quite enough to bar an ordinary fox from escape. But nature had taught Lady Pitchdark more than she teaches the ordinary fox. She was one of the rare vulpines born with climbing genius.

Up she scrambled, her fierce momentum carrying her to the very top of the fence, to the spot where it merged with the eight-inch overhang. Here, by every rule, the vixen should have yielded to the immutable law of gravity and should have tumbled back to the ground with a breath-expelling flop.

This is precisely what she did not do. Still helped by her momentum, she clawed frantically with both forefeet at the edge of the overhang. Her claws hooked in its end meshes. Her hindfeet released their hold on the in-slanting fence and she swung for an instant between moon and earth—a glowing black swirl of fur, shot with a myriad silver threads.

Then lithely she drew herself up on the overhang. A pause for breath and she was skidding down the steep slope of the fence's outer side. A dart across the yard and she reached the kennel's boundary fence just as Whitefoot was squirming to freedom through the second and shorter tunnel he had made that night.

Diving through, so close behind him that her outthrust muzzle brushed his sensitive tailtip, Pitchdark reached the safety of the outer world at almost the same instant as did he. Whitefoot felt the light touch at his tail. He spun around, snarling murderously, his razor-keen teeth bared. He had won his way to liberty by no slight exercise of brain and of muscle. He was not minded to surrender tamely to any possible pursuer.

But as he confronted the slender young vixen in her royal splendor of pelt and with her unafraid, excited eyes fixed so mischievously upon him, the dog-fox's lips slipped down from their snarling curl, sheathing the fearsome array of teeth. For a fraction of a second Whitefoot and Pitchdark faced each other there under the dazzling white moon, twin ebony blotches on the frost-strewn grass. Twenty-two pairs of yellow-fire eyes were upon them.

Then on impulse the two refugees touched noses. As though by this act they established common understanding, they wheeled about as one and galloped silently, shoulder to shoulder, across the frosted meadow to the safety of the black mountainside forest.

Sportsmanship can go only just so far, even in cool-nerved foxes. As the couple vanished through the night, a shrilly hideous multiple clamor of barking went up from twenty-two furry black throats. The tense hush was broken by a bedlam of raucous noise. The prisoners dashed themselves against the springy sides of their wire runs. One and another of them made desperate scrambling attempts to climb the inslanting walls that encircled them—only to fall back to the frozen ground and add their quota once more to the universal din.

Rance and Ethan Venner came tumbling out of the nearby house, grasping their flashlights and shouting confusedly to each other.

Instantly blank silence overspread the yards. The foxes crouched low, eyes aflame, staring mutely at the belated humans.

The briefest of inspections told the brothers what had happened. First they found the tunnel leading forth from Whitefoot's run. Then they discovered that Pitchdark's run was empty, though they could find no clue to its occupant's mysterious vanishing until next morning's sunrise showed them a tuft of finespun black fur stuck to a point of wire on the overhang, ten feet above ground. Last of all the partners came upon the hole under the fence which divided the kennel from the meadow.

"Whitefoot was worth an easy six hundred dollars as he stood," grunted Rance Venner, miserably, as his flashlight's ray explored the hole under the fence. "Nearer seven hundred dollars, in the coat he's carrying this fall. And Pitchdark isn't more'n a couple of hundred dollars behind him. Two of the best we had. A hundred percent loss—just as we're getting started."

"Nope," contradicted Ethan. "Not a hundred percent loss. Only about fifty. The pelt of either one of 'em will bring three hundred dollars, dressed. Any of a dozen dealers will pay us that for it."

"If they was to pay us three million, we wouldn't be any richer," complained Rance. "We haven't got the pelts to sell. You're talking plumb foolish, Ethan."

"We'll have 'em both by noon tomorrow," declared Ethan. "Those two foxes were born in a kennel. They don't know anything else. They're as tame as pet squirrels. We'll start out gunning for 'em at sunrise. We'll take Ruby along. She'll scent 'em, double quick. Then all we'll have to do is plant the shots where they won't muss the pelt too much."

"We'll do better'n that," supplemented Rance, his spirits rising at his brother's tone of confidence. "We won't shoot 'em. We'll get out the traps, instead. They're both tame and neither of 'em ever had to hustle for a meal. They'll walk right into the traps, as quick as they get the sniff of cooked food. C'mon in and help me put the traps in shape. We ought to be setting 'em before sunrise. The two foxes will be scouting for breakfast by that time."

The newly optimistic Rance was mistaken in all his forecasts. The two fugitives were not scouting for breakfast at sunrise. Hours earlier they twisted their way in through the narrow little opening of an unguarded chicken house belonging to a farm six miles from the kennel, drawn there by the delicious odor of living prey.

There, like a million foxes since the birth of time, they slew without noise or turmoil. There they glutted themselves, each carrying away a heavy fowl for future feasting, bearing off their plunder in true vulpine fashion with the weight of the bird slung scientifically over the bearer's shoulders.

Daybreak found them lying snugly asleep in a hollow windfall tree that was open at either end and which lay lengthwise in the nick of a hillside, with briars forming an effective hedge all about it.

Nor did the best casting efforts of Ruby, the partners' foxhound, succeed in following their cleverly confused trail across a pool and two brooks. In the latter brook, they had waded for nearly two-hundred yards before emerging on dry ground at the same side.

Thus set in a winter of bare sustenance for the runaways. They kept to no settled abiding place, but drifted across country, feasting at such few farmsteads as had penetrable hencoops, doing wondrous teamwork in the catching of rabbits and partridges, holing in under windfalls or in rock clefts when blizzards made the going bad.

It was the season when foxes as a rule run solitary. Seldom in early winter do they hunt in pairs and never at any season in packs. But these two black and silver waifs were bound together not only by early association but by mutual inexperience of the wild. And while this inexperience did not blur or flaw their marvelous instinct, they found it more profitable to hunt together than alone.

Only once or twice in their winter's foraging did they chance upon any of the high-country's native red foxes. A heavy hunting season had shifted most of the reds to a distant part of the county, as is the way with foxes that are overpressed by the attentions of trappers and hounds. In that region, pink coats and hunting horses and foxhound packs were unknown. But many a mountain farmer eked out his lean income by faring afield with a brace of disreputable but reliable mongrel hounds and a fowling piece as disreputably reliable, eager for the price of skins offered by the nearest wholesale dealer. This sum, of course, was for the common red fox; silver foxes being as unknown to the region at large as were dinosaurs.

The two silver foxes had the forest and farmland largely to themselves. The few reds they met did not attack them or affiliate with them at that hungry time of year.

The winter winds and the ice storms made Whitefoot's coat shine and thicken as never had it done on scientifically balanced rations. The life of the wild put new depth to Pitchdark's narrow chest and gave her muscular power and sinew to spare. Mother Nature had lifted them from man's wisest care, as though as an object lesson in her own infinitely more efficient methods for conditioning her children.

Late January brought a sore-throat thaw and with it a melting of drift and ice pack. Incidentally it ushered in the yearly vulpine mating season.

Spring was early that year. But before the frost was out of the ground, Pitchdark had chosen her nursery. It was by no means as elaborate or as sanitary as had been the costly brood nests at the kennel. Indeed it would have struck horror to the heart of any scientific breeder.

For it was merely a woodchuck hole in an upland meadow at the forest edge, a short mile from a straggling farmstead. Even here Whitefoot's inspired prowess as a digger was not called into play. His sole share toward securing the home was to thrash the asthmatically indignant old woodchuck that had dug the burrow. Then Pitchdark made her way cautiously down the hole and proceeded to enlarge it a little at the shallow bottom. That was all the homemaking done by the pair.

Then, of a windy night, just before the first of April, the vixen did not join her mate in his expedition for loot. And as he panted homeward before dawn with a broken-winged quail between his jaws, he found her lying in the burrow's hollow, with five indeterminate-looking babies nuzzling close to her soft side.

Then began days, or rather nights, of double foraging for Whitefoot.

For it is no light thing to provide food for a den-ridden mate and, indirectly, for five hungry and husky cubs.

Nor was the season propitious for food finding. The migratory birds, for the most part, had not shifted north. The rabbits for some silly reason of their own had changed their feeding grounds to the opposite valley. Farmers had suffered too many depredations from Whitefoot and Pitchdark during the past month to leave their henroosts as hospitably open as of yore.

The first day's hunting netted only a sick crow that had tumbled from a tree. Whitefoot turned with disgust from this find. For, though he would have been delighted to dine on the rankest of carrion, yet in common with all foxes, he could not be induced to touch any bird of prey.

That night he foraged again, in spite of having departed from his regular custom by hunting in daylight. There was no fun in hunting this night. For a wild torrent of rain had burst out of the black clouds which all day had been butting their way across the windy sky.

Foxes detest rain, and this rain was a veritable deluge, a flood that started the spring freshets and turned miles of bottomland into soggy lakes. Yet Whitefoot kept on. Grey dawn found him midway between his lair and the farmstead at the foot of the hill.

This farm he and Pitchdark had avoided. It was too near their den for safe plundering. Its human occupants might well be expected to seek the despoilers. And just then those despoilers were in no condition to elude the chase. Therefore, fox-fashion, the two had ranged far afield and had reserved the nearby farm for later emergencies.

Now the emergency appeared to call for such a visit from Whitefoot. A moment or so he hesitated, irresolute whether to return empty-mouthed to his mate or to go first to the farm for possible food. He decided on the farm.

Had he gone to the burrow he would have known there was no further need to forage for those five beautiful baby silvers, so different in aspect from the slate-gray infants of the red fox. A swelling rivulet of rain had been deflected from its downhill course by a wrinkle in the soil; and had poured, swishing, down the opening of the woodchuck warren and thence down into the ill-constructed brood nest at its bottom.

For the safeguarding of newborn fox babies, as of the babies of every race, dry warmth is all-essential. Chilled and soaked, despite their young mother's frantic efforts to protect them, the five ill-nourished and perilously inbred cubs ceased to nurse and began to squeak right dolefully. Then, one by one, they died. The last of them stiffened out just before daybreak.

Rance and Ethan Venner would have cursed luridly at loss of so many hundreds of dollars in potential pelts. But the bereft little mother only cuddled her ice-cold babies the closer, crooning piteously to them. They were her first litter. She could not realize what had befallen them, nor why one and all of them had ceased to nurse.

Meantime, her mate was drifting like an unobtrusive black shadow through the rain toward the clutter of farm buildings at the base of the hill pasture. His scent told him there was a dog somewhere in that welter of sheds and barns and houses. But his scent told him also that there were fowls aplenty. Preparing to match his speed and his wit against any dog's, he crept close and closer, taking due advantage of every patch of cover, unchecked even by the somewhat more distant man-scent, and urged on by that ever stronger odor of live chickens.

Presently he was skirting the chicken yard. It and its coop were too fast-locked for him to hope to enter with less than a half-hour's clever digging. He had not a half hour. He had not a half minute to spare.

Slinking from the coop, he rounded a toolhouse. There he halted. For to his nostrils came again the smell of living food, though of a sort vaguely unpleasant to him. Hunger and the need to feed his brood formed too strong a combination for this faint distaste to combat.

He peered around the corner of the half-open door of the toolhouse. From the interior arose the hated dog smell, ten times stronger than before. But he knew by nose and by hearing that the dog was no longer in there.

He was correct in this, as in most of his surmises. Not five minutes earlier, the early-rising Dick Logan had opened the toolhouse door and

convoyed thence his pedigreed collie, Jean, to the kitchen for her breakfast.

In the corner of the toolhouse was a box half filled with rags. Down
among the rags nestled and squirmed and muttered a litter of seven
pure-bred collie pups, scarce a fortnight old.

Man-scent and dog-scent filled the air, scaring and disgusting the
hesitant Whitefoot. Stark hunger spurred him on. A fleeting black
shadow slipped noiselessly swift into the toolhouse and then out again.

Through the welter of rain, Whitefoot was making for his mile-distant lair, at top speed, pausing not to glance over his shoulder, straining
every muscle to get away from that place of double peril and to his
waiting family. No need to waste time in confusing the trail. The sluicing rain was doing that.

Between his teeth the fox carried a squealing and struggling fat collie
puppy.

Keen as was his own need for food, he did not pause to devour or
even to kill the plump morsel he had snatched up. Nor did his pinpoint
teeth so much as prick through the fuzzy fat sides of his prey. Holding
the puppy as daintily as a bird dog might retrieve a wounded partridge,
he sped on.

At the mouth of the warren, Pitchdark was waiting for him. She had
brought her babies out of the death hole, though too late. They lay
strewn on the rain-sick ground in front of her. She herself was crouched
for shelter in the lee of a rock that stood beside the hole.

Whitefoot dropped the collie pup in front of his mate, and prepared
to join her in the banquet. Pitchdark nosed the blind, helpless atom of
babyhood, as though trying to make out what it might be.

The puppy, finding himself close to something warm and soft and
furry, crept instinctively toward this barrier from the cold and wet which
were striking through to the very heart of him. At his forward motion,
Pitchdark snarled down at him. But as his poking nose chanced to touch
her, the snarl merged suddenly into a croon. With her own sharp nose,
she pushed him closer to her and interposed her body between him and
the rain.

Whitefoot, the water cascading from his splendid coat, stood dripping and staring. Failing to make any sense of his mate's delay in beginning to devour the breakfast he had brought along at such danger to himself, he took a step forward, his jaws parting for the first mouthful of the feast. Pitchdark growled hideously at him and slashed at his advancing face.

Piqued and amazed at her ungrateful treatment, he hesitated a moment longer, then trotted glumly off into the rain, leaving Pitchdark crooningly nursing the queer substitute for her five dead infants. As he ran, he all but collided with a rain-dazed rabbit that hopped out of a briar clump to avoid him.

Five minutes later he and Pitchdark were lying side by side in the lee of the rock, crunching unctuously the bones of the luckless bunny, while the collie pup feasted as happily in his own fashion as did they, nuzzling deep into the soft hair of his foster mother's warm underbody.

Why the exposure to rain and cold did not kill the puppy is as much a mystery as why Pitchdark did not kill him. Nevertheless—as is the odd way of one collie pup in twenty—he took no harm from the mile of rainy gallop to which Whitefoot had treated him. More—he thrived mainly on the milk which had been destined for five fox cubs.

The downpour was followed by weeks of unseasonably dry and warm weather. The porous earth of the warren was dry within a few hours. The lair bed proved as comfortable for the new baby as it was to have been to his luckless predecessors.

By the time May brought the warm nights and the long bright days, the puppy weighed more than twice as much as any fox cub of his age. He had ceased to look like a sleek dun-colored rat and resembled rather a golden-and-white teddy bear.

On the moonlit May nights and in the red dawning and in the soft afterglow, he and his pretty mother would frisk and gambol in the lush young meadow grass around the lair. It was sweet to see the lithe black beauty's complete devotion to her clumsy baby and the jealous care wherewith she guarded him. From the first she was teaching him the cunning caution which is a fox's world-old birthright and which is foreign to a man-owned collie. With his foster mother's milk and from his foster mother's example he drank in the secrets of the wild and the fact that man is the dread foe of the beast.

Gaily as the two might play in the moonlit grass, the first distant whiff of man-scent was enough to send Pitchdark scuttling silently into the burrow, driving the shambling pup ahead of her. There the two would lie, noiseless, almost without breathing, while man or dog or both passed by.

This was not the season for hunting foxes. Their pelts were off prime —in no condition for the market. Thus, the pair in the burrow were not sought out or harried.

Back at the Logan farm there was bewilderment at the puppy's mysterious vanishing. His dam, returning from the kitchen after breakfast, had broken into a growl of sudden wrath and had changed her trot for a handgallop as she neared the toolshed. Into the shed she had dashed, abristle and growling, then out again, sniffing the earth, casting in ever widening circles, and setting off presently on a trail which the deluging rain wiped out before she could follow it for a hundred yards.

The stolen pup was the only one in the litter which had not been sold or else bespoken. For the Logan collies had a just fame in the region. But that one pup had been set aside by Dick Logan as a future housedog. This because he was the largest and strongest and liveliest of the seven, and because of the unusually wide white ruff which encircled his broad shoulders like a shawl.

Dick had named the youngster "Ruff," because of this adornment. And now he was liked to have no use for the name.

Ruff, meantime, was gaining his education, such as it was, far more quickly than his super-domesticated collie mother and Dick together could have imparted it to him.

By example and by swift punishment in the event of disobedience, Pitchdark was teaching him to crouch, flattened and noiseless, at sound or scent of man or of alien beast. She was teaching him to worm his pudgy little body snakelike through grass and undergrowth and to make wise use of every bit of cover. She was teaching him—as foxes have taught their young for a million years—the incredible cunning of her race and the fear of man.

By the time his legs could fairly support him on the briefest of journeys, she was teaching him to stalk game—to creep up on foolish field-mice, to confuse and head off young rabbits, and the like. Before he was fairly weaned she made him try his awkward prowess at finishing a rabbit-kill she had begun. With Ruff it was a case of kill or starve. For Pitchdark cut off natural supplies from him a full week earlier than his own gentle mother would have done.

Pitchdark was a born schoolmistress in Nature's grim woodland course of "eat or be eaten." To her stern teachings the puppy brought a brain such as no fox could hope to possess. Ruff was a collie—member of a breed which can assimilate practically any mental or physical teachings, if taught rightly and at an early enough age. Pitchdark was teaching him rightly, if rigidly. Assuredly, too, she was beginning early enough.

To the imparted cunning of the fox, Ruff added the brain of a highly sensitized collie. The combination was a triumph. He learned nearly as fast as Pitchdark could teach. If nine-tenths of the things she taught him were as reprehensible as they were needful, he deserved no less credit for his speed in mastering them and for his native ability to add to them.

At an age when his brothers and sisters, back at the farm, were still playing aimlessly around the dooryard, Ruff was grasping the weird secrets of the wild. While they were still at the teddy bear stage of appealing helplessness, his fat body was turning lean and supple from raw food and from much exercise and from the nature of that exercise. While they were romping merrily with an old shoe, Ruff was creeping up on fieldmouse nests and on crouching quail, or he was heading off witlessly racing rabbits which his foster mother drove toward the cul-de-sacs where she had stationed him.

For a pup situated like Ruff, there were two open courses—abnormal thriving or quick starvation. Ruff thrived.

By the time he was three months old he weighed nearly eighteen pounds. He was more than a third heavier than Pitchdark, though the silvered black vixen had the appearance of being fully twice his size. A fox is the most deceptive creature on earth in regard to bulk. Pitchdark, for instance, gave the impression of being as large as any thirty-pound terrier, if of far different build. Yet, stripped of her pelt, her slim carcass would not have weighed eleven pounds. Perhaps it would not have weighed more than ten pounds, for she was not large for her kind.

Before Ruff was six weeks old, Whitefoot had tired of domesticity—especially with so perplexing a canine slant to it—and had deserted his mate and foster son.

The warm days were coming on. The woods at last were alive with catchable game. The chickens on many a farm were perching out of doors at night. Life was gloriously livable. There seemed no sense in fettering himself to a family, or in helping to provide for a huge youngster in whom his own interest was purely gastronomical.

More than once Whitefoot had sought to slay and eat the changeling. But always, at such times, Pitchdark was at him, ravening and raging in defense of her suckling.

Then crept the influx of spring food into the valley and mountain. There was dinner to be gotten more easily than by battling a ferocious mate for it, a mate who no longer felt even her oldtime lonely comradeship for the dog-fox, and whose every thought and care was for the sprawling puppy. Apart from this, the inherently hated dog-scent on Ruff was a continual irritation to Whitefoot, though maternal care had long since accustomed Pitchdark to it.

Thus on a morning in late April Whitefoot wandered away and neglected to return. His mate was forced to forage for herself and for Ruff. But the task was easy in this new time of food lushness. She did not seem to miss her recreant spouse.

She and Ruff shifted their abode from the burrow whose narrow sides the fast-growing pup could scarcely squeeze through. They took up changeable quarters in the hinterland forest. There Ruff's training began in grim earnest.

So the sweet spring and the long drowsy summer wore themselves away. Through the fat months Pitchdark and Ruff lived together, drawn toward each other by the queerly strong tie that so often knits foster mother and child, in the fourfoot kingdom—a tie that is prone to be far stronger than that of normal brute mother and offspring.

This chumship now was wholly a thing of choice. For no longer did Ruff depend on the vixen to teach him how to catch his daily bread. True, he still profited by her experience and her abnormal cunning, and he assimilated it and improved on it—as is the way with a collie when he is taught something that catches his bright fancy. But he was self-supporting.

He continued to live with Pitchdark and to travel with her and to hunt with her; not because he needed to, but because he loved her. To this temperamental black-and-silver vixen went out all the loyal devotion and hero-worship and innate protectiveness which a normal collie lavishes on the human who is his god.

Together they roved the mountain, where Pitchdark's technique and craft bagged unlimited game for them. Together on dark nights they scouted the farm valleys, where Ruff's strength and odd audacity won them access to hencoop after hencoop whose rickety door would have resisted a fox's onslaught.

Twice, Ruff forced his way through the rotting palings of a sheepfold and bore thence to his admiring foster mother a lamb that was twice as heavy as Pitchdark. Once in open field he fought and outmaneuvred and thrashed a sheep-herding mongrel, dragging off in triumph a half-grown sheep.

There were things about Pitchdark the young collie could not understand, just as there were traits of his which baffled her keen wits. To him a grape vineyard was a place whose sole interest centered about any possible field mouse nests in its mould. An apple orchard had as little significance to him. He would pause and look in questioning surprise as Pitchdark stopped, during their progress through an orchard, to munch happily at a fallen harvest apple, or while she stood daintily on her hind legs to strip grapevines of their ripening clusters.

The fable of the fox and the sour grapes had its basis in natural history. For the fox, almost alone of carnivors, loves fruit. Ruff cared nothing for it. Few collies do.

Also, he could see no reason for Pitchdark's rapture when they chanced upon the rotting carcasses of animals. True, he felt an esthetic thrill in rubbing first one shoulder and then the other in such rotting carrion and then in rolling luxuriously over on his back in it. But it was not good to eat. Ruff knew that. Yet Pitchdark devoured it in delight. On the other hand, when the two came upon a young hawk that had fallen from its pine-top nest, Pitchdark gave one sniff at the broken bird of prey, and then pattered on, leaving it alone. Ruff killed and ate it with relish.

By the first cool days of autumn, Ruff stood twenty-four inches at the shoulder. He would have tipped the scales at a fraction above fifty pounds. His gold-red winter coat was beginning to come in, luxuriantly and with a sheen such as only the pelt of a forest-dweller can boast. His young chest was deep. His shoulders were broad and sinewy. His build was that of a wild beast, not of a domesticated dog. Diet and tremendous exercise and his mode of life had wrought that vast difference.

He had the noiselessly padding gait and the furtive air of a fox. Mentally and morally he was a fox, with the keener and finer brain of a collie. His dark and deepset eyes had the glint of the wild, rather than the straightforward gaze of a collie. Yet those eyes were a dog's and not a fox's. A fox has the eye of a cat, not of a dog. The iris is not round, but is long and slitted, like a cat's. In bright sunlight it closes to a vertical line, and does not contract to a tiny circle, like dog's or man's.

Nor did Ruff have the long and crouching hind legs and short catlike forelegs of Pitchdark. His were the honestly sturdy legs and sturdy pads of a collie.

The wolf is the dog's brother. They are of one blood. They can and do mate as readily as dog and dog. Dog and fox are far different. Their cousinship is remote. Their physique is remoter—too remote to permit blending. There is almost as much of the cat as of the dog in a fox's makeup—too much of it to permit of interbreeding with the cat-detesting dog.

Yet Ruff and Pitchdark were loving pals. They profited materially from their association, so far as food-getting went. They were inseparable comrades, through the fat summer and autumn and in the lean winter which followed.

In the bitter weather, when rabbits were few and when most birds had flown south and when rodents were holed in, it was young Ruff whose daring and strength enabled them to snatch fawns from snow-lined deer yards in the mountain creases and to raid sheepfolds and rip through flimsy hencoop doors. He kept them alive and he kept them in good condition. Daily he grew larger and stronger and wilier.

At a year, he weighed a full sixty pounds, and he had the strength and uncanny quickness of a tiger-cat. It was now he who led, while Pitchdark followed in meek adoration. Such foxes as they chanced to meet fled in sullen terror before the collie's assault. Ruff did not like foxes.

The next autumn brought forth the hunters. A few city folk and farm boys ranged the hills with rifles and with or without birddog or rabbit hound. These novices were ridiculously easy for Ruff and Pitchdark to avoid. They offered still less menace to Whitefoot ranging in solitary comfort on the other side of the mountain wall.

But the real hunters of the region were a more serious obstacle to smug comfort and to safety. They were lanky or stumpy men in wooly old clothes and accompanied by businesslike hounds. These men did not bother with mere sport or pot hunting. Red fox pelts brought a good price, even uncured, from the wholesaler down at Heckettville. Fox hunting was a recognized form of livelihood here in the upland valley district.

It was not like quail shooting or other sport open to any amateur. It was an art. It called for craft and for experience and for a rudimentary knowledge of the habits of foxes and for perfect marksmanship. Also it required the aid of a well-trained foxhound—not the type of foxhound the pink coats trail after, in conventional hunting fields—not the spruce foxhound on exhibition at dogshows—but rangy and stringy and wise and tireless dogs of dubious pedigree but vast fox-sense.

A veteran hunter with a good hound, in that part of the country and in those days, could readily pay the year's taxes and improvements on his farm by the fox pelts he was able to secure in a single month's roaming of the hills. Therefore, now that the year's farmwork was done, these few experts began their season of lucrative and sportless sport.

Time and again that fall, some gaunt and sad-faced hound hit Pitchdark's confused trail, only to veer from it presently when his nostrils caught the unmistakable dog-scent along with it. Still more often did a hound cling tenaciously to that trail, only to be outwitted by the vixen's cleverer maneuvres.

Pitchdark had as much genius for eluding pursuit as for climbing unclimbable fences. There are such foxes.

In these retreats from pursuing hounds it was she who took up afresh the leadership she had laid down. Ruff followed her implicitly in her many mazelike twists and doublings. At first he followed blindly. But gradually he began to get the hang of it, and to devise collie improvements on the hide-and-seek game.

He and she were alone in their wanderings, especially since the hunting season forced them higher among the almost inaccessible peaks of the range. Foxes that crossed their path or happened to sight or scent them fled as ever in terror at the dog-smell.

In midwinter, the day after a tracking snow had fallen, one Jeffreys Holt, an aged fox hunter, tramping home with his tired hound at his heels, chanced upon an incredible sight.

An animal rounded a bend of rock on a hillside perhaps a hundred yards in front of him, and stood there, stock still for a few seconds, sharply outlined against the snow. Then, as Holt stared slackjawed, the creature oozed from sight into a crevice. Holt plunged ahead, urging his weary hound to the chase. But by the time he reached the crevice there was no sign of the quarry.

The cleft led through to an opening on the far side of a rocky outcrop. From there a hundred-yard rib of rock jutted above the snow. Along this, presumably, had the prey fled, for there were no further marks of him in the whiteness. Hold cast his dog futilely upon the trail. He studied the footprints in the snow at the point where first the beast had been standing. Then he plodded home.

Whitefoot, from the safety of another double-entry rock lair, two hundred yards away, watched him depart. Long immunity had made the big dog-fox overbold. Yet this was the first time human eyes had focused on him for two years.

At the store that night, Rance Venner glanced up from his task of ordering supplies for the Stippled Silver Kennels and listened with sudden interest to the harangue of an oldster among the group around the stove.

"I'm telling you," Holt was insisting, in reply to a doubter, "I'm telling you I saw him as plain as I see you. Jet black he was, only his tailtip was white, and one of his hind feet, and there was shiny gray hairs sticking out from his shoulders and over his eyebrows. He—"

"Somebody's black dog, most likely," suggested the doubter.

"Dog nothing!" snorted Holt. "I've killed too many foxes not to know 'em from dogs. This was a fox. A reg'lar ol' he-one. A corker. And I'm telling you he was coal black, all but the tip of his tail and them hairs sprinkled all over his mask and—"

"Well," soothed the doubter, seeking to calm Holt's vexed vehemence, "I'm not saying there mayn't be black foxes with white tails and white hind feet and gray masks. For all I know, there's maybe foxes that's bright green and foxes that's red-white-and-blue, or speckled with pink. There may be. Only nobody's ever seen 'em. Any more'n anybody's ever seen a black-and-white-and-gray one, till you seen that one today, Jeff. I—"

Rance Venner came into the circle of disputants. He did not mingle with the folk of this village, six miles from his fox farm. This was his first visit to the store. The store nearest his home had burned down that week. Therefore his need to go farther afield for supplies.

"You say you saw a silver fox?" he asked excitedly, confronting Holt.

Holt stared truculently at him, suspecting further banter and not relishing it from a stranger.

"Nope," solemnly spoke up the doubter. "Not silver. Rainbow color,

with a streak of this here radium you've likely heard tell of. Jeff Holt
don't see queer things often. But when he does, he sure sees 'em plenty
vivid."

"My name is Venner," went on Rance, still addressing Holt. "My
brother and I run the Stippled Silver Fox Farm, up above Croziers. Two
years ago a couple of our silver foxes got loose on us. They—"

"Sure they wasn't di'mond foxes?" asked the doubter, politely.

The audience snickered at this scintillating flash of native wit. But
Rance went on, unheeding. Briefly, he explained the appearance and
general nature and value of silver foxes, and expanded upon the loss of
the two that had escaped from his kennel.

His oration gained scant personal interest; until he made a substantial
cash offer to anyone who would bring him Whitefoot's or Pitchdark's
pelt in good condition. He made an even higher offer for either fox if
captured alive and undamaged.

At this point incredulity reached its climax among his hearers. But
when Venner pulled a down payment from his hip pocket and deposited
it with the postmaster-storekeeper in evidence of good faith, the sight of
real money caused a wholesale conversion.

This conversion became rockbound conviction when, next night, Holt
returned from a call upon the wholesale pelt buyer at Heckettville, fifteen miles away.

"Say!" reported Holt, to the group of idling men at the stove side.
"That Venner cuss ain't loony, after all. Gannett told me all about them
silver foxes. They're true, all right. Showed me a picture of one. The
spitting image of the one I seen. Gave me this circ'lar to prove it. It was
sent to him by the gov'ment or by some sort of association. Listen
here."

Drawing out a folder, he began to read at random:

"Some silver foxes are cheap at a thousand dollars. If every silver fox
in the world should be pelted in November or December, when the fur
is prime, they could all be disposed of in a city the size of New York, in
less than a week, at a fab—at a fab'lous sum."

Impressively and for the most part taking the more unfamiliar words in his stride, Jeffreys Holt continued to read. Nor did he cease until he had made his eager audience acquainted with every line of the folder, including the printer's name and address at the foot of the fourth page.

Next morning all available fox traps for some miles around were on duty in the woods and among the hilltop rock barrens. Every man who understood the first thing about fox hunting was abroad with gun and dog, as well as local wealth seekers to whom the fine art of tracking foxes was merely a thing of hearsay. In that meager community and in that meager time of a meager year, the lure of the cash was irresistible. The village went afield.

Rance Venner and his brother were among the hunters, they and their little mixed-blood foxhound, Ruby.

Before dawn, Ruff and Pitchdark caught the distant signs of the chase, and they denned in, far among the peak rocks, for the day. At that, the chase might perhaps have neared their lofty eyrie before sunset, but for Whitefoot.

The big dog-fox had enjoyed long immunity from harm. He lacked Pitchdark's super caution. His adventure with man and dog, two days earlier, had resulted in no harm to himself. With entire ease he had blurred pursuit. Seeking rabbits again, in the clefts of the same rockridge, at sunrise on this day of universal hunting, he heard hounds baying futilely in far quarters of the valley and foothills below him.

Instead of denning in, as had his former mate and Ruff, he went on with his own hunt. Lacking a confederate like the collie to help him find food which was beyond his own vulpine powers to capture or slay, Whitefoot had begun to feel the pinch of winter hunger. Unappeasable appetite made him take chances from which the vixen would have recoiled.

For example, the sound and smell of the distant hunt this morning did not send him to cover. All autumn and early winter he had been hearing such faroff sounds, had been catching the man-and-dog scent. Never had he come to harm from any of it. He had been able to keep out of its way. Until that afternoon when Holt chanced upon him, no human eye had seen him. And even then there had been no trouble about getting away clean.

There were rabbits hiding in these clefts and crevices along the ridge side. Whitefoot could smell them. With luck he might be able to stampede one of them into a cul-de-sac cranny big enough to admit his own slim body.

An empty and gnawing stomach urged him on. It urged him on even after he caught the scent of human footprints which had passed that way, not an hour ago. It urged him on, even when, in a cranny, he came upon a contrivance of wood and iron which fairly reeked of human touch. The thing reeked of something else—of an excessively dead chicken which lay just beyond it in the cleft.

Too crafty to go past such a manmade and man-scented contrivance; yet Whitefoot felt his mouth water at the ancient odor of the chicken. He craved it beyond anything. Detouring the top of the ridge, he entered the cleft from the other side. No visible object of man's workmanship checked him here or stood between him and the tempting food. Of course the man-scent was as strong here as at the opposite end. But the morning wind was shifting through the cleft, bearing the reek with it.

Cautiously the half-starved fox padded forward through the drift of dead leaves toward the chicken which itself was half buried in leafage. His jaws closed on it.

As he backed out with his treasure trove, steel jaws closed on his left forefoot.

An hour later, Rance Venner and Holt climbed the ridge to visit the former's newfangled patent foxtrap. In the centre of a patch of bloody trampled snow lay a magnificent silver fox, motionless, his eyes rolled back, his teeth curled away from his upper jaw. Limp and pitifully still he lay.

Venner ran forward with a cry of joy and knelt to unfasten the trap jaws from the lifeless creature's paw.

"It's our King Whitefoot II!" he exulted, laying the supine body in his lap and smoothing the rumpled glory of pelt. "But I can't figure why he's dead. Maybe the shock killed him, or else he broke a blood vessel in his brain trying to tear loose. He—"

The rambling conjecture ended in a hoot of pain. There was an indescribably swift whirl of the inert black body. Rance Venner's thumb received a lightning bite from teeth which scraped sickeningly into its very bone. Whitefoot was flying like mad for the nearest available rock cranny.

Venner once more was increasing his knowledge of fox character. Apart from being prodigies at digging and at climbing, it appeared now that foxes, in emergency, understood to perfection the trick of playing dead.

Away flashed Whitefoot, his lacerated forepaw marring his speed not at all. Jeffreys Holt was an old enough huntsman to act on sheer instinct. Through no conscious volition of his own he whipped to his shoulder the gun that had hung idle in his grasp while he watched Rance open the trap. Taking quick aim, he pulled trigger.

Whitefoot did not stop at once his panic flight. He continued it for two yards longer, rolling over and over like a mechanical toy, before thumping against the rockside, stone dead.

"There's another good stunt we done, in getting that ol' feller," remarked Holt, ten minutes later, as he and Venner made their way downhill with their prize. "I'll bet my share of his pelt he's the fox that's been working the hencoops all along the valley this winter. He's a whopping big cuss. And no common-size fox could 'a busted in the coop doors like he did at a couple of places. Now that we got the fox, I s'pose it's up to us to get the wolf."

"What wolf?" mumbled Venner, still sucking his bitten thumb.

"Why, the one the reward is out for, of course," answered Holt in surprise at such ignorance. "First wolf that's been in this section in thutty years or more. He's been at sheepfolds, all over. At hencoops, too. First off folks thought maybe it was a stray cur. But no dog c'd do the smart wolf stunts that feller's done. It's a wolf, all right, all right."

The store was jammed that evening, by folk who came to stare at the wonder-fox. Next day and the next the whole community was out in quest of the priceless vixen.

All the second day, after a night of successful forage, Ruff and Pitch-dark denned amid the rocks of their peak. At nightfall they went forth again, as usual. But as they were padding contentedly back to their safe eyrie at gray dawn, Pitchdark failed to note a deadfall which had been placed in a hillside gully three months earlier.

Going back and forth—always of course by different routes—during the past three days, she and Ruff had scented and avoided a score of shrewdly laid traps scattered here and there. But this clumsy deadfall had been in place since November, when a farm lad had set it and then forgotten all about it. Rains and snow and winds had rubbed it clean of any vestige of man-scent. It seemed nothing but a fallen log propped against a tree trunk.

By way of a shortcut, Pitchdark ran under it.

There was a thump, followed at once by an astounded yell. The vixen, flattened out, lay whimpering under the tumbled log.

Ruff was trotting along a yard or so behind her. The fall of the log had made him spring instinctively sideways. Now he went over to where Pitchdark lay moaning and writhing. Tenderly he sniffed at her, then he walked around the log and her pinioned body. In another second he was at work clawing and shoving at the weight that imprisoned her.

The log was too light for its purpose. Also the boy who made and set the trap was a novice. The end of the log had come to rest on a knot of wood near the tree base. Ruff's weight and applied strength set it rolling. Off from the vixen it bumped, while she cried out again in agony.

Ruff turned to greet her as she should leap joyously to her feet. But she did not leap. The impact of the falling log had injured her spine. The best she could do was to crawl painfully along, stomach to the ground, whining with pain at every step. Her hind legs sagged, useless. Her forepaws made all the progress.

Yet she was a gallant sufferer. Keenly aware that she was in no condition to face or flee any possible dangers of the open, she made pluckily for the eyrie on the distant peak. The great collie slackened his pace to hers. At a windfall too high for her to clamber over, he caught her gently by the nape of the neck with his mighty jaws and scrambled over the impediment, carrying her with him.

Thus, at a snail's pace, they made their way homeward, the collie close beside his crippled chum, quivering from head to foot in distress as now and then the pain forced from her a sharp outcry.

Dawn deepened into daylight. Up came the winter sun, shouldering its sulky way through horizon mists. The day was on. And Ruff and Pitchdark were not yet within a mile of their hiding place.

The last mile promised to be the worst; rising as it did, almost precipice-like, to the summit, and strewn with boulder and rift. To the light-footed pair, such a clamber had ever been childishly easy. Now it threatened to be one long torment to the vixen.

No longer, since the accident, did they seek as usual to confuse or obliterate their homeward trail. There was no question now of wasting a step or of delaying the critical moment of safety.

Then, as they came to a ten-foot cliff at the base of the peak's last stiff climb, they halted and looked miserably upward. Along the face of this rock wall a narrow, rudimentary trail ran, from bottom to top, a widened rock fissure. The fox and the collie were accustomed to taking it almost at a bound.

But now there was no question of bounding. Nor was the collie able to navigate the tricky climb with Pitchdark suspended from his jaws. It was not a matter of weight but of leverage and of balance. He had sense enough to know that.

For the past half mile he had been carrying the vixen, her helpless hind legs dragging along the ground. Very tenderly, by the nape of the neck, he had borne her along. Yet the wrenching motion had forced cries from her, so that once and again he had set her down and stared in pitiful sorrow at her.

Now Pitchdark took matters into her own hands. At the base of the cliff was an alcove niche of rock, perhaps two feet deep and eighteen inches wide, roofed over by a slant of half-fallen stone. It was bedded with dead leaves. There were worse holes into which to crawl to die than this natural den. Into it, painfully, wearily, the vixen dragged her racked body. There she laid herself down on the leaf couch, spent and in torture. She had come to the end of her journey, though still a mile on the other side of the den where she and Ruff would hide.

It was no hiding place, no safe refuge, this niche of rock where she lay. But it was the best substitute. Panting, she settled down to bear her anguish as best she might. Above her, at the opening of the niche, stood the heartsick dog that loved her.

Puzzled, miserable, tormented, he stood there. At times he would bend down to lick the sufferer, crooning softly to her. But she gave him scant heed.

A rabbit scuttled across the snowy open space in front of the cliff. With a dash, Ruff was after him. Several yards away the chase ended in a reddened swirl of snow. Back to Pitchdark trotted Ruff, the rabbit in his mouth. He laid the offering in front of her. But she was past eating or even noticing food.

Then, as he watched her, his deepset dark eyes sick with pity and grief, he stiffened to attention, and his lip curled away from his curving white teeth. The morning breeze bore to him a scent and a sound that had but one meaning.

The scent was of dogs. The sound was of multiple baying.

Instinctively he glanced at the cliff trail—the trail he could surmount so quickly and easily, to the safety of the peak's upper reaches. Then his unhappy gaze fell on Pitchdark. The baying and the odor had reached her even more keenly than it had reached Ruff. She read it right, and the realization brought her out of the pained daze into which she had fallen. She tried to get to her feet. Failing, she fell to whimpering softly.

Once she peered up questioningly at Ruff. The big collie was standing in front of the niche, shielding it with his strong body. His head was high and his eye had the look of eagles. Gone from his expression was the furtiveness of the wild. In this crisis he was all collie. The sun blazed on his flaming red-gold coat and his snowy mass of ruff and frill. Every muscle was tense. Every faculty was alert.

Zeb Harlow knew nothing about fox hunting. Indeed, he knew little enough about anything. But at the store conclave the preceding night, his fancy had been fired by tales of the silver foxhunt. He had an inspiration.

Before daybreak he was abroad, gun in hand. Going from one sleeping neighbor's to another's, he loosed and took along with him no fewer than five chained foxhounds.

The dogs all knew him well enough to let him handle them. There was not one of the five that would not have followed anybody who carried a gun. So his one-man hunt was organized. He and the five hounds made for the ridge where, two days before, Whitefoot had been caught.

From reading fictional tales of nature, Zeb argued that the slain fox's mate would be haunting the scene of her spouse's death. It was a pretty theory, as pretty as it was asinine. Like many another wholly idiotic premise it led to large results—of a sort.

As Zeb was traversing a wooded gully on the way to the ridge, the lead hound gave tongue. The pack had come to the spot where Pitchdark had been crippled. From that point a blind mongrel puppy could have followed the pungent trail.

Oblivious of Harlow, for whom they had all a dog's amusedly tolerant contempt for an inefficient human leader, the quintet swept away on the track. Zeb made to follow as best he could. Not being a woodsman, his progress was slow.

Up the gully they roared and out into the hillside birch woods beyond and then to the patch of broken ground over which Ruff had carried Pitchdark so tenderly. The scent was rankly strong now. It was breast high. No longer was there need to work with nostrils to earth. The dragging hind feet of the vixen were easier to follow than a deliberately laid trail.

Out into the cleared space they swung—the clearing with the ten-foot cliff behind it. There, not fifty yards in front of them, clearly visible between the braced legs of a shimmering gold-and-white collie on guard at the niche opening, crouched their prey.

Deliriously they rushed to the kill.

The kill was there. But so was the killer.

Perhaps there are two foxhounds on earth which together can down a normal collie. Assuredly there is no one foxhound that can hope to achieve the deed. Most assuredly such a hound was not the half-breed, black-and-yellow leader of that impromptu pack.

The black-and-yellow made for the niche, a clean dozen lengths ahead of his nearest follower. Blind to all but the lust of slaughter, he dived between the braced legs of the waiting collie, and struck for the cowering vixen.

Ruff drove downward at him as the hound dived. The collie's terrible jaws clamped shut behind the base of the leader's skull. The aim, made accurate by a thousand snaps at fleeing rabbits and rising birds, was flawless. The jaws had been strengthened past normal by the daily grinding of bony food.

Ruff tossed high his head. The black-and-yellow was flung in air and fell back amid his onrushing fellows, his neck broken, his spinal cord severed.

But that was Ruff's last opportunity for individual fighting. The four following hounds were upon him in one solid battling mass. Noting their leader's fate they did not make the error of trying to jostle past to the vixen. Instead, they sought to clear the way by flinging themselves ravenously on her solitary guard.

The rest was horror.

There was no scope for scientific fighting or for craft. The four fastened upon the collie in murderous unison. They might more wisely have fastened upon a hornet nest.

Down under their avalanche of weight went Ruff, battling as he fell. But a collie down is not a collie beaten. As he fell, he slashed to the bone the nearest gaunt shoulder. By the time he had struck ground on his back, he lunged upward for one flying spotted hind leg that chanced to flounder nearest to his jaws. The fighting tricks of his long-ago wolf ancestors came to him in his hour of stress. Catching the leg midway between hock and body he gave a sidewise wrench to it that nearly heaved off the pack that piled upon him. The possessor of the spotted hind leg screeched aloud and fell back, tumbling out of the ruck with a fractured and useless limb.

Up from the tangle of fighting hounds rose Ruff, his golden coat smeared with blood. High he reared above the surrounding heads. Slashing, tearing, dodging, wheeling, he fought clear of his mangled foes.

For an instant, as they gathered their force for a new charge at this tigerlike adversary, the great collie stood clear of them all. A single bound would have carried him to the cliff trail. Then to its top would have been a climb of less than half a second. At the summit he could have fought back an army of dogs or he could have made his escape to the safety beyond. Never was there a foxhound that could keep pace with a racing collie.

The coast was clear, if only for an instant. There was time—just time —for the leap. Ruff made the leap.

But he did not make it in the direction of the inviting trail. Instead, he sprang back again in front of the trembling vixen as she crouched in her niche.

A fox would have fled. So would any creature of the wild. But no longer was Ruff a creature of the wild. In his supreme moment he was all collie.

Whirling to face his oncoming enemies he took his stand. And there the charge of the hounds crashed into him.

By footwork, by dodging, by leading his foes into a chase where they should string out, he could have conquered them. But this he dared not do. He knew well what must befall Pitchdark the moment he should leave the niche unguarded. So he stood where he was and went down once more under the rush.

There were but three opponents on top of him this time. The spotted hound was out of the fight with a crunched leg and a craven heart. Nor were any of the three others unmarked by slash or nip or tear.

As Ruff fell he pulled one of the three down with him, his awful fangs busy at the hound's throat. A second of the trio rolled over with them, the forequarters of his inverted body sprawled within the niche. While he bit and roared at the fast-rolling Ruff, the vixen saw her chance.

Darting her head forward, she set her needle teeth deep in the hound's throat. Instantly, seared by the hurt, he was atop her, ripping away at her unprotected back, tearing it to ribbons. But with death upon her and the rear half of her paralyzed, she did not abate the merciless grinding at the hound's throat. Presently, the needle teeth found their goal.

Ruff was up again, one of his assailants gasping out his life beneath him, the other with Pitchdark clinging in death to his throat. Torn and bleeding and panting as he was, Ruff flew at the fourth dog, the only one of the five still in fighting condition.

Before that one-to-one onset the mongrel hound's heart went back on him. He turned and fled, but not before Ruff's madly twisting jaws had lamed him for life.

The battle was fought and won. Of the five hounds, one lay dead, two more were dying, a fourth was lying helpless with a crunched hind leg. The fifth was in limping flight.

The young collie staggered, then righted himself. Crossing to Pitchdark, he bent painfully down and licked her face—the face whose teeth were locked in her oppressor's throat.

Never now would that glorious pelt sell for hundreds of dollars, or even for hundreds of cents. The dying hound had seen to that. So had the dog now limping away. This latter had taken advantage of Ruff's preoccupation with his two fellows, as they rolled in the snow, to tear destructively at the silken coat as the vixen's teeth were finding their way to his comrade's jugular.

Crooning, licking, Ruff sought to make his loved little foster mother awaken. Then he lifted his head and wheeled wearily about to face a new intruder.

Across the snow toward him was clumping a slack-faced man who gripped in both hands a cocked gun and who was shouting foolishly in his excitement. Zeb Harlow had caught up to the hunt at last.

Ruff had not been so near to any human since he was two weeks old. The carefully taught lessons of Pitchdark warned him to turn and flee. The cliff trail was still open to him. But into the brain that was once again all collie there seeped a queer sensation the big dog could not analyze.

His dear little comrade was dead. Without her the old life would be empty. His was the collie heritage—the stark need for comradeship coupled with the unconscious craving to be owned by man and to give his devotion to man, his god.

Still unable to analyze his own unaccustomed feelings, Ruff bent again and licked Pitchdark's dead face. Then, hesitant, he took a step toward the stormily advancing Harlow. He took another irresolute step, paused again and wagged his plumy tail.

"Attacked me, he did!" bragged Zeb Harlow, that night at the store. "Come straight for me, like he was going to eat me alive. But I stopped him, all right, all right. I stood my ground. After the second step he took, I let him have both bar'ls. You saw for yourselves what he looked like after he tried to tackle *me.*"

THE COMING OF LAD

In the mile away village of Hampton, there had been a veritable epidemic of burglaries—ranging from the theft of a brand-new trash can from the steps of the Methodist chapel to the ravaging of Mrs. Blauvelt's whole lineful of clothes, on a washday dusk.

Up the valley and down it, from Tuxedo to Ridgewood, there had been a dozen robberies of a very different order—depredations wrought, obviously by professionals, thieves whose cars served the twentieth-century purpose of such historic steeds as Dick Turpin's Black Bess and Jack Shepard's Ranter. These thefts were in the line of jewelry and the like, and were as daringly executed as were the modest local operators' raids on trash can and laundry.

It is the easiest thing in the world to stir humankind's ever tense burglar nerves into hysterical jangling. In house after house, for miles of the peaceful North Jersey region, old pistols were cleaned and loaded,

33

window fastenings and door locks were inspected and new hiding places found for portable family treasures.

Across the lake from the village, and down the valley from a dozen country homes, seeped the tide of precautions. And it swirled at last around the Place—a thirty-acre homestead, isolated and sweet, whose grounds ran from highway to lake, and whose wisteria-clad gray house drowsed among big oaks midway between road and water, two hundred yards or more distant from either.

The Place's family dog—a pointer—had died, rich in years and honor. And the new peril of burglary made it highly necessary to choose a successor for him.

The master talked of buying a whalebone-and-steel-and-snow bull terrier, or a more formidable if more greedy Great Dane. But the mistress wanted a collie. So they compromised by getting the collie.

He reached the Place in a cramped and smelly crate, preceded by a long envelope containing an intricate and imposing pedigree. The burglary-preventing problem seemed solved.

But when the crate was opened and its occupant stepped gravely forth on the Place's veranda, the problem was revived.

All the master and the mistress had known about the newcomer— apart from his price and his lofty lineage—was that his breeder had named him Lad.

From these meager facts they had somehow built up a picture of a huge and grimly ferocious animal that should be a terror to all intruders and that might in time be induced to make friends with the Place's occupants. In view of this, they had had a stout kennel made and to it they had affixed with double staples a chain strong enough to restrain a bull.

(It may as well be said here that never in all the sixteen years of his beautiful life did Lad occupy that or any other kennel nor wear that or any other chain.)

Even the crate which brought the new dog to the Place failed somehow to destroy the illusion of size and fierceness. But, the moment the crate door was opened the delusion was wrecked by Lad himself.

Out on to the porch he walked. The ramshackle crate behind him had a ridiculous air of a chrysalis from which some bright thing had departed. For a shaft of sunlight was shimmering across the veranda floor. And into the middle of the warm bar of radiance Laddie stepped—and stood.

His fluffy puppy-coat of wavy mahogany-and-white caught a million sunbeams, reflecting them back in tawny-orange glints and in a dazzle as of snow. His forepaws were absurdly small, even for a puppy's. Above them the ridging of the stocky leg bones gave as clear promise of mighty size and strength as did the amazingly deep little chest and square shoulders.

Here one day would stand a giant among dogs, powerful as a timber wolf, lithe as a cat, as dangerous to foes as an angry tiger; a dog without fear or treachery; a dog of uncanny brain and great lovingly loyal heart, and a dancing sense of fun, as well—a dog with a soul.

All this, any canine physiologist might have read from the compact frame, the proud head carriage, the smolder in the deep-set sorrowful dark eyes. To the casual observer, he was but a beautiful and appealing and wonderfully cuddleable bunch of puppyhood.

Lad's dark eyes swept the porch, the soft swelling green of the lawn, the flash of fire-blue lake among the trees below. Then he deigned to look at the group of humans at one side of him. Gravely, impersonally, he surveyed them, not at all cowed or strange in his new surroundings, courteously inquisitive as to the twist of luck that had set him down here and as to the people who, presumably, were to be his future companions.

Perhaps the stout little heart quivered just a bit, if memory went back to his home kennel and to the rowdy throng of brothers and sisters and, most of all, to the soft furry mother against whose side he had nestled every night since he was born. But if so, Lad was too valiant to show homesickness by so much as a whimper. And, assuredly, this house of peace was infinitely better than the miserable crate in which he had spent twenty horrible and jouncing and smelly and noisy hours.

From one to another of the group strayed the level, sorrowful gaze.

After the swift inspection, Laddie's eyes rested again on the mistress. For an instant, he stood, looking at her in that mildly polite curiosity which held no hint of personal interest.

Then all at once his plumy tail began to wave. Into his sad eyes sprang a flicker of warm friendliness. Unbidden—oblivious of every one else—he trotted across to where the mistress sat. He put one tiny white paw in her lap and stood thus, looking up lovingly into her face, tail awag, eyes shining.

"There's no question whose dog he's going to be," laughed the master. "He's elected you—by acclamation."

The mistress caught up into her arms the half-grown youngster, petting his silken head, running her white fingers through his shining mahogany coat, making crooning little friendly noises to him. Lad forgot he was a dignified and stately pocket-edition of a collie. Under this spell, he changed in a second to an excessively loving and nestling and adoring puppy.

"Just the same," interposed the master, "we've been stung. I wanted a dog to guard the place and to be a menace to burglars and all that sort of thing. And they've sent us a teddy bear. I think I'll ship him back and get a grown one. What sort of use is—?"

"He is going to be all those things," eagerly prophesied the mistress. "And a hundred more. See how he loves to have me pet him! And—look —he's learned, already, to shake hands, and—"

"Fine!" applauded the master. "So when it comes our turn to be visited by this roving burglar, the puppy will shake hands with him, and register love of petting, and the burly marauder will be so touched by Lad's friendliness that he'll not only spare our house but lead an upright life ever after. I—"

"Don't send him back!" she pleaded. "He'll grow up soon, and—"

"And if only the courteous burglars will wait till he's a couple of years old," suggested the master, "he—"

Set gently on the floor by the mistress, Laddie had crossed to where the master stood. The man, glancing down, met the puppy's gaze. For an instant he scowled at the miniature watchdog, so ludicrously different from the ferocious brute he had expected. Then—for some queer reason—he stooped and ran his hand roughly over the tawny coat, letting it rest at last on the shapely head that did not flinch or wriggle at his touch.

"All right," he decreed. "Let him stay. He'll be an amusing pet for you, anyhow. And his eye has the true thoroughbred expression—'the look of eagles.' He may amount to something after all. Let him stay. We'll take a chance on burglars."

So it was that Lad came to the Place. So it was that he demanded and received due welcome—which was ever Lad's way. The master had been right about the pup's proving an amusing pet for the mistress. From that first hour, Lad was never willingly out of her sight. He had adopted her. The master, too—in only a little lesser wholeheartedness—he adopted. Toward the rest of the world, from the first, he was friendly but more or less indifferent.

Almost at once his owners noted an odd trait in the dog's nature. He would of course get into any or all of the thousand mischief-scrapes which are the heritage of puppies. But a single reproof was enough to cure him forever of the particular form of mischief for which he had just been chided. He was one of those rare dogs that learn by instinct, and that remember for all time a command or a prohibition given them but once.

For example: On his second day at the Place, he made a furious rush at a neurotic mother hen and her golden convoy of chicks. The mistress —luckily for all concerned—was within call. At her sharp summons the puppy wheeled, midway in his charge, and trotted back to her. Severely, yet trying not to laugh at his worried aspect, she scolded Lad for his misdeed.

An hour later, as Lad was scampering ahead of her past the stables, they rounded a corner and came flush upon the same nerve-wracked hen and her brood. Lad halted in his scamper with a suddenness that made him skid. Then, as though walking on eggs, he made an idiotically wide circle about the feathered dam and her silly chicks. Never thereafter did he assail any of the Place's fowls.

It was the same when he sprang up merrily at a line of laundry, flapping in alluring invitation from the clothesline. A single word of rebuke—and from then on the family wash was safe from him.

And so on with the myriad perplexing "don'ts" which spatter the career of a fun-loving collie pup. Versed in the patience-fraying ways of pups in general, the mistress and the master marveled and bragged and praised.

All day and every day, life was a delight to the little dog. He had friends everywhere willing to romp with him. He had squirrels to chase among the oaks. He had the lake to splash in ecstatically. He had all he wanted to eat, and he had all the petting his hungry little heart craved.

He was even allowed, with certain restrictions, to come into the mysterious house itself. And, neither after one defiant bark at a leopardskin rug, did he molest anything there. In the house, too, he found a genuine cave—a wonderful place to lie and watch the world at large, and to stay cool in and to pretend he was a wolf. The cave was the deep space beneath the piano in the music room. It seemed to have a peculiar charm for Lad. To the end of his days, by the way, this cave was his chosen resting place. And, during his lifetime, no other dog ever set foot in that spot.

So much for all day and every day. But the nights were different.

Lad hated the nights. In the first place, everybody went to bed and left him alone. In the second, his hard-hearted owners made him sleep on a fluffy rug in a corner of the veranda instead of in his delectable piano cave. What's more, there was no food at night. And there was nobody to play with or to go for walks with or to listen to. There was nothing but gloom and silence and dullness.

When a puppy takes fifty cat naps in the course of the day, he cannot always be expected to sleep the night through. It is too much to ask. And Lad's waking hours at night were times of desolation and of utter boredom. True, he might have consoled himself, as does many a lesser pup, with voicing his woes in a series of melancholy howls. That, in time, would have drawn plenty of human attention to the lonely youngster, even if the attention were not wholly flattering.

But Lad did not belong to the howling type. When he was unhappy, he grew silent. And his sorrowful eyes took on a deeper woe. By the way, if there is anything more sorrowful than the eyes of a collie pup that has never known sorrow, I have yet to see it.

No, Lad could not howl. And he could not hunt for squirrels. For these enemies of his were not content with the unfairness of climbing out of his reach in the daytime when he chased them; but they added to their sins by joining the rest of the world—except Lad—in sleeping all night. Even the lake that was so friendly by day was a chilly and forbidding playfellow during the cool North Jersey nights.

There was nothing for a poor lonely pup to do but stretch out on his rug and stare in unhappy silence up the driveway, in the impossible hope that some one might happen along through the darkness to play with him.

At such an hour and in such lonesomeness, Lad would gladly have tossed aside all prejudices of caste—and all his natural dislikes—and would have frolicked in mad joy with the most unknown stranger. Anything was better than this dreary solitude throughout the million hours before the first of the maids would be stirring or the first of the farmhands reported for work. Yes, night was a disgusting time, and it had not one single redeeming trait for the puppy.

Lad was not even consoled by the knowledge that he was guarding the slumbering house. He was not guarding it. He had not even the remotest idea what it meant to be a watchdog. In all his five months he had never learned that there is unfriendliness in the world, or that there is anything to guard a house against.

True, it was instinctive with him to bark when people came down the drive, or appeared at the gates without warning. But more than once the master had bidden him be silent when a rackety puppy salvo of barking had broken in on the arrival of some guest. And Lad was still in perplexed doubt as to whether barking was something forbidden or merely limited.

One night—a solemn, black, breathless August night, when half-visible heat lightning turned the murk of the western horizon to pulses of dirty sulphur—Lad awoke from a fitful dream of chasing squirrels which had never learned to climb.

He sat up on his rug, blinking around through the gloom in the half hope that some of those non-climbing squirrels might still be in sight. As they were not, he sighed unhappily and prepared to lay his classic young head back again on the rug for another spell of night-shortening sleep.

But before his head could touch the rug, he reared it and half of his small body from the floor, and focused his nearsighted eyes on the driveway. At the same time, his tail began to wag a thumping welcome.

Now, by day, a dog cannot see as far or as clearly as can a human. But by night—for comparatively short distances—he can see much better than can his master. By day or by darkness, his keen hearing and keener scent make up for all defects of eyesight.

And now three of Lad's senses told him he was no longer alone in his tedious vigil. Down the drive, moving with amusing slowness and silence, a man was coming. He was on foot. And he was fairly well dressed. Dogs—the foremost snobs in creation—are quick to note the difference between a well-clad and a disreputable stranger.

Here unquestionably was a visitor—some such man as so often came to the Place and paid such flattering attention to the puppy. No longer need Lad be bored by the solitude of this particular night. Someone was coming toward the house and carrying a small bag under his arm. Someone to make friends with. Lad was very happy.

Deep in his throat a welcoming bark was born. But he stilled it. Once, when he had barked at the approach of a stranger, the stranger had gone away. If this stranger were to go away, all the night's fun would go with him. Also, no later than yesterday, the master had scolded Lad for barking at a man who had come. Therefore, the dog held his peace.

Getting to his feet and stretching himself from head to tail in true collie fashion, the pup gamboled up the drive to meet the visitor.

The man was feeling his way through the pitch darkness, groping cautiously, halting once or twice for a smolder of lightning to silhouette the house he was nearing. In a wooded lane, a quarter mile away, his lightless motor car waited.

Lad trotted up to him, the tiny white feet noiseless in the soft dust of the drive. The man did not see him, but passed so close to the dog's hospitably upthrust nose that he all but touched it.

Only slightly rebuffed at such chill lack of cordiality, Lad fell in behind him, tail wagging, and followed him to the porch. When a guest rang the bell, the master or one of the maids would come to the door. There would be lights and talk, and perhaps Laddie himself might be allowed to slip into his beloved cave.

But the man did not ring. He did not stop at the door at all. On tiptoe he skirted the veranda to the old-fashioned bay windows at the south side of the living room—windows with old-fashioned catches and simple to open.

Lad padded along, a pace or so to the rear—still hopeful of being petted or perhaps even romped with. The man gave a faint but promising sign of intent to romp by swinging his small and very shiny brown bag to and fro as he walked. So did the master swing Lad's precious flannel doll before throwing it for him to retrieve. Lad made a tentative snap at the bag, his tail wagging harder than ever. But he missed it. And in another moment, the man stopped swinging the bag and tucked it under his arm again as he began to fumble with a bit of steel.

There was the very faintest of clicks. Then, noiselessly, the window slid upward. A second fumbling sent the inside wooden shutters ajar. The man worked with no uncertainty. Ever since his visit to the Place a week earlier, under cover of a big and bright and newly forged telephone-inspector badge, he had carried in his trained memory the location of windows and of obstructing furniture and of the primitive small safe in the living room wall, with its pitifully pickable lock—the safe in which the Place's few bits of valuable jewelry and other small treasures were kept at night.

Lad was tempted to follow the creeping body and the hypnotically swinging bag indoors. But his one effort to enter the house—with muddy paws—by way of an open window, had been rebuked by the

Lawgivers. He had been led to understand that really well-bred little dogs come in by way of the door, and then only with permission.

So he waited doubtfully at the veranda edge, in the hope that his new friend might reappear or that the master might perhaps want to show off his pup to the caller, as so often the master liked to do.

Head cocked to one side, tulip ears alert, Laddie stood listening. To the keenest human ears the thief's soft progress across the wide living room to the wall safe would have been all but inaudible. But Lad could follow every phase of it—the cautious skirting of each chair; the hesitant pause as a bit of ancient furniture creaked; the halt in front of the safe; the queer grinding noise, muffled but persevering, at the lock; then the faint creak of the swinging iron door, and the deft groping of fingers.

Soon, the man started back toward the paler oblong of gloom which marked the window's outlines from the surrounding black. Lad's tail began to wag again. Apparently, this eccentric person was coming out, after all, to keep him company. Now the man was kneeling on the window seat. Now, carefully, he reached forward and set the small bag down on the veranda before negotiating the climb across the broad seat —a climb that might well call for the use of both his hands.

Lad was entranced. Here was a game he understood. Thus, more than once, had the mistress tossed out to him his flannel doll, as he had stood in pathetic invitation on the porch, looking in at her as she read or talked. She had laughed at his wild tossings and other maltreatments of the limp doll. He had felt he was scoring a real hit. And this hit he decided to repeat.

Snatching up the swollen little satchel, almost before it left the intruder's hand, Lad shook it, joyously, reveling in the faint clink and jingle of the contents. He backed playfully away, the bag handle swinging in his jaws. Crouching low, he wagged his tail in ardent invitation to the stranger to chase him and to get back the satchel. Thus did the master romp with Lad when the flannel doll was the prize of their game. And Lad loved such races.

Yes, the stranger was accepting the invitation. The moment he had crawled out on the veranda he reached down for the bag. As it was not where he thought he had left it, he swung his groping hand forward in a half-circle, his fingers sweeping the floor.

Make that enticing motion directly in front of a playful collie pup—especially if he has something he doesn't want you to take from him—and watch the effect.

Instantly, Lad was alive with the spirit of the game. In one scurrying backward jump, he was off the veranda and on the lawn, tail vibrating, eyes dancing, the satchel held tantalizingly towards its would-be possessor.

The light sound of his body touching ground reached the man. Reasoning that the sweep of his own arm had somehow knocked the bag off the porch, he ventured off the edge of the veranda and flashed a ray of his pocketlight along the ground in search of it.

The flashlight's lens was cleverly shaded in a way to give forth but a single subdued finger of illumination. That one brief glimmer was enough to show the thief an impossible sight. The glow struck answering lights from the polished sides of the brown bag. The bag was hanging in the air some six inches above the grass and perhaps five feet away from him. Then he saw it swing to one side and vanish in the night.

The astonished man had seen more. The flashlight's beam was feeble—too feeble to outline against the night the small dark body behind the shining brown bag. But that same ray caught and reflected back to the incredulous beholder two splashes of pale fire—glints from a pair of deep-set collie eyes.

As the bag disappeared, the eerie points of light were gone. The thief all but dropped his flashlight. He gaped in nervous dread and sought vainly to explain the witchery he had witnessed.

He had plenty of nerve. He had plenty of experience along his chosen line of endeavor. But while a crook may control his nerve, he cannot make it cool or steady. Always, he must be conscious of holding it in check, as a clever rider checks and steadies and keeps in check a plunging horse. Let the vigilance slacken and there is a runaway.

Now this particular thief had long ago keyed his nerve to the chance of interruption from some gun-brandishing householder, and to the possible pursuit of police, and to the need of fighting or of fleeing. But all his preparations had not taken into account this newest emergency. He had not steeled himself to watch unmoved the gliding away of a loot bag apparently moving of its own will, or the shimmer of two greenish sparks in the air just above it. And, for an instant, the man had to battle against a cowardly desire to bolt.

Lad, meanwhile, was having a beautiful time. He really appreciated the playful grab his nocturnal friend had made in his general direction. Lad had countered this by frisking away for another five or six feet and then wheeling about to face once more his playfellow and to await the next move in the carefree romp. The pup could see tolerably well in the darkness—quite well enough to play the game his guest had devised. And of course he had no way of knowing that the man could not see equally well.

Shaking off his momentary terror, the thief once more pressed the button of his flashlight, swinging the torch in a swift semicircle and extinguishing it at once, lest the dim glow be seen by any wakeful member of the family.

That one quick sweep revealed to his gaze the shiny brown bag a half-dozen feet ahead of him, still swinging several inches above ground. He flung himself forward at it, refusing to believe he also saw that queer double glow of pale light just above. He dived for the satchel with the speed and the accuracy of a football tackle. And that was all the good it did him.

Perhaps there is something in nature more agile and dismayingly elusive than a romping young collie. But that something is not a mortal man. As the thief sprang, Lad sprang in unison with him, darting to the left and a yard or so backward. He came to an expectant standstill once more, his tail wildly vibrating, his entire furry body tingling with the glad excitement of the game. This playful visitor of his was a veritable godsend. If only he could be coaxed into coming to play with him every night!

But presently he noted that the other seemed to have wearied of the game. After plunging through the air and landing on all fours with his grasping hands closing on nothingness, the man had remained thus, as if dazed, for a second or so. Then he had felt the ground all about him. Then, bewildered, he had scrambled to his feet. Now he was standing motionless, his lips working.

Yes, he seemed to be tired of the lovely game—and just when Laddie was beginning to enter into the full spirit of it. Once in a while, the mistress or the master stopped playing during the romps with the flannel doll. And Laddie had long since hit on a trick for reviving their interest. He employed this ruse now.

As the man stood, puzzled and scared, something brushed very lightly —even flirtatiously—against his knuckles. He started in nervous fright. An instant later, the same thing brushed his knuckles again, this time more insistently. The man, in a spurt of fear-driven rage, grabbed at the invisible object. His fingers slipped along the smooth sides of the bewitched bag that Lad was shoving invitingly at him.

Brief as was the contact, it was long enough for the thief's sensitive finger tips to recognize what they touched. And both hands were brought suddenly into play in a mad snatch for the prize. The ten avid fingers missed the bag and came together with clawing force. But, before they met, the finger tips of the left hand telegraphed to the man's brain that they had had momentary contact with something hairy and warm—something that had slipped, eel-like, past them into the night— something that most assuredly was no satchel, but *alive!*

The man's throat contracted in gagging fright. And, as before, fear spurred him to feverish rage.

Recklessly he pressed the flashlight's button and swung the muffled bar of light in every direction. In his other hand he leveled the pistol he had drawn. This time the shaded ray revealed to him not only his bag, but—vaguely—the thing that held it.

He could not make out what manner of creature it was which gripped the satchel's handle and whose eyes pulsed back greenish flares into the torch's dim glow. But it was an animal of some kind—distorted and formless in the wavering finger of blunted light, but still an animal—not a ghost.

And fear departed. The intruder feared nothing mortal. The mystery in part explained, he did not bother to puzzle out the remainder of it. Impossible as it seemed, his bag was carried by some living thing. All that remained for him was to capture the thing and recover his bag. The weak light still turned on, he gave chase.

Lad's spirits arose with a bound. His ruse had succeeded. He had reawakened in this easily discouraged chum a new interest in the game. And he gamboled across the lawn, fairly wriggling with delight. He did not wish to make his friend lose interest again. So instead of dashing off at full speed, he frisked daintily, just out of reach of the clawing hand.

And in this pleasant fashion the two playfellows covered a hundred yards of ground. More than once the man came within an inch of his quarry. But always, by the most minute spurt of speed, Laddie arranged to keep himself and his dear satchel from capture.

Then, in no time at all, the game ended, and with it ended Lad's baby faith in the friendliness and trustworthiness of all human nature.

Realizing that the sound of his own stumbling running feet and the intermittent flashes of his torch might well awaken some light sleeper in the house, the thief resolved on a daring move. This creature in front of him—dog or bear or goat, or whatever it was—was uncatchable. But by sending a bullet through it, he could bring the animal to a sudden and permanent stop.

Then, snatching up his bag and running at top speed, he himself could easily get clear of the place before anyone in the household should appear. And his car would be a mile away before the neighborhood could be aroused. Fury at the weird beast and the wrenching strain on his own nerves made the idea all the more attractive.

He reached back again for his pistol, whipped it out, and, coming to a standstill, aimed at the pup. Lad, waiting only to bound over an obstruction in his path, came to a corresponding pause, not ten feet ahead of his playmate.

It was an easy shot. Yet the bullet went several inches above the waiting dog's back. Nine men out of ten, shooting by moonlight or by flashlight, aim too high. The thief had heard this old maxim fifty times.

But, like most hearers of maxims, he had forgotten it at the one time in his career when it might have been of any use to him.

He had fired. He had missed. In another second, every sleeper in the house would be out of bed. His night's work was a blank, unless—

With a mad rush he hurled himself forward at the waiting Lad. And, as he sprang, he fired again. Then several things happened.

Everyone, except movie actors and newly appointed policemen, knows that a man on foot cannot shoot straight unless he is standing stock still. Yet, as luck would have it, this second shot found a mark where the first and better aimed bullet had gone wild.

Lad had leaped the narrow and deep ditch left along the lawn's edge by workers who were putting in a new watermain for the Place. On the far side of this obstacle he had stopped and had waited for his friend to follow. But the friend had not followed. Instead he had been somehow responsible for a spurt of red flame and for a most thrilling noise. Lad was more impressed than ever by the man's wondrous possibilities as a midnight entertainer. He waited, gaily expectant, for more. He got it.

There was a second noisy explosion and a second puff of lightning from the man's outflung hand. But this time, something like a red-hot whiplash struck Lad with horribly agonizing force across the right hip.

The man had done this—the man whom Laddie had thought so friendly and playful!

He had not done it by accident. For his hand had been outflung directly at the pup, just as once had been the arm of the kennel man, back at Lad's birthplace, in beating a disobedient mongrel. It was the only beating Lad had ever seen. And it had stuck horribly in his uncannily sensitive memory. And now he himself had just had a like experience.

In an instant, the pup's trustful friendliness was gone. The man had come on the Place, in the dead of night, and had struck him. That must be paid for! Never would the pup forget his agonizing lesson that night intruders are not to be trusted or even to be tolerated. Within a single second, he had graduated from a little friend of all the world into a vigilant watchdog.

With a snarl, he dropped the bag and whizzed forward at his assailant. Needle-sharp milkteeth bared, head low, ruff abristle, friendly soft eyes as ferocious as a wolf's, he charged.

There had been scarce a breathing space between the second report of the pistol and the collie's counterattack. But there had been time enough for the onward-plunging thief to step into the narrow lip of the waterpipe ditch. The momentum of his own rush hurled the upper part of his body forward. But his left leg, caught between the ditch sides, did not keep pace with the rest of him. There was a hideous snapping sound, a screech of mortal anguish and the man crashed to earth in a dead faint of pain and shock—his broken left leg still thrust at an impossible angle in the ditch.

Lad checked himself midway in his own fierce charge. Teeth bared, throat agrowl, he hesitated. It had seemed to him right and natural to assail the man who had struck him so painfully. But now this same man was lying still and helpless under him. And the sporting instincts of a hundred generations of thoroughbreds cried out to him not to mangle the defenseless.

Therefore, he stood, irresolute, alert for sign of movement on the part of his foe. But there was no such sign. And the light bullet graze on his hip was hurting terribly.

What's more, every window in the house beyond was blossoming forth into lights. There were sounds—reassuring human sounds. And doors were opening. His gods were coming forth.

All at once, Laddie stopped being a vengeful beast of prey and remembered that he was a very small and very much hurt and very lonely and worried puppy. He craved the mistress's dear touch on his wound, and a word of crooning comfort from her soft voice. This yearning was mingled with a doubt that perhaps he had been transgressing the Place's Law, in some new way; and that he might have let himself in for a scolding. The Law was still so queer and so illogical!

Lad started toward the house. Then, pausing, he picked up the bag which had been so exhilarating a plaything for him this past few minutes and which he had forgotten in his pain.

It was Lad's collie way to pick up offerings (ranging from slippers to very dead fish) and to carry them to the mistress. Sometimes he was petted for this. Sometimes the offering was lifted gingerly between delicate fingers and tossed back into the lake. But nobody could well refuse so jingly and pretty a gift as this satchel.

The master, scantily attired, came running down the lawn, flashlight in hand. Past him, unnoticed, as he sped toward the ditch, a collie pup limped—a very unhappy and comfort-seeking puppy who carried in his mouth a blood-spattered brown bag.

"It doesn't make sense to me!" complained the master, next day, as he told the story for the dozenth time to a new group of callers. "I heard the shots and I went out to investigate. There he was lying half in and half out of the ditch. The fellow was unconscious. He didn't get his senses back till after the police came. Then he told some babbling yarn about a creature that had stolen his bag of loot and that had lured him to the ditch. He was all unnerved and upset, and almost out of his head with pain. So the police had little enough trouble in getting him to confess. He told everything he knew. And there's a wholesale roundup of the gang going on this afternoon as a result of it. But what I can't understand—"

"It's as clear as day," insisted the mistress, stroking a silken head that pressed lovingly against her knee. "As clear as day. I was standing in the doorway here when Laddie came pattering up to me and laid a little satchel at my feet. I opened it, and—well, it had everything of value in it that had been in the safe over there. That and the thief's story make it perfectly plain. Laddie caught the man as he was climbing out of that window. He got the bag away from him, and the man chased him, firing as he went. And he stumbled into the ditch and—"

"Nonsense!" laughed the master. "I'll grant all you say about Lad's being the most marvelous puppy on earth. And I'll even believe all the miracles of his cleverness. But when it comes to taking a bag of jewelry from a burglar and then enticing him to a ditch and then coming back here to you with the bag—"

"Then how do you account—?"

"I don't. None of it makes sense to me. As I just said. But whatever happened, it's turned Laddie into a real watchdog. Did you notice how he went for the police when they started down the drive last night? We've got a watchdog at last."

"We've got more than a watchdog," amended the mistress. "An ordinary watchdog would just scare away thieves or bite them. Lad captured the thief and then brought the stolen jewelry back to us. No other dog could have done that."

Lad, enraptured by the note of praise in the mistress's soft voice, looked adoringly up into the face that smiled so proudly down at him. Then, catching the sound of a step on the drive, he dashed out to bark in murderous fashion at a wholly harmless delivery boy whom he had seen every day for weeks.

A watchdog can't afford to relax vigilance, for a single instant—especially at the responsible age of five months.

Into the middle of the warm bar of radiance
Laddie stepped—and stood.
The Coming of Lad, page 35

"The pup's a wonder, but the old dog is still
the best of the lot."
"Youth Will Be Served!" page 61

"YOUTH WILL BE SERVED!"

Bruce was a collie—physically and in many other ways a super-collie. Twenty-six inches at the shoulder, seventy-five pounds in weight, his great frame had no more hint of coarseness than had his classic head and foreface.

His mighty coat was stippled black at its edges, like Seedley Stirling's, giving the dog almost the look of a "tricolor" rather than of a "dark-sable-and-white." There was an air of majesty, of perfect breeding, about Bruce—an intangible something that lent him the bearing of a monarch. He was, in brief, such a dog as one sees perhaps three times in a generation.

At the Place, after old Lad's death, Bruce ruled as king. He was no mere kennel dog—reared and cared for like some prize ox—but was part and parcel of the household, a member of the family, as befitted a dog of his beauty and brain and soul.

It was when Bruce was less than a year old that he was taken to his first American Kennel Club bench show. The master was eager that the dog-show world should acclaim his grand young dog, and that the puppy—like the youthful knights of old—should have fair chance to prove his mettle against the champions of his kind. For it is in these shows that a dog's rating is determined; that he is pitted against the best in dogdom, before judges who are almost always competent and still more often honest in their decisions.

The goal of the show dog is the championship, whose fifteen points must be awarded under no less than three judges, at three different times; in ratings that range from one point to five points, according to the number of dogs exhibited. To only the show's best dog of his or her special breed and sex are points awarded.

The master took Bruce to his first A.K.C. show with much nervousness. He knew how perfect was this splendid young collie of his. But he also knew that the judge might turn out to be some ultra-modernist who preferred daintiness of head and smallness of bone to Bruce's wealth of bone and thickness of coat and unusual size.

Modestly, therefore, he entered his dog only in the puppy and novice classes, and strove to cure his own show-fever by ceaseless grooming and rubbing and brushing of the youngster, whose burnished coat already stood out like the hair of an exotic beauty and who was fit in every way to make the showing of his life.

In intervals of polishing the bored puppy's coat, the master spent much time in covertly studying the collie judge, who was chatting with a group of friends at the ring's edge, waiting for his breed's classes to be called.

The master was partly puzzled, partly reassured, by the appearance of the little judge.

Angus McGilead's Scottish origins were still apparent in the very faintest burr of his speech and in the shrewd, pale eyes that peered, terrier-like, above his lean face and huge thatch of grizzling red beard. He was a man whose forebears had known collies as well as they knew their own children, and who rated a true collie above the price of mere money.

From childhood McGilead had made a life study of this, his favorite breed. As a result, he was admittedly the chief collie authority on either side of the ocean. This fact, and his solid honesty, made him a judge to be looked up to with a reverent faith which had in it a tinge of fear.

Such was the man who, at this three-point show, was to pass judgment on Bruce.

After an eternity of waiting, the last Airedale was led from the judging ring. The first collie class—"Puppies, male—" was chalked on the blackboard. The master, with one final ministration of the brush, snapped a ring leash on Bruce's collar, and led him down the collie section into the ring.

Four other puppies were already there. McGilead, his shrewd pale eyes half shut, was lounging in one end of the enclosure, apparently listening to something the ring steward was saying, but with his seemingly careless gaze and his keen mind wholly absorbed in watching the little procession of pups as it filed into the ring. Under the sandy lashes, his eyes caressed or criticized all the entrants in turn, boring into their very souls.

Then, as the last of the five walked in and the gate was shut behind them, he came to life. Approaching the huddle of dogs and their handlers, he singled out a shivering little puppy whose baby fur had not yet been lost in the rough coat of maturity and whose body was still pudgy and formless.

"How old is this pup?" he asked the woman who was tugging at the excited baby's leash.

"Six months, yesterday!" was the answer. "Isn't he a little beauty, Judge? Two days younger and he'd have been too young to show. He just comes in under the law. It's lucky he wasn't born two days later."

"No," gently contradicted McGilead, petting the downy little chap. "It's unlucky. Both for you and for him. The rules admit a pup to the show ring at six months. The rules are harsh, for they make him compete with dogs almost double his age. The puppy limit is from six to twelve months in shows. I don't want you to feel bad when I refuse to judge this little fellow. It isn't your fault, or his, that he hasn't begun to develop. But it would be like putting a child of five into competitive examination at school with a lad of twenty."

Motioning her gently to a far corner, he rasped at the others, "Walk your dogs, please!"

The procession started around the ring. Presently, McGilead waved the master to take Bruce to one side. Then he placed one after another of the remaining dogs on the central block and went over them with infinite care. At the end of the inspection, he beckoned the worried master to bring Bruce to the block. After running his hands lightly over and under the pup, he turned to the ring steward, who stood waiting with a ledger and a handful of ribbons.

Writing down four numbers in the book, McGilead took a blue and a red and a yellow and a white ribbon and advanced again toward the waiting exhibitors.

(And this, by the way, is the Big Moment to any dog handler—this instant when the judge is approaching with the ribbons. For sheer thrill, it makes roulette and horseracing seem childish.)

To the master, the little judge handed the blue ribbon. Then he awarded the red "second" and the yellow "third" and the white "reserve" to three others.

The recipient of the reserve snorted loudly.

"Say!" he complained. "Better judges than you have said this pup of mine is the finest collie of his age in America. What do you mean by giving him a measly reserve? What's the matter with him?"

"Compared with what's the matter with *you*," drawled McGilead, unruffled, "there's nothing at all the matter with him. Didn't anybody ever tell you how unsportsmanlike it is to argue a judge's decision in the ring? It's against the A.K.C. rules, too. I'm always glad, later, to explain my rulings to any one who asks me civilly. Since you want to know what's the matter with your dog, I'll tell you. He has spaniel ears. Fault number one. He is cow-hocked. Fault number two. He is apple-domed, and he's cheeky and he has a snipe-nose. Faults three, four, and five. He's long-bodied and swaybacked and over-shot and his undercoat is as thin as your own sportsmanship. He carries his tail high over his back, too. And his outer coat is almost curly. Those are all the faults I can see about him just now. He'll never win anything in any A.K.C. show. It's only fair to tell you that, to save you further money and to save you from another such breach of sportsmanship. That's all."

The master, quietly petting Bruce and telling him in a whisper what a grand dog he was, waited at an end of the ring for the next class—the novice—to be called.

Here the competition was somewhat keener. Yet the result was the same. And Bruce found himself with another dark blue ribbon in token of his second victory.

Then, when the winning dogs of every class were brought into the ring for "Winners"—to decide on the best male collie—Bruce received the winner's rosette and found himself advanced three points on his fifteen-point journey toward the championship.

When the collie judging was over and the master sat on the bench edge petting his victorious dog, Angus McGilead strolled over to where the winner lay and stood staring down on him.

"How old?" he asked, curtly.

"Twelve months next Tuesday," returned the Master.

"If he keeps on," pursued the dryly rasping voice, "you can say you own the greatest collie Angus McGilead has seen in ten years. It's a privilege to look at such a dog. A privilege. I'm not speaking, mind you, as the collie judge of this show, but as a man who has spent some fifty-odd years in studying the breed. I've not seen his like in many a day. I'll keep my eye on him."

And he was as good as his word. At every succeeding show to which the master took Bruce, he was certain to run into McGilead, there as a spectator, standing with head on one side, brooding over the physical perfections of Bruce. Always the little judge was brief in his conversation with the master. But always, he gazed upon Bruce as might an inspired artist on some still more inspired painting.

McGilead had been right in his prophecy as to the collie's future. Not only did Bruce keep on, but the passing months added new wealth and luster to his huge coat and new grace and shapeliness to his massive body, and a clearer and cleaner set of lines to his classic head.

Three more shows, two of them three-point exhibitions and one a single-pointer, brought him seven more points toward the championship. Then, on the day of the Collie Club of the Union's annual show, came the crowning triumph.

Thirty-two dogs were on hand, precisely the number, under the new rulings, to make it a five-point show. And Angus McGilead was the judge.

When McGilead gave Bruce the winner's rosette, which marked also his winning of the championship, the pale and shrewd old eyes were misted ever so little, and the hard and thin mouth was set like a gash.

It was as proud a moment in the little judge's life as it was in the master's. America once more had a champion collie—a young dog at that—at which McGilead could point with inordinate pride, when collie folk fell to bewailing the decadence of the breed in the Scottish man's adopted country.

"I gave him his first winners!" he bragged that night to a group of fellow countrymen, in a rare fit of expansiveness. "I gave him his first winners, first time he ever was showed. I said to myself when he swung into the ring that day—under twelve months old, mind you—I said, 'Angus, lad, yon's a *dog!*' I said. 'Watch him, Angus!' I said. 'For he's going far, is yon tyke,' I said. And what's he done? Won his championship in five shows. In less'n a year. And I'm the man who gave him the 'winners' that got him his championship. Watch him! He's due to last for years longer and to clean up wherever he goes. Remember I said so, when you see him going through every bunch he's shown against. He's the grandest dog in America today, is Brucie."

Again was the Scotsman's forecast justified. At the few shows that the master found time to take him to, during the next six years, Bruce won prize after prize. Age did not seem to lessen his physical perfection. And the years added to the regal dignity that shone about him like an almost visible atmosphere.

Watching from the ringside or presiding in the ring, Angus McGilead thrilled to the dog's every victory as if to the triumph of some beloved friend. There was an odd bond between the great dog and the little judge. Except for the mistress and the master, the collie felt scant interest in humanity at large. A one-man dog, he received the pettings of outsiders and the handling of judges with lofty coldness.

But at sight of McGilead, the plumed tail was at once awag. The deepset eyes would soften and brighten, and the long nose would wrinkle into a most engaging smile. Bruce loved to be talked to and petted by Angus. He carried his affection for the inordinately tickled judge to the point of trying to shake hands with him or romp with him in the ring, to the outward scandal and inward delight of the somber Scot.

"Can't you keep the beast from acting like he belonged to me when I'm judging him?" McGilead, once complained grumpily to the master. "A fine impression it makes on strangers, don't it, when they see him come wagging and grinning up to me and wanting to shake hands, or to roll over for me to play with him? One fool asked me, was it my own dog I gave the prize to. He said no outsider's dog would be making such a fuss over a judge. Try to keep him in better order in the ring, or I'll prove he isn't mine by 'giving him the gate' one of these days. See if I don't."

But he never did. And the master knew well that he never would. So it was that Bruce's career as a winner continued unbrokenly, while other champions came and went.

With dogs, as with horses, youth will be served. By the time a horse is six, his racing days are past, and he has something like twenty years of cart or carriage mediocrity ahead of him. His glory as a track king has fled forever.

And with dogs—whose average life of activity runs little beyond ten years—ring honors usually come in youth or not at all. Yes, and they depart with youth. The dog remains handsome and useful for years thereafter. But his head has coarsened. His figure has lost its perfection. His gait stiffens. In a score of ways he drops back from the standard required of winners. Younger dogs are put above him. And that is life—whether in kennel, or in stable, or in office, or in the courts of love. Youth wins.

Yet the passing years seemed to take no perceptible toll on Bruce. His classic head lost none of its fineness. His body remained limber and graceful and shapely. His coat was mightier than ever. Even McGilead's apprehensive and super-piercing glance could find no flaw, no sign of oncoming age.

The years had, before this, been nearly as kind to Angus, himself. Dry and wiry and small, he had neither shown nor felt the weight of advancing age. Yet now, passing his sixtieth milestone, an attack of rheumatic fever left him oddly heavy and slothful. Instead of taking the stairs two at a time, he set a foot on every step. And at the top of any very long flight, he was annoyed to find himself breathing absurdly hard.

He found himself, for the first time in his life, sneering at youth's gay spirits, and snubbing the vitality of his growing sons.

"Youth!" he snarled grimly once to the master, as they met at a show. "Everything's for youth, these days. It was plenty different when I was young. Just as a man begins to get seasoned and to know his way around, folks call him an oldster and fix up a place for him in the corner. Youth isn't the only thing in this world. Not by a long sight. Take Bruce here, for instance. (Yes, I'm talking about you, you big ruffian! Give me your paw, now, and listen to me tell how good you are!) Take Bruce here, for instance. Nearly eight years old. Eight in August, isn't it? As old, that is, as fifty-odd for a human. And look at him! Is there one of the young bunch of dogs that can win against him—under any judge that knows his business? Not a one of 'em. He's finer today than he was when he came out at his first show. Us oldsters can still hold our own, and a little more. Bring on your youngsters! Me and Brucie are ready for 'em all. (Hey, Big Boy? Gimme your other paw, like a gentleman! Not the left one.) Why, first time I set eyes on this dog I said to myself—"

"I've got something up at the Place that's due to give Bruce the tussle of his life in the show ring some day," bragged the master. "He's Bruce's own son, and grandson. That means he's pretty nearly seventy-five percent Bruce. And he shows it. His kennel name's 'Jock.' He's only eight months old now, and he's the living image of what Bruce was at his age. Best head I ever saw. Great coat, too, and carriage. He's the best of all

Bruce's dozens of pups, by far. I'm going to show him at the 'Charity' in September."

"Are you, though?" sniffed McGilead. "It happens I'm judging at the Charity. (Some liars can say I'm beginning to show my age. But I take note they keep on wanting me to judge, oftener'n ever.) And I'll be on the lookout for that wonderful pup of yours. All pups are wonderful, I notice. Till they get in the ring. Being old Bruce's son, this youngster of yours can't be altogether bad. I grant that. But I'll gamble he'll never be what his Dad is."

"You'll have the first say-so on that," answered the master. "I'm entering Bruce for 'Open, Any Color,' at the 'Charity.' (By the way, it's the old fellow's last show. I'm going to retire him from the game while he's still good.) Little Jock is entered for 'Puppy and Novice.' It's a cinch they'll come together before you, in 'Winners'!"

"And when they do," scoffed McGilead, "don't feel too bad if Bruce gets winners and the pup don't get a look in. Jock may never see a winners' class. Plenty of these promising world-beaters never do. You're as daft on this 'youth' notion as any of 'em. Here you've got the grandest collie in the States. And you turn your silly back on him and go cracking your jaw about an upstart pup of his that most likely has more flaws than fleas—and a bushel basketful of both. Grrh!"

Often, during the next three months, Angus found his mind dwelling reluctantly upon the newcomer. He was anxious to see the near-paragon. He realized he was all but prejudiced against the youngster by the master's boastful praise.

Then McGilead would pull himself up short. For he prided himself on his four-square honesty and his lack of prejudice in show ring matters. This absolute squareness had brought him where he was today—to the very foremost place among all dog-show judges. It had kept him respected and had kept his services in constant demand for decades, while showier and lesser judges had come and gone and had been forgotten.

This honesty of his was McGilead's obsession and pride in life. Yet, here he was, sight unseen, prejudiced against a dog, and that dog his adored Bruce's own son!

McGilead brought himself together sharply, cursed himself for an old blackguard, and sought to put the whole matter out of his mind. Yet somehow he found himself looking forward to the five-point Charity show more interestedly than to any such event in years.

It was one of McGilead's many points of professional ethics never to go near the collie section of any show until after his share of the judging should be over. Thus it was, on the day of the Charity show, his first glimpse of Jock was when the master led the youngster into the ring, when the puppy class was called.

Six other pups also were brought into the ring. McGilead, as ever, surveyed them with breathless keenness, from between his half-shut eyes—pretending all the while to be talking interestedly with the ring steward—while the procession filed in through the gate.

But his eyes, once singling out Jock, refused to focus on any other entrant. And he set his teeth in a twinge of wonder and admiration for the newcomer. What's more, he observed in him none of the fright, or curiosity, or awkwardness that is common for so many puppies on their first entrance to the show ring. The youngster seemed comfortably at home in the strange surroundings.

Nor was this unnatural. The master had made use of a simple trick that he had employed more than once before. Arriving at the show long before the judging had begun and while the first spectators were trailing in, he had led Jock at once to the ring, where, of course, neither the master nor the dog had, technically, any right to be at such a time.

First unleashing Jock, the master had let him roam at will for a few minutes around the strange enclosure, then had called the wandering collie over to him, fed him bits of fried liver and lured him into a romp. After which, the Master had sat down on the edge of the judging block, calling Jock to him, petting and feeding him for a few moments, and then persuading the pup to fall asleep at his feet.

Thus, when they re-entered the ring for the judging, Jock no longer regarded it as a strange and possibly terrifying place. To him the ring was now a familiar and friendly place, where he had played and slept and been fed and made much of. All its associations were pleasant in the puppy's memory. And he was mildly pleased to be there again.

McGilead's veiled eyes were minutely studying every motion and every inch of Bruce's young son. And as a dog lover he rejoiced at what he saw. The pup was all the master had said and far more. Nearly as tall and as strong of frame as his sire, Jock had Bruce's classic head and wondrous coat and the older dog's perfect and short-backed body, ear carriage, flawless foreface, true collie expression and grace of action, soundness, and build. Above all, Bruce had transmitted to him that same elusive air of regal dignity and nobility.

"Walk your dogs, please!" rasped the judge, starting out of his daze to a realization that the seven exhibitors were waiting for him to come to earth again.

As, seven years earlier, he had waved Bruce aside, that he might not be bothered in his judging of the lesser contestants, so, now, he bade the master take Jock into a corner while the parade and the preliminary examining went on. The master—this time not worried—obeyed.

And the scene of Bruce's debut was re-enacted, both in puppy and in novice classes. Not one competitor was worthy of a second's hesitation between himself and Jock.

Then, for a while, the tawny debutante was allowed to go back in peace to his bench, and the other classes were called. When "Open, Any Color," came up for judging, this most crucial of all classes had fine representation. Four sables, two tri-colors and two black dogs competed.

Yet, in all honesty, not one of the rest could equal old Bruce. The great dog stood forth, preeminently their superior. And, with the customary little tug of pleasure at his aged heart, McGilead awarded to his old favorite the squarely earned blue ribbon.

"The pup's a wonder," he told himself. "But the old dog is still the best of the lot. The best of *any* lot."

The regular classes were judged, and the best dog in each came into the ring for winners. At last, Bruce and Jock stood side by side on the judging block. The contest had narrowed down to them.

And now, for the first time, McGilead was able to concentrate all his attention and his judging prowess on a comparison of the two. For several minutes he eyed them. He made their handlers shift the dogs' positions. He went over them, like an inspired surgeon with his sensitive old fingers, though Bruce's body was already as familiar to his touch as is the keyboard to a pianist. He made them "show." He studied them from fifty angles.

Now to casual observers, Angus McGilead was going through his task with a perfunctory deftness that verged on boredom. The tired, half-shut eyes and the wrinkled brown face gave no hint of emotion. Yet, within the Scotsman's heart, a veritable hell of emotion was surging.

This prolonged examination was not necessary. He had known it was not necessary from the first instant he had seen the two dogs, sire and son, standing side by side on the block before him. He was dragging out the judging, partly in the vain hope of finding something to make him reverse his first opinion, but chiefly to settle, one way or another, the battle that was waging within him.

For, at once, his acutely practiced eye had discerned that Jock was the better dog. Not that he was better, necessarily, than Bruce had been a few years earlier. But previously unnoted marks of time on the older dog had sprung into sudden and merciless relief by comparison with the flawless youngster.

Seen alone, or with the average opponent, these would not have been noticeable. But alongside of Jock, the latter's perfection brought out every beginning flaw of age in his sire.

All this had been obvious to McGilead at his first critical glance. The younger dog was the better—only a shade the better, thus far, it is true. But by such shades are contests won—and lost.

No outsider—few professional judges—could have recognized the superiority of one of the competitors over the other. Yet McGilead recognized it as clearly as a lightning flash. And he saw his duty—the duty that lay plain before him.

He had given Bruce his earliest ring award. He had awarded Bruce the prize that gave the dog his championship. And now he must uncrown this collie he loved. For the first time he must pass Bruce over and give winners to another and younger dog. Youth will be served! His heart as sore as an ulcer, his pale and half-shut eyes smarting, the hot and impotent fury of old age boiling in his brain, Angus McGilead continued his meaningless and seemingly bored inspection of the two dogs.

He loved Bruce—better than ever before he had realized. He had always felt himself the marvelous collie's sponsor. And now—

Oh, why hadn't the dog's fool of an owner had sense enough to retire him from the ring before this inevitable downfall had come—this fate that lies craftily in wait for dog and horse and man who stay in the game too long?

The master had said this was to be the old dog's last show. His last show! And he must leave the ring—beaten! Beaten by a youngster, at that! A pup who had years and years of triumphs ahead of him. Surely the smugly perfect little tyke could have waited till his sire's retirement, before beginning his own career of conquest! He needn't have started out by winning dear old Bruce's scalp and by smashing the old dog's long record of victories!

Bruce! Glorious old Brucie, whose progress had been McGilead's own life monument! To slink out of the ring—at his very last show, too—defeated by a puppy! Oh, this rotten cult of youth—youth—*youth!* He and Bruce were both old numbers at last.

But were they?

Bruce, bored by the long wait, nudged the Scotsman's unmoving fist with his cold nose, and sought to shake hands. This diversion brought the judge back to earth.

A gust of red rage set McGilead's blood to swirling. On fierce impulse he straightened his bent figure and unveiled his sleepy-looking eyes in a glare of fury.

He laid both hands on the head of the gallant old dog whom he idolized.

"Bruce wins!" he proclaimed, his rasping voice as harsh as a file on rusty iron. "Bruce *wins!*"

Wheeling on the master, he croaked, in that same strained, rasping shout, the scrap of a schoolboy's quotation which had come often to his memory of late.

" 'It's safer playing with the lion's whelp than with the old lion dying!' " he mouthed. "Bruce wins! Retire him, now! 'Youth will be served.' But not till us oldsters are out of the way. Clear the ring!"

As he stomped from the enclosure he was buttonholed by a sporty-looking man whom he had met at many a show.

"Mr. McGilead," began the man, respectfully, "the Collie Club of the Union has appointed me a committee of one to engage you for judge at our annual show in November. Some of the members suggested a younger man. But the Old Guard held out for *you*. I was going to write, but—"

"It'd have done you no good!" growled McGilead, sick with shame. "Let me alone!"

"If it's a question of price—" urged the puzzled man.

"Price?" snarled McGilead, turning on him in fury. *"Price?* There's only one price. And I've paid it. I won't judge at your show! I'll never judge again at any show! My judging days are over! I'm a dead one! I'm an old, *old* man, I tell you! I'm in my dotage! I—why, I couldn't even trust myself any more to judge squarely. I'm *through!*"

LOCHINVAR BOBBY

W hen the first Angus Mackellar left his ancestral Lochbuy moors, he brought to America the big, shaggy, broad-headed collie dog he loved—the dog that had helped him herd his employer's sheep for the past five years.

Man and dog landed at Castle Garden, in New York, half a century before. From that time on, as for three hundred years earlier, no member of the Mackellar family was without a collie, the best and wisest to be found.

Evolution narrowed the heads and lightened the stocky frames of these collies as the decades crawled past.

Evolution changed the successive generations of Mackellars not at all, except to rub smoother their Highland burr and to make them serve America as ardently as ever their forefathers had served Scotland. But not one of them lost his hereditary love for the dog of the moors.

Which brings us by degrees to Jamie Mackellar, grandson of the emigrating Angus. Jamie was twenty-eight. His tough little body was so meagerly spare that his big heart and bigger soul were almost indecently exposed. For the rest, his speech still held an occasional word or two of handed-down ancestral dialect. In moments of excitement these inherited phrases came thicker, and with them a tang of Scots accent.

Jamie lived in a suburb of Midwestburg and in one of the suburb's least expensive houses. But the house had a yard. And the yard harbored a glorious old collie, a rare prize winner in his day. The house in front of the yard, by the way, harbored Jamie's Yorkshire wife and their two children, Elspeth and Donald.

Jamie divided his home time between the house and the open. So—after true Highland fashion—did the collie.

There were long rambles in the forests and the wild half-cleared land beyond the suburb—walks that meant as much to Jamie as to the dog, after the Scot had been driving a contractor's truck six days of the week for an adequate monthly wage.

Now, on Jamie's wages, the Mackellar family lived in comfort. But they had scant margin for the less practical luxuries of life. And in a sheepless and law-abiding region a high-quality collie is a nonpractical luxury. Yet Jamie would almost as soon have thought of selling one of his thick-legged children as of accepting any of the several good offers made him for the beautiful dog which had been his chum for so many years, the dog whose prize ribbons and cups from a score of local shows filled the trophy corner of the Mackellar living room.

Then, on a late afternoon—when the grand old collie was galloping delightedly across the street to meet his home-returning master—a delivery truck driven by a speed-drunk boy whizzed around the corner on the wrong side of the street.

The big dog died as he had lived—gallantly and without a whine. Gathering himself up from the muck of the road he walked steadfastly forward to meet the running Mackellar. As Jamie bent down to search the muddled body for injuries, the collie licked his master's dear hand, shivered slightly and fell limp across the man's feet.

When the judge heard the next morning that a raving little Scot had sprung to the door of the truck and had hauled from it a youth twice his size and had hammered the said youth into one hundred percent eligibility for a hospital bed, he listened gravely to the other side of the story and merely ordered Jamie to pay a minimal fine.

The released prisoner returned with bent head and scraped knuckles to a house which all at once had been left desolate. For the first time in centuries a Mackellar was without a collie.

During the next week the Midwestburg Kennel Association's annual dog show was held at the Fourth Regiment Armory. This show was one of the banner events of the year throughout western dog circles. Its rich cash prizes and its prestige drew breeders even from the Atlantic states to exhibit the best their kennels had to offer.

There, still hot and sore of heart, went Jamie Mackellar. Always during the three days of the Midwestburg dog show Jamie took a triple holiday and haunted the collie section and the ringside. Here more than once his dead chum had won a blue ribbon and cash over the show dogs from larger and richer kennels. And at such times Jamie Mackellar had rejoiced with a joy that was too big for words, and which could express itself only in a furtive hug of his collie's shaggy ruff.

Today, as usual, Jamie entered the barnlike armory among the very first handful of spectators. To his ears the reverberating clangor of a thousand barks was like battle music, as it echoed from the girdered roof and yammered incessantly on the eardrums.

As ever, he made his way at once to the collie section. A famous New York judge was to pass judgement upon this breed. And there was a turnout of nearly sixty collies, including no less than five from the east. Four of these came from New Jersey, which breeds more high-class collies than do any three other states in the Union.

It was Jamie's rule to stroll through the whole section for a casual glance over the collies, before stopping at any of the benches for a closer appraisal. But today he came to a halt before he had passed the first row of stalls. His pale-blue eyes were riveted on a single dog.

Lying at lazily majestic ease on the straw of a double-size bench was a huge dark-sable collie. A full twenty-six inches high at the shoulder and weighing perhaps seventy-five pounds, this dog gave no hint of coarseness or of oversize. He was moulded as by a super-sculptor. His wellsprung ribs and mighty chest and lion-like shoulders were fit complements to the classically exquisite yet splendidly strong head.

His tawny coat was as heavy as a lion's mane. The outer coat—save where it turned to spun silk on the head—was harsh and wavy. The undercoat was as impenetrably soft as the breast of an eider duck. From gladiator shoulders the graceful, powerful body sloped back to hips which spoke of lightning speed and endurance. The tulip ears had never known weights or pincers. The head was a true wedge, from every viewpoint. The deep-set dark eyes were unbelievably perfect in expression and placement.

Here was a collie! Here was a dog whose sheer perfection made Jamie Mackellar catch his breath in wonder, and then begin pawing frantically at his show catalogue. He read, half aloud:

729: *Lochinvar Kennels.* CHAMPION LOCHINVAR KING. *Lochinvar Peerless—Lochinvar Queen*

Then followed the birth date and the words "Breeder owner."

Jamie Mackellar's pale eyes opened yet wider and he stared at the collie with tenfold interest, an interest which held in it a splash of reverence. Jamie was a faithful reader of the dog press. And for the past two years Champion Lochinvar King's many pictures and infinitely more victories had stirred his admiration. He knew the dog, as a million Americans know Man-o'-War, the champion racehorse.

Now he eagerly scanned the wonder collie. Every detail—from the level mouth and chiselled, wedge-shaped head and stern eyes with their true "look of eagles," to the fox-brush tail with its sidewise swirl at the tip—Jamie scanned with the delight of an artist who comes for the first time on a Velasquez of which he has read and dreamed. Never in his dog-starred life had the little man beheld so perfect a collie. It was an education to him to study such a marvel.

Two more men came up to the bench. One was wearing a linen jacket, and fell to grooming King's incredibly massive coat with expert hands. The other—a plump giant in exaggeratedly vivid clothes—chirped to the dog and ran careless fingers over the silken head. The collie waved his plumed tail in response to the caress. Recalling how coldly King had ignored his own friendly advances, Jamie Mackellar addressed the plump man in deep respect.

"Excuse me, sir," said he humbly, "but might you be Mr. Frayne— Mr. Lucius Frayne?"

The man turned with insolent laziness, eyed the shabby little figure from head to foot, and nodded. Then he went back to his inspection of King.

Not to be rebuffed, Mackellar continued:

"I remember reading about you when you started the Lochinvar Kennels, sir. That'll be—let's see—that'll be the best part of eight years ago. And three years back you showed Lochinvar Peerless out here—this great feller's sire. I'm proud to meet you, sir."

Frayne acknowledged this tribute by another nod, this time not even bothering to turn toward his admirer.

Mackellar pattered on:

"Peerless got Americanbred and Limit, that year, and he went to Reserve Winners. If I'd 'a' been judging, I'd of gave him Winners over Rivers Pride, that topped him. Pride was a good inch-and-a-half too short in the brush. And the sable grew away too far from his eyes. Gave 'em a roundish, big look. He was just a wee bit overshot too. And your Peerless outshowed him, besides. But good as Peerless was, he wasn't a patch on this son of his you've got here today. Gee, but it sure looks like you was due to make a killing, Mr. Frayne."

And now the breeder deigned to face the man whose words were pattering so meekly into his unhearing ears. Frayne realized this little chap was not one of the ignorant bores who pester exhibitors at every big show; but that he spoke, and spoke well, the language of the initiate. No breeder is above catering to intelligent praise of his dog. And Frayne warmed mildly toward the devotee.

"Like him, do you?" he asked, indulgently.

"Like him?" echoed Mackellar. "*Like* him? Man, he's fifty percent the best I've set eyes on. And I've seen a hantle of 'em."

"Take him down, Roke," Frayne bade his linen-coated kennel man. "Let him move about a bit. You can get a real idea of him when you see his action," he continued to the dazzled Mackellar. "How about that? Hey?"

At the unfastening of his chain, Lochinvar King stepped majestically to the floor and for an instant stood gazing up at his master. He stood as might an idealized statue of a collie. Mackellar caught his breath and stared. Then with expert eyes he watched the dog's perfect action as the kennel man led him up and down for half a dozen steps.

"He's—he's better even than I thought he could be," sighed Jamie. "He looked too good to be true. Lord, it does tickle a man's heartstrings to see such a dog! I—I lost a mighty fine collie a few days back," he went on confidingly. "Not in King's class, of course, sir. But a grand old dog. And—and he was my chum, too. I'm fair sick with grief over him. It kind of crumples a feller, don't it, to lose a chum collie? One reason I wanted to come here early today was to look around and see were any of the for-sale ones inside my means. I've never been without a collie before. And I want to get me one—a reg'lar first-rater, like the old dog— as quick as I can. It's lonesome-like not to have a collie laying at my feet, evening times, or running out to meet me."

Lucius Frayne listened now with real interest to the little man's timid complaint.

As Mackellar paused, shamefaced at his own show of feeling, the owner of the Lochinvar Kennels asked suavely:

"What were you counting on paying for a new dog? Or hadn't you made up your mind?"

"Once in a blue moon," replied Mackellar, "a pretty good one is for sale cheap. Either before the judging or if the judge don't happen to fancy his type. I—well, if I had to, I was willing to spend a thousand—if I could get the right dog. But I thought maybe I could get one for less."

With still more interest Frayne beamed down on the earnest little Mackellar.

"It's a pity you can't go higher," said he with elaborate nonconcern. "Especially since King here has caught your fancy. You see, I've got a four-month-old pup of King's back home. Out of my winning Lochinvar Lassie, at that. I sold all the other six in the litter. Sold 'em at gilt-edge prices, on account of their breeding. This little four-monther I'm speaking about—he was so much the best of the lot that I was planning to keep him. He's the dead image of what King was at his age. He's got 'future champion' written all over him. But—well, since you've lost your chum dog and since you know enough of collies to treat him right— well, if you were back east where you could look him over, I'd—well, I'd listen to your offer for him."

He turned toward his kennel man as if ending the talk. Like a well-cued phonograph, the linen-clad functionary spoke up.

"Oh, Mr. Frayne!" he blathered, ceasing to groom King's wondrous coat and clasping both dirty hands together. "You wouldn't ever go and sell the little 'un? Not Lochinvar Bobby, sir? Not the best pup we ever bred? Why, he's twenty percent. better than what King here was at his age. You'll make a champion of him by the time he's ten months old. Just like Doc Burrows did with his Queen Betty. He's a second Howgill Rival, that pup is—a second Sunnybank Sigurd! You sure wouldn't go selling him? Not Bobby?"

"There'll be other Lochinvar King pups along in a few weeks, Roke," argued Frayne. "And this man has just lost his only dog. If—What a pair of fools we are!" he broke off, laughing loudly. "Here we go gabbling about selling Bobby, and our friend here isn't willing to go above a thousand dollars for a dog!"

The kennel man, visibly relieved, resumed operations on King with brush and cloth. But Mackellar stood looking up at Frayne as a hungry pup might plead dumbly with some human who had just taken from him his dinner bone.

"If—if he's due to be a second Lochinvar King," faltered Jamie, "I—I s'pose he'd be way beyond me. I'm a truck driver, you see, sir. And I've got a wife and a couple of kids. So I wouldn't have any right to spend too much, just for a dog—even if I had the cash. But—gee, but it's a chance!"

Sighing softly in resignation, he took another long and admiring gaze at the glorious Lochinvar King, and then made as though to move away. But Lucius Frayne's dog-loving heart evidently was touched by Jamie's admiration for the champion and by the hinted tale of his chum dog's death. He stopped the sadly departing Mackellar.

"Tell me more about that collie you lost," he urged. "How'd he die? What was his breeding? Ever show him?"

Now perhaps there breathes some collie man who can resist one of those three questions about his favorite dog. Assuredly none lives who can resist all three. Mackellar, in a couple of seconds, found himself prattling eagerly to this sympathetic giant, telling of his dog's points and wisdom and lovableness, and of the prizes he had won, and, last of all, the tale of his ending.

Frayne listened avidly, nodding his head and grunting consolation from time to time. At last he burst forth, on impulse:

"Look here! You know dogs. You know collies. I see that. I'd rather have a Lochinvar pup go to a man who can appreciate him, as you would, and who'd give him the sort of home you'd give him, than to sell him for three times as much, to some mucker. I'm in this game for love of the breed, not to skin my neighbors. Lochinvar Bobby is yours, friend, for fifteen hundred dollars. I hope you'll say no," he added with his loud laugh, "because I'd rather part with one of my back teeth. But anyhow I feel more decent for making the offer."

Popeyed and scarlet and breathing fast, Jamie Mackellar did some mental arithmetic. Fifteen hundred dollars was a breathtaking sum. Nobody knew it better than did he. But—oh, there stood Lochinvar King! And King's best pup could be Jamie's for that amount.

Then Mackellar bethought him of an extra job that was afloat just now in Midwestburg—a job at trucking explosives by night from the dynamite factory over on the heights to the railroad. It was a job few people cared for. The roads were bumpy. And dynamite was a ticklish explosive. Even the company's offer of high wages and short hours had not brought forth many eager drivers.

Yet Jamie was a careful driver. He knew he could minimize the risk. And by working three hours a night for three weeks he could clean up the price of the wonderful pup without going down into the family's slim funds.

"You're—you're on!" he babbled, shaking all over with pure happiness. "In three weeks I'll send you a money order. Here's—here's—let's see—here's twenty-seven dollars to bind the bargain."

"Roke," said Frayne, ignoring his kennel man's almost weeping protests, "scribble out a bill of sale for Lochinvar Bobby. And see he's shipped here the day we get this gentleman's money order for the balance of the price. And don't forget to send him Bobby's papers at the same time. Seeing it's such a golden bargain for him, he'll not grudge paying the shipping, too. I suppose I'm a fool, but—say! Hasn't a man got to do a generous action once in a while? Besides, it's all for the good of the breed."

Ten minutes later Mackellar tore away his ardent eyes from inspection of the grand dog whose best pup he was so soon to earn, and pattered on down the collie section.

Then and then only did Lucius Frayne and Roke look at each other. Long and earnestly they looked. And Frayne reached out his thick hand and shook his kennel man's soiled fingers. He shook them with much heartiness. He was a democratic sportsman, this owner of the famed Lochinvar Kennels. He did not disdain to grasp the toil-hardened hand of his honest servitor, especially at a time like this.

Lochinvar King that day cut his path straight through "Open, Sable-and-White" and "Open, Any Color" to "Winners," in a division of fifty-eight collies. Then he won the cup and the cash awards for Best of Breed, also four other cash prizes. And in the classic special for Best Dog in Show he came as near to winning as ever a present-day collie can hope to at so large a show. Jamie Mackellar, with a vibrating pride and a sense of personal importance, watched and applauded every win of his pup's matchless sire.

"In another year," he mused raptly, "I'll be scooping up them same specials with King's gorgeous little son. This man Frayne is sure one of the best fellers on earth."

Four weeks and two days later, an old slatted crate labeled "Lochinvar Collie Kennels," was delivered at Jamie's door. It arrived a bare ten minutes after Mackellar came home from work. All the family gathered around it in the kitchen, while, with hands that would not stay steady, the head of the house proceeded to unfasten the clamps which held down its top.

It was Jamie Mackellar's great moment, and his wife and children were touched almost to hysteria by his long-sustained excitement.

Back went the crate lid. Out onto the kitchen floor shambled a dog.

For a long minute, as the newly arrived collie stood blinking and trembling in the light, everybody peered at him without word or motion. Jamie's jaw had gone slack at first sight of him, and it still hung open.

The puppy was undersized. He was scrawny and angular and all but shapeless. At a glance, he might have belonged to any breed or to many breeds or to none. His coat was sparse and short and kinky, and through it glared patches of lately healed eczema. The coat's color was indeterminate—what there was of it. Nor had four days in a tight crate improved its looks.

The puppy's chest was pitifully narrow. The sprawling legs were out at elbow and cow-hocked. The shoulders were noteworthy by the absence of any visible sign of them. The brush was an almost hairless rat-tail. The spine was sagged and slightly awry.

But the head was the most awful part of the newcomer. Its expressionless eyes were sore and dull. Its ears hung limp as a setter's. The nose and foreface were as snubbed and broad as a Saint Bernard's. The slack jaw was badly overshot. The jowls showed a marked tendency to cheekiness and the skull seemed to be developing an apple-shaped dome in place of the semi-platform which the top of a collie's head ought to present.

Breed dogs as carefully and as scientifically as you will; once in a while some such specimen will be born into even the most blue-blooded litter

—a specimen whose looks defy all laws of clean heredity; a specimen which it would be gross flattery to call a mutt.

One of three courses at such times can be followed by the luckless breeder: To kill the unfortunate misfit; to give it away to some child who may or may not maul it; or to swindle a buyer into paying a respectable price for it.

Lucius Frayne had chosen the third course. And no law could touch him for the deal. He had played safe in his dirty trade.

Mackellar had bought the dog, sight unseen. Frayne had guaranteed nothing save the pedigree, which was flawless. He had said the creature was the image of King at the same age. But he had said it in the presence of no witness save his own kennel man.

No—Frayne, like many another shrewd professional dog breeder, had played safe. And he had gained fifteen hundred dollars, in hard-earned hoardings, for a beast whose true cash value was less than almost nothing. He had not even bothered to give the cur a high-sounding pedigree name.

There stood, or crouched, the trembling and whimpering wisp of worthlessness, while the Mackellar family looked on in shocked horror. To add to the pup's ludicrous aspect, an enormous collar hung dangling from his neck. Frayne had been thrifty in even this minor detail. Following the letter of the transportation rules, he had "equipped the dog with suitable collar and chain." But the chain, which Jamie had unclasped in releasing the pup from the crate, had been rusty and flimsy. The collar had been cast off by some grown dog. To keep it from slipping off over the puppy's head Roke had fastened to it a twist of wire whose other end was enmeshed in the scattering short hairs of the youngster's neck. From this collar's ring still swung the last year's license tag of its former wearer.

It was little Elspeth who broke the awful spell of silence.

"Looks—looks kind of—of measly, don't he?" she volunteered.

"*Jamie Mackellar!*" shrilled her mother, finding voice and wrath in one swift gasp. "You—you went and gambled with your life on them explosion trucks—and never told me a word about it till it was over—just to earn money to buy—to buy—*that!*"

Then Jamie spoke. And at his first sputtered sentence his wife shooed the children out of the room in scandalized haste. But from the cottage's farthest end she could hear her spouse's light voice still raised to shrill falsetto. He seemed to be in earnest conversation with his Maker, and the absence of his wife and children from the room lent luster and scope to his vocabulary.

Outside, the night was settling in bitterly cold. A drifting snow was sifting over the frozen earth. The winter's worst cold spell was beginning. But in the firelit kitchen a hope-blasted and swindled man was gripped by a boiling rage that all the frigid outer world could not have cooled.

Presently, through his sputtering soliloquy, Mackellar found time and justice to note that Lochinvar Bobby was still shaking with the cold of his long ride through the snow from the station. And sullenly the man went to the refrigerator in the back areaway for milk to warm for the sufferer.

He left the door open behind him. Into the kitchen seeped the deadly chill of night. It struck the miserable Bobby and roused him from the apathy of fright into which his entry to the bright room had immersed him.

The fright remained, but the inability to move was gone. Fear had been born in his cringing soul from the harsh treatment meted out to him in the place of his birth by kennel men who scoffed at his worthlessness. Fear had increased fiftyfold by his long and noisy journey across half the continent. Now fear came to a climax.

He had cowered in helpless terror before these strangers, here in the closed room. He had sensed their hostility. But now for an instant the strangers had left him. Yes, and the back door was standing ajar—the door to possible escape from the unknown dangers which beset him on all sides.

Tucking his ratlike tail between his cow-hocks, Bobby put down his head and bolted. Through the doorway he scurried, dodging behind the legs of Jamie Mackellar as he fled through the areaway. Jamie heard the scrambling footfalls, and turned in time to make a belated grab for the fleeing dog.

He missed Bobby by an inch, and the man's gesture seemed to the pup a new menace. Thus had Roke and the other kennel men struck him in early days, or had seized him by tail or hind leg as he fled in terror from their beatings.

Out into the unfenced yard galloped the panic-driven Bobby. And through the pitch blackness Mackellar stumbled in futile pursuit. The sound of Jamie's following feet lent new speed to the cowed youngster. Instead of stopping after a few moments, he galloped on, with his ridiculous wavering and sidewise gait.

Mackellar lived on the outskirts of the suburb, which, in turn, was on the outskirts of the city. By chance or by instinct Bobby struck out for the rocky ridge which divided denser civilization from the uncleared wilderness and the patches of farm country to the north. The puppy did not stop running until, puffing, he had topped the ridge's summit. There he came to a shambling halt and peered fearfully around him.

On the ridge crest the wind was blowing with razor sharpness. It cut like a billion whiplashes through the sparse coat and against the sagging ribs of the pup. It drove the snow needles into his watering eyes, and it stung the blown-back insides of his sensitive ears. He cowered under its pitiless might as under a thrashing, and again he began to whimper and to sob.

Below him, in the direction from which he had wormed his slippery way up the ridge, lay the squalid, flat bit of plain with its sprinkle of mean houses; behind it, the straggling suburb whence he had escaped; and behind that, the far-reaching tangle of glare and blackness which was Midwestburg, with miles of lurid light reflection on the low-hanging clouds.

Turning, the puppy looked down the farther slope of his ridge to the rolling miles of forest and clearing, with wide-scattered farmsteads and cottages. The wilds seemed less actively and noisily terrifying than the glare and muffled roar of the city behind him. And, since anything was better than to cower freezing there in the wind's full path, Bobby slunk down the ridge's northern flank and toward the naked black woodlands beyond its base.

The rock edges and the ice cut his uncallused splay feet. Even out of the wind, the chill gnawed through coat and skin. The world was a miserable place to do one's living in. What's more, Bobby had not eaten in more than twenty-four hours, although a pup of his age is supposed to be fed no fewer than four times a day.

The rock-strewn ridge having been passed, the going became easier. Here, on the more level ground, a snow carpet made it softer, if colder. No longer running, but at a loose-jointed wolf trot, Bobby entered the woods. A quarter mile farther on, he stopped again, at the sight of something which loomed up at a height of perhaps three feet above the half-acre of cleared ground about it.

He had strayed into the once-popular Blake's Woods picnic grove, and the thing which arrested his sick glance was the dancing platform which had been erected at the grove's geometrical center.

Years ago, Blake's Woods had been a favorite outing ground for Midwestburg's workers. The coming of the interurban bus, which brought Boone Lake Beach within half an hour of the city, had turned these woods into a dead loss as far as local pleasure seekers were concerned. The benches had been split up or stolen or had rotted. The trim central patch of green grass had been left to grow successive unmown harvests of ragweed.

The dancing platform, with its once-smooth floor and the bright-painted lattice which ran around its base, was sharing the fate of the rest of the grove. The floor was sunken and pitted. The laths of the lattice had fallen away in one or two places, and everywhere they had been washed free of paint.

Bobby's aimless course took him past one end of the platform, as soon as he discovered it was harmless and deserted. A furtive sidelong glance at the latticed stretch showed him a weed-masked hole some two feet square, where the laths had been ripped away or had been kicked in. The sight awoke vague memories, centuries old, in the artificially reared pup. Thus had his wolf forbears seen, and explored for den purposes, gaps between rocks or under windfalls. Bobby, moving with scared caution, crept up to the opening, sniffed its musty interior, and, step by step, ventured in under the platform.

Here it was still bitter cold, yet it was noticeably warmer than in the open. Year after year, dead leaves had drifted through the gap. Piles of them lay ankle deep near the entrance. Down into the thickest of the piles the wretched puppy wiggled his shivering way. There he lay, still shaking, but gaining what scant comfort he might from the warmth of the leaves beneath and around him.

Presently from sheer nervous fatigue he slept.

It was past midnight when Bobby awoke. He was awakened less by cold than by ravening hunger. His was not the normal increase of appetite that had come upon him at such times as the Lochinvar kennel men had been an hour or so late with his dinner. This was the first phase of famine.

Fear and discomfort had robbed him of hunger throughout the train journey. But now he was safely away from the strangers who had seemed to menace his every move, and he had had a few hours of sleep to knit his frayed nerves. He was more than hungry. He was famished. All his nature cried out for food.

Now, never in his brief life had Lochinvar Bobby found his own meals. Never had he so much as caught a mouse or rifled a garbage pail. He had passed all his time in a sanitary man-made kennel run and hutch. He had not had the human companionship which sharpens a collie's brain as much as does stark need. And he had no experience with food, except that which had been served him in a dish. He did not know that food grows in any other form or place.

But here there was no dish heaped with scientifically balanced, if uninspired, rations. Here there was no manner of food at all. Bobby nosed about among the dead leaves and the mold of his new-found den. Nothing was there which his sense of smell recognized as edible. And goaded by the scourge of hunger he ventured out again into the night.

The wind had dropped. But the cold had only intensified, and a light snow was still sifting down.

Bobby stood and sniffed. Far off, his sensitive nostrils told him, was human habitation. Presumably that meant food was there, too. Humans and food, in Bobby's experience, always went together. The pup followed the command of his scent and trotted dubiously toward the distant man-scent.

In another quarter-hour the starving pup was sniffing about the locked kitchen door of a farmhouse. Within, he could smell milk and meat and bread. But that was all the good it did him. Timidly he skirted the house for a way in. He had almost completed the round when a stronger odor struck his senses. It was a smell which in the past he would have disregarded. But, with the primal impulse of famine, other long-buried traits were stirring in the back of his necessity-sharpened brain.

His new scent was not of prepared food, but of hot and living prey. Bobby paused by the unlatched door of the farm chicken coop. Tentatively he scratched at the whitewashed panel. Under the pressure the door swung inward. Out gushed a pleasant warmth and a greatly increased repetition of the whiff which had drawn him to the henhouse.

Just above him, well within reach, perched fifteen or twenty feathery balls of varicolored fluff. And famine did the rest.

Acting on some impulse wholly beyond his understanding, Bobby sprang up and drove his white teeth deep into the breast of a Plymouth Rock hen.

Instantly, his ears were assailed by a most unearthly racket. The quiet hencoop was filled with high-pitched squawks and was alive with feathers. All Bobby's natural fear urged him to drop this flapping and squawking hen and to run for his life.

But something infinitely more potent than fear had taken hold of him. Through his fright surged a sensation of mad rapture. He had set teeth in live prey. Blood was hot in his nostrils. Quivering flesh was twisting and struggling between his tense jaws. For the moment he was a primitive forest beast.

Still gripping his noisy five-pound burden, he galloped out of the hencoop and across the barnyard, heading instinctively for the lair in which he had found a soft bed and safety from human intruders. As he fled he heard a man's bellowing voice. A light showed in an upper window of the house. Bobby ran the faster.

The hen was heavy, for so spindly a killer. But Bobby's overshot jaws held firm. He dared not pause to eat his kill until he should be safely away from the shouting man.

Stumbling into his platform den, half dead with hunger and fatigue, the dog sought his bed of leaves. And there he feasted, rather than ate. For never before had he known such a meal. And when the last edible morsel of it was swallowed, he snuggled happily down in his nest and slept.

Poultry bones are the worst and most dangerous fare for any domesticated dog. Their slivers tear murderously at throat and stomach and intestines, and have claimed their victims by the hundred. Yet since the beginning of time, wild animals such as foxes and wolves, have fed with impunity on such bones. No naturalist knows just why. And for some reason Bobby was no more the worse for his orgy of crunched chicken bones than a coyote would have been.

He awoke late in the morning. Some newborn sense, in addition to his normal fear, warned him to stay in his den throughout the daylight hours. And he did so, sleeping part of the time and part of the time nosing about amid the flurry of feathers in vain search for some overlooked bone or fragment of meat.

Dusk and hunger drove him forth again. And, as before, he sought the farmstead which had furnished him with so delicious a meal. But as he drew near, the sound of voices from indoors and the passing of an occasional silhouette across the bright window shades of the kitchen warned him of danger.

When the kitchen light was blown out, he ventured to the chicken coop where he found the door too well closed to yield to his hardest scratch. Miserably hungry and disappointed, he slunk away.

Bobby visited three farms that night before he found another with an unlatched henhouse door. There the events of the preceding evening were repeated. Lugging an eight-pound Dominic rooster, Bobby made for his mile-distant lair. Behind him again raged sound and fury. The eight-pound bird with its dangling legs and tail feathers kept tripping up the fleeing dog, until, acting again on instinct, Bobby slung the swaying body over his shoulder, fox fashion, and thus made his way with less discomfort.

By the third night the collie had taken another long step on his journey backward to the wild. When a dog kills a chicken everyone within half a mile is likely to be drawn by the sound. When a fox or wolf or coyote kills a chicken, the deed is done in skillful silence, with no squawks or flurry of feathers to tell the story. Nature teaches the killer this secret. And Nature taught it to Bobby, as she has taught it to other gone-wild dogs.

As a result, his further depredations left no uproar behind them. Also, he soon learned the vulpine art of hoarding—in other words, when safety permitted, to stay on the ground until he had not only slain but eaten one chicken, and then to carry another bird back to his lair for future use. It cut down the peril of too many trips to neighboring coops.

In time he learned to rely less and less on the closely guarded chickens in the vicinity of his den, and to roam the farm country for a radius of ten or more miles in search of food. The same queer new instinct taught him infinite craft in keeping away from humans and in covering his tracks.

He was doing no more than do thousands of foxes throughout the world. There was no miracle in his newly found deftness as a forager. Nature was merely telling her ancient and simple secrets to a wise little brain no longer too clogged by association with mankind to learn them.

There was a profitable sideline to Bobby's chicken hunts. The wilder woods back of Midwestburg abounded in rabbits for such as had the wit to find them. And Bobby acquired the wit.

Incredibly soon, he learned the wolf's art of tracking a cottontail and of stalking the prey until the moment that a lightning dash and a blood-streaked swirl in the snow marked the end of the chase. Squirrels, too,

The police dog halted, growling far down
in his throat.
Lochinvar Bobby, page 85

He was red-gold and white of coat—
a big, slender youngster.
"One Minute Longer," page 99

and an occasional unwary partridge or smaller bird, were added to the collie's menu. And more than once, as he grew stronger, Bobby lugged homeward over his shoulder a twenty-pound lamb from some distant sheepfold.

Nature had played a cruel trick on Lochinvar Bobby by bringing him into the world as the puny and defective runt of a royal litter. It had threatened his life by casting him loose in the winter woods. But at that point Nature seemed to repent of the unkindness to the poor helpless atom of colliehood. It taught him the closely guarded secrets of the awful Live-on-One-Another ritual.

As winter grew soggy at the far approach of spring, Bobby found less and less trouble in making a nightly run of thirty miles in search of meals or in carrying back to his lair the heaviest of burdens.

Feasting on raw meat—and plenty of it—living in the open, with the icy cold for his bedfellow, he was taking one of the only two courses left to those who must forage or die. Readily enough he might have dwindled and starved. The chill weather might have snuffed out his gangling life. Instead, the cold and the exposure, and the necessary exercise, and the life according to forest nature, and the rich supply of meat that was his for the catching—all these had worked wonders on the spindly runt.

His narrow chest had filled out from much lung work. His shoulders, from the same cause and from incessant night running, had taken on a splendid breadth. His gawky, shambling body grew rapidly. The overshot puppy jaw was leveling. And as his frame grew it shaped itself along lines of powerful grace, such as Nature gives to the leopard and to the stag. Incessant exposure to the cold had changed his sparse covering of hair to a coat whose thickness and length and texture would have been the wonder of the dog-show world. In brief, his mode of life was achieving for him what all the kennel experts and vets could not have accomplished.

It had been a case of kill or cure. Bobby was cured.

After the departure of the snows and the zero-degree nights, and before the leaves made secret progress safe through forest and meadow,

Bobby knew a period of leanness. True, he foraged as before, but he did it at far greater risk and with less certainty of results.

For—he could not guess why—the countryside was infested nowadays with armed men, men who carried rifles or shotguns and who not only scoured hill and valley by daylight but also lurked outside chicken coops and sheepfolds by night.

Of course, by day Bobby could avoid them—and he did—by lying close in his den. And at night his amazingly keen sense of smell enabled him to skirt them, out of gunshot range, as they waited at barn door or at fold gate. But such necessity for caution played havoc with his chances for easily acquired food. And for the most part he had to fall back on rabbit-catching or to traveling far afield—until the thickening of foliage made his hunting excursions safer from detection by human eye.

There was sufficient reason for all this patrolling of the district. During the past few months word had seeped through the farm country that a wolf was at large in the long-wolfless region, and that he was slaughtering all manner of livestock, from pullets to newborn calves.

No dog, it was argued, could be the killer. For no known dog could slay so silently and cover his tracks with such consummate skill. Nor could a fox carry away a lamb of double its own weight. The marauder must be a wolf. And old-timers raked up yarns of the superhumanly clever exploits of lone wolves, in the days when populous Midwestburg was a trading post.

The county farmers' association took up the matter and offered a bounty for the wolf's scalp and ears. It was a slack time on the farms— the period between woodcutting and early planting. It was a slack time in Midwestburg, too; several mills having shut down for a couple of months.

Thus, farmers and factory workers amused themselves by making a try for the bounty and for the honor of bagging the super-wolf. It was pleasant if profitless sport for the hunters. But it cut down Bobby's rations, until farm work and reopening mills called off the quest. Then

life went on as before—after a buckshot graze on the hip had taught the
collie to beware of guns and to know their scent.

So the fat summer drowsed along. And so autumn brought again to
the northern air the tang which started afresh the splendid luxuriance of
the tawny coat which Bobby had shed during the first weeks of spring.

Late in December the dog had a narrow escape from death. A farmer,
furious at the demise of his best Jersey calf, went gunning for the mysterious wolf. With him he took along a German shepherd. He had borrowed the dog for the hunt, lured by its master's tales of his pet's
invincible ferocity.

Man and dog had searched the woods in vain all day, some five miles
to the north of Bobby's cave. At early dusk they were heading homeward
through a rock gulch.

The wind was blowing strongly from the north. Midway through the
gulch the dog halted, back abristle, growling far down in his throat. The
man looked up.

As he did so, Bobby topped the cliff which formed the gulch's
northerly side. The collie was on his way to a farm in the valley beyond
which he had not visited for so long a time that its occupants might
reasonably be supposed to have relaxed some of their unneighborly vigilance. The wind from the north kept him from smelling or hearing the
two in the gully a hundred feet to the south of him.

Yet reaching the summit, Bobby paused, his usual caution bidding
him to search the lower grounds for signs of danger, before traveling
farther by fading daylight in such an exposed position.

It was then that the farmer saw him clearly for the best part of two
seconds, silhouetted against the dying sunset. The man knew little
enough of collies, and less of wolves. And his mental vision was set for a
wolf. Thus, to the best of his belief, a wolf was what he saw. But he saw
also something he had not expected to see.

The last rays of the sun glinted on a bit of metal that swung beneath
Bobby's shaggy throat; metal that had been worn bright by constant
friction with the dog's ruff.

Thanks to the twist of wire which had been fastened into his hair,

Bobby had not slipped the leather collar with which Frayne had equipped him. And later his swelling muscular neck had been large enough to hold it on. From its ring the old license tag still dangled.

Up went the farmer's gun. He fired both barrels. As he pressed the two triggers at once, the dog made a rush for the collie. The farmer chanced to be just in front of his canine companion. The dog sought a shortcut to reach his foe by diving between the marksman's slightly spread legs. The two gun barrels were fired straight upward into the sky, and the tripped-up hunter sat down with extreme suddenness on a pointed jut of rock.

By the time he could focus his maddened gaze on the cliff top again, Bobby had vanished. The other dog was charging over the summit at express-train speed. The farmer shook an impotent fist after the disappearing spoiler of his aim.

"I hope he licks the life out of you if you ever catch up with him, you bunglin' fool!" he bellowed.

His wish came true. Next day, in a hollow a mile farther on, the body of the German shepherd was found, twenty slashes on his grayish hide and one through his jugular. No German shepherd ever lived that could catch up with a galloping collie who did not want to be caught. Bobby had varied a career of profit with a moment or two of real pleasure.

Two days later, in the Midwestburg *Herald*, Jamie Mackellar read the account of this fragmentary drama. He scanned it with no deep interest. Tales of the wolf had grown stale to *Herald* readers. But suddenly his attention focused itself on the line:

"Mr. Gierson declares that a small disk of metal was suspended from the throat of the brute."

Jamie laid down the paper and went into executive session with his own memories. A disk of metal suspended from the throat of an animal means but one thing: It is a license tag. Never has such a tag been fastened to a wolf.

Back into Mackellar's memory came the picture of a poor shivering waif from whose meager and almost naked throat hung a huge collar—a collar affixed by wire which was wound into such sparse strands of hair as could be made to support it.

On the morning after the next snowfall, Jamie took a day off. Carrying only a collar and chain and a muzzle, he fared forth into the woods. All day he hunted. He found nothing.

A week later came another snowfall in the night. Next morning Mackellar set forth again, this time letting his little son Donald come along. He had told his family the farfetched suspicion that had dawned upon him, and Donald had begged to join the hunt.

On his first search, Jamie had covered the country to west of the ridge. Today he climbed the rocks and made his way into the rolling land below. Skirting Blake's Woods, he was moving on toward the farms when, in the fresh snow, he came upon the tracks he sought. For an hour he followed them. Apparently they led nowhere. At least they doubled twice upon themselves and then vanished on a long outcrop of snowless rock which stretched back into Blake's Woods.

Tiring of this fruitless way of spending the morning, Donald strayed from his father. Into the woods he wandered. And presently he sighted the dancing platform amid its tangle of dead weeds. Running over to it, the boy climbed on it. Then, striking an attitude, he began to address an invisible audience from the platform edge.

"My friends!" he shrilled, "our anc'st'rs fit fer the lib'ty we enjoy! Are we goin' to—? *Ouch! Hey, Daddy!*"

One rhetorically stamping little foot had smashed through the rotten boarding. Donald could not pull it out. At the yell of fright, Jamie came running. But a few yards from his son, Mackellar slid to a stop. His eyes were fixed on an opening just below the boy's imprisoned foot, an opening from which the passage of Donald's advancing body had cleared aside some of the tangled weeds. From the tip of a ragged lath, at the edge of his aperture, fluttered a tuft of tawny hair.

Pulling Donald free, Mackellar got down on all fours and peered into the space beneath the platform. For a few seconds he could see nothing. Then, as his eyes accustomed themselves to the dimness, he saw two greenish points of light turned toward him from the farthest corner of the lair.

"Bobby?" called the man doubtfully.

The cornered dog heard the name. It roused vague half memories. The memories were not pleasant, though the voice had in it a friendliness that stirred the collie strangely.

Bobby crouched the closer to the earth and his lips writhed back from murderous white teeth. The man called again, in the same friendly, coaxing voice. Then he began to crawl forward a foot or so. Behind him the excited boy was blocking the only way out of the den.

The Lochinvar Bobby of ten months ago would have cowered whimperingly in his corner, waiting for capture. He might even have pleaded for mercy by rolling over on his back.

The Lochinvar Bobby of today was quite another creature. He laid out his plan of campaign, and then in the wink of an eye he carried it into effect.

With a rabid snarl he charged the advancing man. As Jamie braced himself to fend off the ravening jaws, the dog veered sharply to one side and dashed for the opening. Instinct told him the boy would be easier to break past than the man.

But it was not Jamie Mackellar's first experience with fighting or playing dogs. As Bobby veered, Jamie threw his own body to the same side and made a grab for the fast-flying collie. His fingers closed and tightened around Bobby's left hind leg, just below the hock.

With a snarl, Bobby wheeled and drove his jaws at the captor's wrist in a slash which might well have severed an artery. But, expecting just such a move, Jamie was ready with his free hand. Its fingers buried themselves in the avalanche of fur to one side of Bobby's throat. The slashing eye-teeth barely grazed the pinioning wrist. And Bobby thrashed furiously from side to side to free himself and to tear at his enemy.

Mackellar's expert hands found grips to either side of the whirling jaws and he held on. Bit by bit, bracing himself with all his wiry strength, he backed out, dragging the frantic beast behind him.

Five minutes later, at the expense of a few half-thwarted bites, he had the muzzle bound in place and was leading the exhausted and foaming collie toward Midwestburg. Bobby held back, he flung himself against the chain, he fought with futile madness against the gentle skill of his master.

Then shuddering all over he gave up the fight. Head and tail drooping, he suffered himself to be led to prison.

"It's Lochinvar Bobby, all right!" the wondering Jamie was saying to his son in intervals of lavishing kindly talk and pats on the luckless dog. "The collar and tag prove that. But if it wasn't for them, I'd swear it couldn't be the same. It's—it's enough to take a body's breath away, Donald! I've followed the dog game from the time I was born, but I never set eyes on such a collie in all my days. Just run your hand through that coat! Was there ever another like it? And did you ever see such bone and head? He's—Lord, to think how he looked when that Frayne crook pawned him off on me! It's a miracle he lived through the first winter. I never heard of but one other case like it. And that happened up in Toronto, if I remember right.

"Now, listen, sonny—I'm not anxious to be sued for damages by every farmer in the county. So let 'em keep on looking for their wolf. This is a dog I bought last year. He's been away in the country till now. That's the truth. And the rest is nobody's business. But—but if it takes me a week to figger it out, I'm going to hit on some way to let Mr. Lucius Frayne, Esquire, see he hasn't stung me so hard as he thought he did!"

For two days Bobby refused to eat or drink. In the stout enclosure built for him in Mackellar's backyard he stood, head and tail drooping, every now and then shivering as if with fever. Then, little by little, Jamie's skilled attentions did their work. The wondrous lure of human fellowship, the joy of cooked food, the sense of security against harm, and, above all, a collie's ancestral love for the one man he chooses for his god—these did their work.

In less than two weeks Bobby was once again a collie. The spirit of the wild beast had departed from him, and he took his rightful place as the chum of the soft-voiced little Scot he was learning to worship. Yes, and he was happy—happier than ever before—happy with a new and strangely sweet contentment. He had come into a collie's eternal heritage.

The Westminster Kennel Club's annual dog show at Madison Square Garden, in New York, is the foremost canine classic in America and in the whole world.

A month before that year's Westminster Show, Lucius Frayne received a letter which made the usually sour sportsman laugh till the tears ran down his face. The joke was too good to keep to himself. So he shouted for Roke, and bade the kennel man share the fun of it with him.

He read aloud, cackling, to the listening Roke:

Mr. Lucius Frayne
My dear Sir:

Last year, out to the Midwestburg show, here, you sold me a fine puppy of your Ch. Lochinvar King. And as soon as I could raise the price you sent him on here to me. I would of written to you when I got him, to thank you and to say how pleased I was with him and how all my friends praised him. But I figured you're a busy man and you haven't got any waste time to spend in reading letters about how good your dogs are. Because you know it already. And so I didn't write to you. But I am writing to you now. Because this is business.

You know what a grand pup Bobby was when you sent him to me? Well to my way of thinking he has developed even better than he gave promise to. And some of my friends say the same. To my way of thinking he is the grandest collie in North America or anywhere else today. He is sure one grand dog. He turned out every bit as good as you said he would. He's better now than he was at five months.

I want to thank you for letting me have such a dog, Mr. Frayne. Just as you said, he is of Champion timber. Now this brings me to the business I spoke about.

Granther used to tell me how the gentry on the other side would bet with each other on their dogs at the shows. Six months ago my Aunt Marjorie died and she willed me nine thousand dollars ($9,000). It is in the bank waiting for a good investment for it. Now here is an investment that seems to me a mighty safe one. Me knowing Bobby as I do. A fine sporting investment. And I hope it may please you as well. I am entering Bobby for Westminster. I read in *Dog News* that you are expecting to enter Champion Lochinvar King there, with others of your string. So here is my proposition.

I propose you enter King for "Open, Sable-and-White" and "Open, Any Color," these being the only regular classes a sable champion is eligible for. I will enter Bobby in the same classes, instead of "Novice" as I was going to. And I will wager you six thousand dollars ($6,000) even, that the judge will place Bobby above King. I am making this offer knowing how fine King is but thinking my dog is even better. For Bobby has really improved since a pup. My wife thinks so too.

If this offer pleases you, will you deposit a certified check of six thousand dollars ($6,000) with the editor of *Dog News*? He is a square man as everyone knows and he will see fair play. He has promised me he will hold the stakes. I am ready to deposit my certified check for six thousand dollars ($6,000) at once. I would like to bet the whole nine thousand dollars ($9,000). Knowing it a safe investment. Knowing Bobby like I do. But my wife doesn't want me to bet it at all and so we are compromising on six thousand dollars ($6,000).

Please let me hear from you on this, Mr. Frayne. And I thank you again for how you treated me as regards Bobby. I hope to repay you at Westminster by letting you see him for yourself.

Your ob't servant,

James A. Mackellar

Yes, it was a long letter. Yet Frayne skipped no word of it. And Roke listened, as if to heavenly music.

"Talk about Lochinvar luck!" chortled Frayne as he finished. "The worst pup we ever bred, and we sold him for fifteen hundred! And now he is due to fetch us another few in dividends. He—"

"You're going to cover his bet?" queried Roke. "Good! I was afraid maybe you'd feel kind of sorry for the poor cuss, and—"

"Unless I break both wrists in the next hour," announced Frayne, "that certified check will start for the *Dog News* office by noon. It's the same old wheeze: A dub has picked up a smattering of dog talk, he thinks he knows it all. He buys a bum pup with a thundering pedigree. The pedigree makes him think the pup is a humdinger. He brags about it to his folks. They think anything that costs so much must be the best ever, no matter how it looks. And he gets to believing he's got a world beater. Then—"

"But, boss," put in Roke happily, "just shut your eyes and try to remember how that poor mutt looked! And the boob says he's 'even better than he gave promise to be.' Do you get that? Gee, but I wish you'd let me have a slice of that bet! I'd—"

"No," said Frayne judicially. "That's my own meat. It was caught in my trap. But I tell you what you can do: Wait till I send my check and till it's covered, and then write to Mackellar and ask him if he's willing to bet another bit on the side, with you. From the way he sounds, you ought to have it easy in getting him to make the side bet. He needn't tell his wife. Try it anyhow, if you like."

Roke tried it. And, after ridiculously small objection on Jamie's part, the side bet was recorded and its checks were posted with the editor of *Dog News*. Once more Lucius Frayne and his faithful kennel man shook hands in perfect happiness.

To the topmost steel rafters, where the gray February shadows hung, old Madison Square Garden echoed and reverberated with the multi-keyed barks of some two thousand dogs. The four-day show had been opened at ten o'clock of a slushy Wednesday morning. And as usual the collies were to be judged on the first day.

Promptly at eleven o'clock the clean-cut collie judge followed his steward into the ring. The runner passed down the double ranks of collie benches, bawling the numbers for the "Male Puppy" Class.

The judge had a reputation for quickness, as well as for accuracy and honesty. The Open classes, for male dogs, were certain to come up for verdict within an hour at most.

Seven benches had been thrown into one for the Frayne dogs. At its back ran a strip of red silk, lettered in silver: "LOCHINVAR COLLIE KENNELS." Seven high-quality dogs lay or sat in this deluxe space. In the center— his name on a bronze plate above his head—reclined Lochinvar King.

In full majesty of conscious perfection he lay there, magnificent as a lion, the target for all eyes. Conditioned and groomed to perfection, he stood out from his high-class kennel-mates like a swan among cygnets.

Frayne, more than once in the show's first hour or so, left his much-admired benches for a glance at a nearby unoccupied space numbered 568. Here, according to the catalogue, should be benched Lochinvar Bobby.

But Bobby was nowhere to be seen.

Congratulating himself on his own craft in having inserted a forfeit clause in the bet agreement, Frayne was nonetheless disappointed that the fifth-rate mutt had not shown up.

He longed for a chance to hear the titter of the onlookers when the out-at-elbow, gangling, semi-hairless little nondescript should shamble into the ring. Bobby's presence would add zest to his own oft-told tale of the wager.

According to American Kennel Club rules, a dog must be on its bench from the moment the exhibition opens until the close, except when it is in the ring or at stated exercise periods. That rule, until recently, has been most flagrantly disregarded by many exhibitors. In view of this, Frayne made a trip to the exercise room and then through the dimly lit stalls under the main floor.

As he came back from a fruitless search for Bobby or for Mackellar, he passed the collie ring. "Limit; Dogs," was chalked on the blackboard. Two classes more—"Open, Merle," and "Open, Tricolor"—and then King must enter the ring for "Open, Sable." Frayne hurried to the Lochinvar benches, where Roke and another kennel man were fast at work putting finishing touches to King's toilet.

The great dog was on his feet, tense and eager for the coming clash.

Close behind the unseeing Roke, and studying King with grave admiration, stood Jamie Mackellar.

"Hello, there!" boomed Frayne with loud cordiality, bearing down upon the little man. "Get cold feet? I see your dog's absent. Remember, you forfeit by absence."

"Yes, sir," said Jamie with meekness, taking off his hat to the renowned sportsman, and too confused in fumbling with its wobbly brim to see the hand which Frayne held out to him. "Yes, sir. I remember the forfeit clause, sir. I'm not forfeiting. Bobby is here."

"Here? Where? I looked all over the—"

"I hired one of the cubbyhole rooms upstairs, sir, to keep him in, nights while he's here. And I haven't brought him down to his bench yet. You see, he—he ain't seen many strangers. And you'll remember, maybe, that he used to be just a wee bit shy. So I'm keeping him there till it is time to show him. My boy, Donald, is up there now, getting him ready. They'll be down presently, sir. I think you'll be real pleased with how Bobby looks."

"I'm counting on a heap of pleasure," was Frayne's cryptic reply, as he turned away to mask a grin of utter joy.

Five gray dogs were coming down the aisle to their benches. The "Merle" Class had been judged and the Tricolors were in the ring. There were only four of these.

In another handful of minutes the "Open, Sable" Class was called. It was the strongest class of the day. It contained no fewer than three champions, in addition to four less famous dogs, like Bobby—seven entries in all.

Six of these dogs were marched into the ring. The judge looked at the steward for the "all-here" signal. As he did so, the seventh entrant made his way past the gate crowd and was piloted into the ring by a small and cheaply clad man.

While the attendant was slipping the number board on Mackellar's arm, Lucius Frayne's eyes fell upon Lochinvar Bobby. So did those of the impatient judge and of ninety out of every hundred of the onlookers.

Through the closely packed ranks of onlookers ran a queer little word-less mutter—the most instinctive and therefore the highest praise that can be accorded.

Alertly calm of nerve, heedless of his surroundings so long as his worshipped god was crooning reassurances to him, Bobby stood at Mac-kellar's side.

His incredible coat was burnished like old bronze. His head was calmly erect, his mighty frame steady. His eyes, with true eagle look, surveyed the staring throng.

Never before, in all the Westminster Club's forty-odd shows, had such a collie been led into the ring. Scientific breeding, wise rationing and tireless human care had gone to the perfecting of other dogs. But Mother Nature herself had made Lochinvar Bobby what he was. She had fed him bountifully upon the all-strengthening ration of the primal beast, and she had given him the exercise-born appetite to eat and profit by it. Her pitiless winter winds had combed and winnowed his coat as could no mortal hand, giving it thickness and length and richness beyond belief. And she had moulded his growing young body into the peerless model of the wild.

Then, because he had the loyal heart of a collie and not the incurable savagery of the wolf, she had awakened his soul and made him bask rapturously in the friendship of a true dog man. The combination was unmatchable.

"Walk your dogs, please," ordered the judge, coming out of his momentary daze.

Before the end of the ring's first turn, he had motioned Frayne and Mackellar to take their dogs into one corner. He proceeded to study the five others, awarding to two of them the yellow third-prize ribbon and the white reserve, and then ordering the quintet from the ring; after which he beckoned Bobby and King to the judging block.

In the interim, Frayne had been staring goggle-eyed at the Midwestburg collie. He tried to speak, but he could not. A hundred thoughts were racing dumbly through his bemused brain. He stood agape, foolish looking.

Jamie Mackellar was pleasantly talkative.

"A grand class, this," he confided to his silent comrade. "But, first crack, Judge Breese had the eye to single out our two as so much the best that he won't size 'em up with the others. How do you like Bobby, sir? Is he very bad? Don't you think, maybe, he's picked up, just a trifle, since you shipped him to me? He's no worse, anyhow, than he was then, is he?"

Frayne babbled wordlessly.

"This is the last time I'll show him for a while, Mr. Frayne," continued Jamie, a rasping note coming into his timid voice. "The cash I'm due to collect from you and Mr. Roke will make enough, with the legacy and what I've saved, to start me in business with a truck of my own. Bobby and I are going into partnership. And we're going to clean up. Bobby is putting our bet and today's cash prizes into the firm. He and I are getting out of the show-end of collie breeding for a time. The more we see of some of you professionals, the better we like cesspools. If dogs weren't the grandest animals ever put on earth, a few of the folks who exploit them would have killed the dog game long ago. It— Judge Breese is beckoning for us!"

Side by side, the two glorious collies advanced to the judging block. Side by side, at their handlers' gestures, they mounted it. And again from the onlookers arose that queer wordless hum. Sire and son, shoulder to shoulder, faced the judge.

And for the first time in his unbroken career of conquests, Lochinvar King looked almost shabby beside the wondrous young giant he had sired. His every good point—and he had no others—was bettered by Bobby.

As a matter of form, Breese went over both dogs with meticulous care, testing coat texture, spring or ribs, action, soundness of bone, carriage, facial expression, and the myriad other details which go into the judging of a show dog. For a long time he faced them, crouching low and staring into their deep-set eyes; marking the set and carriage of the tulip ears; comparing point with point; as becomes a man who is about to give victory to an Unknown over a hitherto Invincible.

Then with a jerk of his head he summoned the steward with the judging book and ribbons. And amid a spontaneous rattle of applause, Jamie Mackellar led his splendid dog to the far end of the ring with one hand, while in the fingers of the other fluttered a strip of gold-lettered dark blue ribbon.

Back came both collies for the "Open, Any Color" Class, and the verdict was repeated, as it was repeated in the supreme "Winners" Class which followed. "Winners" Class carried, with its rosette and cash specials, five points toward Bobby's championship.

Then followed the rich harvest of other cash specials in the collie division, including "Best of Breed," and, for the next three days, even fatter gleanings from among the variety classes and unclassified specials, plus a trunkful of silver cups and other trophies which are more beautiful than valuable.

On Saturday, Jamie Mackellar and Bobby took the midnight train for Midwestburg; richer by a princely sum for their New York sojourn.

Rolling sweetly around in Jamie's memory was a brief talk he had had with Roke an hour before the close of the show. Sent as emissary by Frayne, the kennel manager had offered Mackellar a very high price for the sensational young prize winner.

"We're not parting company, Bobby and I," Jamie had answered. "Thanking you and your boss just as much. But tell Mr. Frayne if ever I breed a pup as good as Bobby was when he came to me, he can have it for an even fifteen hundred. I wouldn't want such a fine chap to think I'm not just as clean a sportsman as what he is!"

"One Minute Longer"

Wolf was a collie, red-gold and white of coat, with a shape more like his long-ago wolf ancestors' than like a domesticated dog's. It was from this ancestral throwback that he was named Wolf.

He looked not at all like his great sire, Sunnybank Lad, nor like his dainty, thoroughbred mother, Lady. Nor was he like them in any other way, except that he inherited old Lad's staunchly gallant spirit and loyalty and uncanny brain. No, in traits as well as in looks, he was more wolf than dog. He almost never barked, his snarl supplying all vocal needs.

The mistress or the master or the boy—any of these three could romp with him, roll him over, tickle him, or subject him to all sorts of playful indignities. And Wolf entered gleefully into the fun of the romp. But let any human, besides these three, lay a hand on his slender body, and a snarling plunge for the offender's throat was Wolf's invariable reply to the caress.

It had been so since his puppyhood. He did not fly at legitimate guests, or, indeed, pay any heed to their presence, so long as they kept their hands off him. But to all of these the boy was forced to say at the very outset of the visit:

"Pat Lad and Bruce all you want to, but please leave Wolf alone. He doesn't care for people. We've taught him to stand for a pat on the head, from guests—but don't touch his body."

Then, to prove his own immunity, the boy would proceed to tumble Wolf about, to the delight of them both.

In romping with humans whom they love, most dogs will bite, more or less gently—or pretend to bite—as a part of the game. Wolf never did this. In his wildest and roughest romps with the boy or with the boy's parents, Wolf did not so much as open his mighty jaws. Perhaps he dared not trust himself to bite gently. Perhaps he realized that a bite is not a joke, but an effort to kill.

There had been only one exception to Wolf's hatred for mauling at strangers' hands. A man came to the Place on a business call, bringing along a chubby two-year-old daughter. The master warned the baby that she must not go near Wolf, although she might pet any of the other collies. Then he became so interested in the business talk that he and his guest forgot all about the child.

Ten minutes later the master chanced to shift his gaze to the far end of the room. And he broke off, with a gasp, in the very middle of a sentence.

The baby was seated astride Wolf's back, her tiny heels digging into the dog's sensitive ribs, and each of her chubby fists gripping one of his ears. Wolf was lying there, with an idiotically happy grin on his face and wagging his tail in ecstasy.

No one knew why he had submitted to the baby's tugging hands, except because she *was* a baby, and because the gallant heart of the dog had gone out to her helplessness.

Wolf was the official watchdog of the Place, and his name carried dread to the thieves and tramps of the region. Also, he was the boy's own special dog. He had been born on the boy's tenth birthday, five years before this story of ours begins, and ever since then the two had been inseparable chums.

One sloppy afternoon in late winter, Wolf and the boy were sprawled side by side on the fur rug in front of the library fire. The mistress and the master had gone to town for the day. The house was lonely and the two chums were left to entertain each other.

The boy was reading a magazine. The dog beside him was blinking in drowsy comfort at the fire. Presently, finishing the story he had been reading, the boy looked across at the sleepy dog.

"Wolf," he said, "here's a story about a dog. I think he must have been something like you. Maybe he was your great-great-great-great-grandfather. He lived an awfully long time ago—in Pompeii. Ever hear of Pompeii?"

Now the boy was fifteen years old, and he had too much sense to imagine that Wolf could possibly understand the story he was about to tell him. But, long since, he had fallen into a way of sometimes talking to his dog as if to another human. It was fun for him to note the almost pathetic eagerness with which Wolf listened and tried to grasp the meaning of what he was saying. Again and again, at sound of some familiar word or voice inflection, the collie would pick up his ears or wag his tail, as if in the joyous hope that he had at last found a clue to his owner's meaning.

"You see," went on the boy, "this dog lived in Pompeii, as I told you. You've never been there, Wolf."

Wolf was looking up at the boy in wistful excitement, seeking vainly to guess what was expected of him.

"And," continued the boy, "the kid who owned him seems to have had a regular knack for getting into trouble all the time. And his dog was always on hand to get him out of it. It's a true story, the magazine says. The kid's father was so grateful to the dog that he bought him a solid silver collar. Solid silver! Get that, Wolfie?"

Wolf did not "get it." But he wagged his tail hopefully, his eyes alight with bewildered interest.

"And," said the boy, "what do you suppose was engraved on the collar? Well, I'll tell you: *'This dog has thrice saved his little master from death. Once by fire, once by flood, and once at the hands of robbers!'* How's that for a record, Wolf? For *one* dog, too!"

At the words "Wolf" and "dog," the collie's tail thumped the floor in glad comprehension. Then he edged closer to the boy as the narrator's voice presently took on a sadder note.

"But at last," resumed the boy, "there came a time when the dog couldn't save the kid. Mount Vesuvius erupted. All the sky was pitch dark, as black as midnight, and Pompeii was buried under lava and ashes. The dog could easily have got away by himself—dogs can see in the dark, can't they, Wolf?—but he couldn't get the kid away. And he wouldn't go without him. You wouldn't have gone without me, either, would you, Wolf? Pretty nearly two thousand years later, some people dug through the lava that covered Pompeii. What do you suppose they found? Of course they found a whole lot of things. One of them was that dog—silver collar and inscription and all. He was lying at the feet of a child. The child he couldn't save. He was one grand dog—hey, Wolf?"

The continued strain of trying to understand began to get on the collie's high-strung nerves. He rose to his feet, quivering, and sought to lick the boy's face, thrusting one upraised white forepaw at him in appeal for a handshake. The boy slammed shut the magazine.

"It's boring in the house here, with nothing to do," he said to his chum. "I'm going up to the lake with my gun to see if any wild ducks have landed in the marshes yet. It's almost time for them. Want to come along?"

The last sentence Wolf understood perfectly. On the instant he was dancing with excitement at the prospect of a walk. Being a collie, he was of no earthly help on a hunting-trip, but on such tramps, as everywhere else, he was the boy's inseparable companion.

Out over the slushy snow the two started, the boy with his light, single-barreled shotgun slung over one shoulder, the dog trotting close at his heels. The March thaw was changing to a sharp freeze. The deep and soggy snow was crusted over, just thick enough to make walking a genuine difficulty for both dog and boy.

The Place was a promontory that ran out into the lake, on the oppo-site bank from the mile-distant village. Behind, across the highroad, lay the winter-choked forest. At the lake's northerly end, two miles beyond the Place, were the reedy marshes where, in a month, wild ducks would congregate. There, with Wolf, the boy plowed his way through the bit-ing cold.

The going got harder and harder. A quarter-mile below the marshes the Boy struck out across the upper corner of the lake. Here the ice was rotten at the top, where the thaw had nibbled at it, but beneath it was still a full eight inches thick, easily strong enough to bear the boy's weight.

Along the gray icefield the two plodded. The skim of water, which the thaw had spread an inch thick over the ice, had frozen in the day's cold spell. It crackled like broken glass as the chums walked over it. The boy had on big hunting boots. So, apart from the extra effort, the glass-like ice did not bother him. To Wolf it gave acute pain. The sharp particles were forever getting between the callous black pads of his feet, pricking and cutting him sharply.

Little smears of blood began to mark the dog's course, but it never occurred to Wolf to turn back, or to betray by any sign that he was suffering. It was all a part of the day's work—a cheap price to pay for the joy of tramping with his adored young master.

Then, forty yards or so on the near side of the marshes, Wolf beheld an amazing phenomenon. The boy had been walking directly in front of him, gun over shoulder. Then, with no warning at all, the youth fell, feet first, out of sight through the ice.

The light shell of newly frozen water that covered the lake's thicker ice also masked an air hole nearly three feet wide. Into this, as he strode carelessly along, the boy had stepped. Straight down he had gone, with all the force of his hundred-and-twenty pounds and with all the impetus of his forward stride.

Instinctively, he threw out his hands to restore his balance. The only effect of this was to send the gun flying ten feet away.

Down went the Boy through less than three feet of water (for the bottom of the lake at this point had started to slope upward towards the marshes) and through nearly two feet more of sticky marsh mud that underlay the lakebed.

His outflung hands struck against the ice on the edges of the air hole, and clung there.

Sputtering and gurgling, the boy brought his head above the surface and tried to raise himself by his hands, high enough to wriggle out upon the surface of the ice. Ordinarily, this would have been simple enough for so strong a lad. But the glue-like mud had imprisoned his feet and the lower part of his legs, and held them powerless.

Try as he would, the boy could not wrench himself free. The water, as he stood upright, was on a level with his mouth. The air hole was too wide for him, at such a depth, to get a good grip on its edges and lift himself bodily to safety.

Gaining such a fingerhold as he could, he heaved with all his might, throwing every muscle of his body into the struggle. One leg was pulled almost free of the mud, but the other was driven deeper into it. And, as the boy's fingers slipped from the smoothly wet ice edge, the attempt to restore his balance drove the free leg back, knee deep into the mire.

Ten minutes of this hopeless fighting left the boy panting and tired out. The icy water was numbing his nerves and chilling his blood. His hands were without sense of feeling as far up as the wrists. Even if he could have shaken his legs free from the mud, now he did not have strength enough left to crawl out of the hole.

He ceased his useless, frantic battle and stood dazed. Then he came sharply to himself. For as he stood, the water crept upward from his lips to his nostrils. He knew why the water seemed to be rising. It was not rising. It was he who was sinking. As soon as he stopped moving, the mud began, very slowly, but very steadily, to suck him downward.

This was not quicksand, but it was a deep mud bed. And only by constant motion could he avoid sinking farther and farther down into it. He had less than two inches to spare, at best, before the water would fill his nostrils; less than two inches of life, even if he could keep the water down to the level of his lips.

There was a moment of utter panic. Then the boy's brain cleared. His only hope was to keep on fighting—to rest when he must, for a moment or so, and then to renew his numbed grip on the ice edge and try to pull his feet a few inches higher out of the mud. He must do this as long as his chilled body could be spurred into obeying his will.

He struggled again, but with virtually no success in raising himself. A second struggle, however, brought him chin-high above the water. He remembered confusedly that some of these earlier struggles had scarcely budged him, while others had gained him two or three inches. Vaguely he wondered why. Then turning his head, he realized why.

Wolf, as he turned, was just loosing his hold on the wide collar of the boy's jacket. His cut forepaws were still braced against a lip of ragged ice on the air hole's edge, and all his tawny body was tense.

His body was dripping wet, too. The boy noted that; and he realized that the repeated effort to draw his master to safety must have resulted, at least once, in pulling the dog down into the water with the floundering boy.

"Once more, Wolfie! *Once more!*" chattered the boy through teeth that clicked together like castanets.

The dog darted forward, caught his grip again on the edge of the boy's collar, and tugged with all his fierce strength, growling and whining ferociously the whole time.

The boy seconded the collie's tuggings by a supreme struggle that lifted him higher than before. He was able to get one arm and shoulder clear. His numb fingers closed about an upthrust tree limb which had been washed down stream in the autumn freshets and had been frozen into the lake ice.

With this new grip, and aided by the dog, the boy tried to drag himself out of the hole. But the chill of the water had done its work. He did not have the strength to move farther. The mud still sucked at his calves and ankles. The big hunting boots were full of water that seemed to weigh a ton.

He lay there, gasping and chattering. Then through the gathering twilight, his eyes fell on the gun, lying ten feet away.

"Wolf!" he ordered, nodding towards the weapon. "Get it! *Get* it!"

Not in vain had the boy talked to Wolf, for years, as if the dog were human. At the words and the nod, the collie trotted over to the gun, lifted it by the stock, and hauled it awkwardly along over the bumpy ice to his master, where he laid it down at the edge of the air hole.

The dog's eyes were cloudy with trouble, and he shivered and whined as with fever. The water on his thick coat was freezing to a mass of ice. But it was from anxiety that he shivered, and not from cold.

Still keeping his numb grasp on the tree branch, the boy balanced himself as best he could, and thrust two fingers of his free hand into his mouth to warm them into feeling again.

When this was done, he reached out to where the gun lay, and pulled the trigger. The shot boomed deafeningly through the twilight winter silences. The recoil sent the weapon sliding sharply back along the ice, spraining the boy's trigger finger and cutting it to the bone.

"That's all I can do," said the boy to himself. "If any one hears it, well and good. I can't get at another cartridge. I couldn't put it into the breech if I had it. My hands are too numb."

For several endless minutes he clung there, listening. But this was a desolate part of the lake, far from any road, and the season was too early for other hunters to be abroad. The bitter cold, in any case, tended to make sane folk hug the fireside rather than to venture so far into the open. Nor was the single report of a gun uncommon enough to call for investigation in such weather.

All this the boy told himself as the minutes dragged by. Then he looked again at Wolf. The dog, head on one side, still stood protectively above him. The dog was cold and in pain. But, being only a dog, it did not occur to him to trot off home to the comfort of the library fire and leave his master to fend for himself.

Presently, with a little sigh, Wolf lay down on the ice, his nose across the boy's arm. Even if he lacked strength to save his beloved master, he could stay and share the boy's sufferings.

But the boy himself thought otherwise. He was not at all minded to freeze to death, nor was he willing to let Wolf imitate the dog of

Pompeii by dying helplessly at his master's side. Controlling for an instant the chattering of his teeth, he called:

"Wolf!"

The dog was on his feet again at the word; alert, eager.

"Wolf!" repeated the boy. "Go! Hear me? Go!"

He pointed homeward.

Wolf stared at him, hesitant. Again the boy called in vehement command, "Go!"

The collie lifted his head to the twilight sky with a wolf howl hideous in its grief and appeal—a howl as wild and discordant as that of any of his savage ancestors. Then, stooping first to lick the numb hand that clung to the branch, Wolf turned and fled.

Across the cruelly sharp film of ice he tore at top speed, head down, whirling through the deepening dusk like a flash of tawny light.

Wolf understood what was wanted of him. Wolf always understood. The pain in his feet was as if nothing. The stiffness of his numbed body was forgotten in the urgency for speed.

The boy looked drearily after the swiftly vanishing figure which the dusk was swallowing. He knew the dog would try to bring help, as has many another and lesser dog in times of need. Whether or not that help could arrive in time, or at all, was a point on which the boy would not let himself dwell. Into his benumbed brain crept the memory of an old Norse proverb he had read in school:

"Heroism consists in hanging on, one minute longer."

Unconsciously he tightened his feeble hold on the tree branch and braced himself.

From the marshes to the Place was a full two miles. Despite the deep and sticky snow, Wolf covered the distance in less than nine minutes. He paused in front of the gate lodge, at the highway entrance to the drive. But the superintendent and his wife had gone shopping to Paterson, that afternoon.

Down the drive to the house he dashed. The maids had taken advantage of their employers' day in New York to walk across the lake to the village, to a movie.

Wise men claim that dogs do not have the power to think or to reason things out in a logical way. So perhaps it was mere chance that next sent Wolf's flying feet across the lake to the village. Perhaps it was chance, and not the knowledge that where there is a village there are people.

Again and again, in the car, he had sat upon the front seat alongside the mistress when she drove to the station to meet guests. There were always people at the station. And to the station Wolf now raced.

The usual group of platform idlers had been dispersed by the cold. A solitary baggageman was hauling a trunk and some boxes onto the platform to be put aboard the five o'clock train from New York.

As the baggageman passed under the clump of station lights, he came to a sudden halt. For out of the darkness dashed a dog. Full tilt, the animal rushed up to him and seized him by the skirt of the overcoat.

The man cried out in scared surprise. He dropped the box he was carrying and struck at the dog to ward off the seemingly murderous attack. He recognized Wolf, and he knew the collie's reputation.

But Wolf was not attacking. Holding tight to the coat, he backed away, trying to draw the man with him, and all the while whimpering aloud like a nervous puppy.

A kick from the heavy-shod boot broke the dog's hold on the coat, even as a second yell from the man brought four or five other people running out from the station waiting room.

One of these, the telegraph operator, took in the scene at a single glance. With great presence of mind he bawled loudly:

"Mad dog!"

This, as Wolf, reeling from the kick, sought to gain another grip on the coat. A second kick sent him rolling over and over on the tracks, while other voices took up the panic cry of "Mad dog!"

Now, a mad dog is supposed to be a dog afflicted by rabies. Once in ten thousand times, at the very most, a mad-dog hue-and-cry is justified —certainly not oftener. A harmless and friendly dog loses his master on the street. He runs about, confused and frightened, looking for the owner he has lost. A boy throws a stone at him. Other boys chase him. His tongue hangs out, and his eyes glaze with terror. Then some fool bellows:

"Mad dog!"

And the cruel chase is on—a chase that ends in the pitiful victim's death. Yes, in every crowd there is a voice ready to raise that idiotic and murderously cruel shout.

So it was with the men who witnessed Wolf's frenzied effort to get help for the imperiled boy.

Voice after voice repeated the cry. Men groped along the platform edge for stones to throw. The village policeman ran puffing to the scene, drawing his revolver.

Finding it useless to make a further attempt to drag the baggageman to the rescue, Wolf leaped back, facing the ever larger group. Back went his head again in that hideous wolf howl. Then he galloped away a few yards, trotted back, howled once more, and again galloped lakeward.

All of which only confirmed the panicky crowd in the belief that they were threatened by a mad dog. A shower of stones hurtled about Wolf as he came back a third time to lure these dull humans into following him.

One pointed rock struck the collie's shoulder, cutting it to the bone. A shot from the policeman's revolver fanned the fur of his ruff as it whizzed past.

Knowing that he faced death, he nevertheless stood his ground, not troubling to dodge the shower of stones, but continuing to run lakeward and then trot back, whining with excitement.

A second pistol shot flew wide. A third grazed the dog's hip. From all directions people were running toward the station. A man darted into a house next door, and emerged carrying a shotgun. This he steadied on the veranda rail not forty feet away from the leaping dog, and made ready to fire.

It was then the train from New York came in. And, momentarily, the sport of "mad-dog" killing was abandoned, while the crowd scattered to each side of the track.

From a front car of the train the mistress and the master emerged into a bedlam of noise and confusion.

"Best hide in the station, Ma'am!" shouted the telegraph operator, at sight of the mistress. "There is a mad dog loose out here! He's chasing folks around, and—"

"Mad dog!" repeated the mistress in high contempt. "If you knew anything about dogs, you'd know mad ones never 'chase folks around,' any more than fever patients do. Then—"

A flash of tawny light beneath the station lamp, a scurrying of frightened idlers, a final wasted shot from the policeman's pistol—as Wolf dived headlong through the frightened crowd towards the voice he heard and recognized.

Up to the mistress and the master galloped Wolf. He was bleeding, his eyes were bloodshot, his fur was rumpled. He seized the astounded master's gloved hand lightly between his teeth and sought to pull him across the tracks and toward the lake.

The master knew dogs. He especially knew Wolf. And without a word he suffered himself to be led. The mistress and one or two inquisitive men followed.

Presently, Wolf loosed his hold on the master's hand and ran on ahead, darting back every few moments to make certain he was followed.

"*Heroism—consists—in—hanging—on—one—minute—longer,*" the boy was whispering deliriously to himself for the hundredth time, as Wolf pattered up to him in triumph across the ice, with the human rescuers a scant ten yards behind.

RUNAWAY

"And there were bears in that dream of mine, Ronny," continued Fay. "Twenty-five bears. They were all cream-colored and they had brown eyes. They were each of them more than seven times as big as you or any other collie, Ronny."

The girl paused to let this amazing statement sink in. Coolharbor Ronald, the mighty-coated, gold-and-white collie, wagged his plumed tail and looked up at her with much interest. He loved this ten-year-old little daughter of his master, and he loved her crooning voice when she talked to him as if he were another child, even though nine-tenths of her actual words meant nothing to him. He loved the way she rumpled his silken ears as she talked. Also, the constant repetition of his name flattered him.

"And, Ronny," went on Fay, "those twenty-five cream-colored bears all lived at the South Pole. I dreamed that it got so hot down there that they all chipped in and bought an airplane, Ronny, and they got into it

111

and they flew clear up to the North Pole, where it was ever so nice and cool, even in summer, Ronny. And they—"

The collie became aware of a malignantly biting flea, feasting in the hollow behind his left ear. He broke in on Fay's narrative by sitting up and scratching the ear-hollow with much intensity. His usually clever face took on a look of idiotic vacuity as he scratched.

"*Ronny!*" rebuked Fay, indignantly. "Do you want to hear the rest of this nice dream of mine, or don't you? It isn't every day anybody has such a wonderful dream. It's worth listening to, I can tell you."

Either at her chiding tone or else because he had abated the supping flea, Ronny settled down again on the veranda floor at her feet, wagging apologetically his plume of a tail and looking in whimsical appeal at the flushed and frowning little face. Appeased, Fay took up again the flea-severed thread of her narrative:

"Well, I dreamed the bears loved it up there, in the cool and the ice and all, after it had been so hot down at their home in the South Pole. But pretty soon it began to get so cold at the North Pole that they were all shivery and chatter-teethed, Ronny. And the bears said, 'Gee, but it's cold, here! Let's get back home where we belong.' So I dreamed they all piled into the airplane again and they stepped on the gas. And, Ronny, what do you suppose happened? The airplane had frozen stiff and it wouldn't move an inch, Ronny.

"So I dreamed they all had to *walk* every step of the whole way home from the North Pole to the South Pole, Ronny. It was pretty near a billion miles. But that was the only way they could get there—by walking. By the time they reached the South Pole again their feet were terribly sore, Ronny. As sore as that new tooth of mine was, last year. Maybe sorer, Ronny."

At the repeated speaking of his name the dog's tail slapped the porch floor anew, and he reached up to lick the gesticulating little brown hand. There was something so confiding and happy in the action that Fay's conscience bothered her. She felt that Ronny not only understood, but believed every word of the tale. Hesitatingly, yet laughing in loud bravado, she added:

"I—I didn't really dream quite every bit of that dream, Ronny. Not just all of it. I—well, I made up a little of it, here and there."

The tail continued to slap the floor and once more the collie sought to lick the hand poised above him. Fay grew red. She avoided the caressing tongue of her canine worshiper and she said in a spurt of self-vexation:

"Now that I come to think it over, Ronny, maybe I didn't even dream any of it at all. But—but wouldn't it have been a perfectly glorious dream if I *had* happened to dream it, Ronny?"

Conscience calmed by confession, she patted remorsefully the classic head at her knee, admonishing her chum:

"You mustn't always believe everything you're told, Ronny. Learn to take a joke, sometimes."

The morning sun was striking across the fire-blue lake. A sluicing rain of the night before had washed the springtime world clean of a week's dust and had filled it with a hundred fresh odors. It was hard, on such a morning, to sit primly on the veranda, in one's best clothes, waiting for the car to come around and keeping Ronny from straying into the lake or over the plowed ground of the rose garden.

Yet this was the brief task assigned to Fay Denning by her father that day. At nine o'clock, Denning, with his wife and daughter, were to start for the hour-distant dog show at Paignton. It was an event, a tremendous event. It was the first outdoor show of the year. It was the show where Coolharbor Ronald was eagerly expected to win the final four points needed for the completion of his championship.

The beautiful young collie had been bathed and brushed and trimmed until his burnished gold-and-white coat gleamed with unusual beauty. For weeks he had been conditioned for the great event. His owners did not believe there was a show collie on earth that could equal in perfection this pet of theirs.

The dog-show virus is as insidious and as potent as an ancient poison. Once let man or woman fall under its spell, and the winning of a blue ribbon seems more important than the winning of a college degree. The purple Winner Rosette is worth a fortune. The annexation of the mystic prefix, "Champion," to a loved dog's name is an honor comparable to the Presidency.

The virus had worked deep into the world of Malcolm Denning and his wife since the day, six months earlier, when they had been persuaded by a friend of theirs to take their home-bred young collie, Coolharbor Ronald, to a neighborhood dog show. The collie had won a spectacular victory there and at ensuing shows, earning with ease eleven of his fifteen championship points. Today's show—if his winning streak should continue—would suffice to gain him his full title.

At daybreak the Dennings had been astir. Ronald had been groomed with all the meticulous care in the world. Then, while Malcolm and his wife were changing into their dog-show clothes, Fay was deputed to stand guard over the collie and to see he did not stray from the veranda.

A single luxurious roll in the rain-wet grass would undo much of his painful grooming. A plunge in the lake and a homeward canter through the loam of the flower borders would necessitate an entire new toilette —the labor of at least an hour. There was not an hour to waste before departing for the show.

For a few minutes Fay found it simple enough to sit on the porch with Ronny, entertaining herself, as ever, with telling him a story. But presently the wait grew tedious. There was a mightily potent call in the sun-blazoned outdoors. Momentarily, to the restless child, the call grew stronger.

"Ronny," she said after a minute of silent fidgeting, "I promised I wouldn't let you get into the lake or on the wet grass or into the flower beds. But I think it would do you good to walk around the gravel paths with me. They are awfully clean and dry, Ronny. Just as clean as this poky old veranda. Daddy says a collie needs lots of exercise. Come along."

She snapped a leash to the dog's collar, so he would not be tempted from the uninspiring gravel to the damp grass. Then she descended the porch steps, Ronny gamboling delightedly around her and tugging at the unaccustomed leash.

Primly she strolled down the wide gravel path to the nearby summer house and back again. Then she struck into the longer and narrower path that led to the vegetable garden behind the stables.

Past the stables she and the dog made their way, and along the central path of the garden. Beyond were the hillside woods—full of enticing sights and sounds, but forbidden ground on this morning. With a sigh Fay turned about at the end of the garden's path and prepared to go houseward again.

Just then, out of a lettuce row whisked something brown and bounding, something with a stumpy white tail and with a fascinatingly bumpy gait as it dashed for the nearby woodland.

At sight and scent of the rabbit the collie yelped his shrill hunt cry. He leaped forward with all his sinewy strength and with the impetus of his sixty pounds of weight. Fay saw the maneuver in time to make an effort to check it. Involuntarily she tightened her grip on the leash, whose loop was around her wrist.

The dog's jump lifted her bodily from her feet and flung her forward. She came to earth prone in the green-and-scarlet center of an early strawberry bed, her pretty white organdy dress at once taking on splashes of scarlet and streaks of rich brown earth.

Checked by her fall, Ronny resorted to guile. Backing away, he slipped his neck out of the loose collar. In the same gesture he wheeled and was off like a gold-white flash, in pursuit of the vanishing rabbit.

Rubbing her chafed palms on her scraped knees, Fay Denning scrambled up from her roll amid the squashy strawberries and soft dirt. Despairingly she blinked after the fast-disappearing collie and at the rabbit that bumped along at full speed some hundred feet in front of him. Then she gave chase.

She was responsible for Coolharbor Ronald's safety and immaculate cleanliness. Both were in peril. All at once her rationalizing—as to the gravel walks being as clean a place for him as the veranda where she had been told to remain—rang thin and cracked. No longer did it seem a convincing argument with which to face her father.

Into the woods she rushed, and through a patch of marshy ground at their border. Her quest was not long. Fifty yards within the woodland the rabbit had dived into a warren, among some stones, on the steep hillside. Around these rocks the collie was dancing, shouting wildly barked insult to his escaped prey. Ronny, too, had traversed the patch of marsh, and at a pace that had spattered his shining coat thick with black mud.

Weeping, Fay called to the dog. Toiling up the slope, she plunged forward under a low-hanging bough to grasp him. Her eyes were blurred with tears. Ronny's were not. Thus it was that the collie, turning around at her call, saw what she missed seeing. He saw and, collie-like, he went into immediate action.

As she ran below the bough the top of her head brushed glancingly against something soft and yielding. It was a hornet nest as large as a hat —the abode of several hundred giant black hornets with white-barred tails.

Scarcely had she touched the nest when Ronny flew at her. His classically chiseled skull smote her with heavy force in the middle of her small body. The girl doubled up and rolled backward down the steep pitch of hillside far more rapidly than she had rolled into the strawberry bed.

Ronald did not so much as glance after her meteorically tumbling body. Slowly, at a deliberate walk, he began to move away in the opposite direction. He knew well what he was doing, as have other collies that have done the same thing. He knew also the price he must pay.

Out of their shaken cone-shaped nest poured the army of hornets, furious to revenge themselves on the intruder who had joggled their home.

In the second or so which had passed since Fay's head had come into contact with the nest, the child had involuntarily put several yards of hillside between herself and the hornets. Even now she was coming to a stop against a bush of mountain laurel.

The hornets saw thus only the nearer moving object—the dog that was walking so deliberately away from them. The whole, buzzing, white-barred troop flew at him settling down above him in a fiercely droning mass.

Now a collie's coat, in its thickest parts, is as impervious to hornet stings as is a suit of armor. But on the head and the feet and under the forelegs there is no such mattress of protection.

While the bulk of the swarm were stabbing vainly at Ronald's back and sides, a dozen or more were driving at the less-guarded parts of him. Their flame-like stings struck deep. Shutting his eyes, the dog broke into a slow canter, still moving in precisely the opposite direction from Fay, and drawing with him the whole furious hornet horde.

Thence, stumblingly, he made his way down the slope and along the water's edge. In a single hurricane dash he could have distanced his torturers. But, baffled, they would have found the weeping child. Therefore, enduring the agony as best he might, he continued for nearly two-hundred yards at the same slow canter before instinct or reason told him he had lured the hornets far enough away from her.

Then, in a spasm of relief, he plunged deep into the lake, freeing himself of his foes and gaining momentary relief from the myriad stings of fire which were swelling his head and feet out of all proportion to the rest of him. But, as collie instinct also told him, mere cold water is not a swift remedy for hornet stings. A better and a quicker cure was at hand. Swimming back alongshore, he landed near the forest-edge strip of marsh. Into the soft cool black mud he thrust himself, shoving his swollen head in it and wallowing deep and luxuriously.

Here Fay came upon him. Herself dirty and torn and rankly disreputable, she peered tearfully down upon an object which by contrast made her look spotlessly well groomed. Coolharbor Ronald was one solid, streaky mass of black mud. Out of the mire his grotesquely swollen head and face arose like some misshapen prehistoric creature. He was horrible to look upon.

Panic drove Fay into action. Regardless of her own appearance, she caught the dog by the collar and dragged him out into the lake. There, the chilly water up to her knees, she strove to scrub Ronald clean of some of his coating of mud. The task was not difficult, for the mire had not yet caked.

A hornet that had become enmeshed in the dog's tangle of hair came to life during the wash, sufficiently to sting her venomously on the hand. Ronny, too, in shifting his position as the cold water sloshed over him, staggered against her and made her lose her footing in the wet ooze.

To her feet she struggled, gasping and dripping, an unlovely, bewildered and unhappy little Venus rising from the mud-stained deep. Pluckily she went on with the task of cleansing the dog.

At last he was superficially clean, his mighty coat sticking dankly to his suddenly attenuated body, his once snowy shirt-frill and ruff grayish with water and with the remnants of mud. His head was still swollen grotesquely. One eye was shut, with a big lump above it. His nose was bulbous; his graceful lower legs and feet were a series of bumps.

As she led the woefully disfigured brute ashore, Fay glanced at her silver wrist watch, the birthday present which was her chief treasure. By some miracle, it was still going. She wished it was not. For it registered ten minutes past nine.

Nine o'clock was the time scheduled for the Dennings' departure for the hour-distant Paignton show, which was to begin—so the premium list said—"promptly at ten"! Paignton was an hour away. The show was to begin in fifty minutes. The hopes of the whole family had rested on Ronny's winning his four points and thus his championship. Already his luxuriant coat was showing first signs of the summer shedding. Before the next show he would be "out of coat." An out-of-coat collie stands slim chance at any show. Six months might pass before he could hope to be "in bloom" once more—perhaps longer.

It was she—she who loved him—who had robbed him of his championship. He had been well content to stay there on the porch with her. It was her own fault they had gone for that miserable walk. She pictured herself trying to explain to her father and mother. And she fell to wishing she were at the South Pole with the twenty-five cream-colored bears of her pseudo dream.

From her drenched pockets she drew forth the envelope she had begged her father to allow her to take charge of, that morning—the yellow envelope containing Ronald's identification card and collar tag for the show. They were wet and a bit pulpy.

Squaring her small shoulders, she drew a long breath. Then, snapping the leash anew on Ronald's smeared collar, she turned homeward. There was only one thing to do. Nothing was to be gained by putting off the evil day of reckoning. It must be faced. There was no least taint of cowardice in the child. Her heart was sick, but her step was steady.

The nearest way to the house, from the curved shore line where she had emerged from the lake, was not through the woods, but by striking straight across to the road and so to the Denning driveway, a quarter-mile distant. To the road she led the drenched collie, the water still dribbling drearily from her own wrecked clothes at every step.

As she went, bits of the nightmare chase began to flit back into her memory. She recalled the route she had taken up the hillside. She wondered at her own blind folly in following that particular course. Not three days earlier she and her father had been rambling through that very part of the woods and Malcolm Denning had pointed out to her the giant hornet nest.

The hornet nest! Then, all at once, she understood. She knew now why her chum, Ronny, had turned on her and had butted her over and sent her rolling down the slope, while he walked so slowly in the other direction. With a catch of her heaving breath, she stooped down and flung both arms around the collie's wet throat.

"Oh, Ronny!" she sobbed. "Of all the dogs that ever were—you're that dog! You're a—a hero, Ronny! That's what you are. A hero. And look what I've gone and done to *you!* I've kept you from being a champion."

To her remorseful senses, just then, her parents' disappointment and anger seemed infinitely less important than did the wrong she had worked on Ronald himself in cheating him out of his golden chance for a championship. From much eager listening to her father's dog talk she had become fiercely imbued with the idea that a championship was the most desirable and most difficult goal in life. And this was the shining goal from which she had deflected her adored pal, Coolharbor Ronald!

She was on the highway now, and pattering toward home. Around a bend in the road chugged a closed car—a car almost as disreputable in aspect as were Fay and the dog. The cleanest thing about its mud-dimmed exterior was the large white linen sign pasted on the wind-shield, a sign that read "TAXI."

It was driven by a grimy-shirted old person with a large pink face—Iry Tevvis, the local hackman. In the backseat of the car were four wicker baskets of generous size and fanciful design.

At sight of the bedraggled girl and her lankly dripping escort, Iry stopped his machine.

"What's wrong, Miss Fay?" he asked, anxiously.

As an accompaniment to his question, a quartet of falsetto barks sounded shrilly from the four wicker baskets in the car. At the sound, Ronald pricked up his ears in mild interest. Even Fay stared wonder-ingly. Iry explained:

"I'm taking Mrs. Biller's four Pekinese over to the show. There isn't room for them in her car. She's gone on ahead. But whatever on earth's happened to you, missy? To the two of you, for that matter? Have you—?"

Stiffly, formally, her jaw set hard, Fay began to tell her story. Then, through no will of her own, she broke down and wailed the rest of the fearsome narrative. Iry listened, open-mouthed. Before he could com-ment, her conscience awoke belatedly. Just because she had ruined Ronny's career, it was no reason why the four basketed Pekes should lose their chances.

"Hurry up!" she exhorted Iry. "You're—you're fifteen minutes late, now. You can't possibly get to Paignton by ten o'clock. And if you don't—"

"If I don't," finished Tevvis, with no trace of anxiety—"if I don't, I'll get there when I do get there. That's all there is to that. But I want you should stop crying. It's rotten hard luck, I know. But—"

"The show begins at ten o'clock," insisted Fay, the fate of the Pekes oppressing her more and more. " 'Promptly at ten.' It says so. And if—"

"And if it does," rumbled Iry, unconcernedly, "there'll be an earth-quake and a new Congress. For there wasn't ever yet a dog show that began anywhere inside of an hour of the time it was scheduled to. I've follered them for a good many years now, with my own dogs and with other folks'. And I haven't found a one of 'em that started before eleven o'clock. So—"

"But that won't do Ronny any good," lamented Fay, her personal griefs coming to the fore again, now she knew the Pekes were not to be made late on her account. "It'll take ever so long to get him clean, and it'll take weeks for those swellings of his to go down. Here I've got his ticket and everything! And he can't even go there, or to any other show till—"

"Hold on!" broke in Iry, eagerly, as her eyes filled anew. "Just don't you go a-crying again, now! There's only two things in this funny old world I can't stand to sit by and watch. And both of 'em is a scared child a-crying. Listen! You're in trouble, anyhow, I s'pose. But the thing you seem unhappiest over is that collie missing his show. Would you as soon take your scolding this afternoon as this morning? Because if you would, hop in here with me, you and your dog."

"I—I don't understand what—"

"You will. Here's the plan: I'm on my way to the show, aren't I? Well, you and the dog can come, too. You got his ticket and everything. If we was to drive all the way back and talk it over with your pa, we'd be late for sure. Besides, if he took one look at that dog, he'd figger there wouldn't be a ghost of a chance for him to ever look decent again. Now *I* know better. I was handling collies before your pa ever saw one. Hop in. As soon as we get to the show, I'll phone your folks. Then they won't worry what's happened to you. And if they want to come over, they can. By that time I'll have the collie a-looking like something. If—"

A veritable squeal of delight interrupted him. Her tear-splotched face transfigured, her imagination fired by the prospect, Fay was swarming up into the car among the baskets, exhorting the willing Ronald to join her there.

"And I'll give you my watch," she promised, gratefully, as they got into motion. "I haven't any money with me except sixteen cents. But you can have my watch for taking us there and back. It's—it's worth ever so many dollars. I—"

"You'll cut out that line of fool talk, missy!" ordained Iry, roughly, "if you and me is to be feller-passengers in this rattly old ark of mine. I'm doing this as a buddy of yours. Not for pay. If your pa wants to slip me something, later, well—why, that's up to *him*. I'll show the dog for you, too, if you like, in the ring. Unless maybe you think he'll show better for you, him not knowing me."

"I'll show him!" she declared, delighted at the prospect. "I know how. I've seen daddy do it at his other dog shows. And I've watched him make Ronny show, for practice, ever so many times, on the lawn at home. I know the words that make him prick up his ears and look all noble. *Please* let me!"

"All right!" agreed Tevvis. "There's no great trick in doing it, if a dog is a natural shower, like this one of yours is. I saw that when I watched him in the ring at Paterson, last fall. Besides, lots of judges kind of favors a dog that's showed by a kid. Go to it!"

To Iry Tevvis there was nothing strikingly amiss in the child's bedraggled costume. True, it was soaking wet. But an hour's drive in sun and wind would dry it. As to its several torn places and its ample brocading of mud and strawberry juice, it was almost neat in comparison with the clothes of his own brood of picturesque grandchildren.

"Besides," he went on, "collies may not be judged till late afternoon. Long before that time your pa and your ma will be there to handle their dog—and maybe to give you a good talking-to," he added.

The prospect of later retribution did not for an instant mar Fay's glittering vision of the show. But she glanced down apprehensively at Ronald as he stood in placid contentment on the floor of the car in front of her. The rush of sunny air from the open windows was drying his lank coat. His fur was beginning to stand out fluffily from chest and sides. Less and less did he look like an emaciated drowned rat.

His face's contour, too, was growing to resemble that of a collie instead of a gargoyle. Fay was learning for the first time the amazing speed with which the swelling of an insect sting can subside from the flesh of a healthy young dog. Already the swollen eye was open. The myriad other lumps were losing size and aggressiveness.

Fay looked disconsolately at her own attire. Then she leaned forward and said primly to Tevvis:

"Iry, will you please promise to keep looking straight ahead at the road? I am going to sit down in the bottom of the car for a little while, and hold my dress out of the window to dry. Then if you can spare some of those pins that are stuck in the front of your shirt, won't you please pass them back to me? I want to do some mending."

By the time the taxi was parked in the tented enclosure where the Paignton dog show was in progress, Coolharbor Ronald was dry and fluffy. His paws and the white portions of his coat were still grayish, and here and there his hair stuck together in bunches. But no longer was he grotesque. The swellings had all but departed.

As Mrs. Biller came forward to collect her baskets full of Pekes, she looked in perplexed disapproval at the daughter of her friend and neighbor, Mrs. Malcolm Denning. Her opinion of that estimable woman declined sharply at sight of the unkempt and altogether wretched condition of Fay's dress and shoes and stockings. The Peke owner could not understand how any mother could let her little girl come to a public place looking like such a mess.

But it was no business of Mrs. Biller's. She told herself so. Later she told several other neighbors so. She gathered up her Pekes and strode away, leaving Iry to pilot Fay and Ronald past the gate and to the collie's numbered stall.

Coolharbor Ronald was anchored on his bench in the collie section—a section which some twenty-seven dogs of his breed already occupied. Owners and handlers were at work over some of them with cloth and dandy brush and talcum and other aids to beauty. Visitors were drifting along the aisles, pausing at one or another of the benches to stare at the dogs or to ask vapid questions of the nervously busy exhibitors.

Iry brought Ronald a pan of fresh drinking water. Then he departed, to telephone the news to Denning. Despite his own brave assurance, assumed for the quelling of Fay's grief and worry, Iry was not wholly at ease in the prospect of explaining to Malcolm Denning that he had kidnapped the girl and the dog. Thus it was with a grin of relief that he heard at the far end of the telephone the voice of one of the Denning maids. Speaking very fast and hanging up the receiver as soon as he had delivered the message, he said:

"This is Iry Tevvis. Tell your boss I've took little Fay and the collie over to the Paignton show, and they're all right and he's not to get sore. Tell him to come on over, quick, and show his dog. I'll have him in shape for the ring before the boss gets here. G'by."

It was another five minutes before Iry returned to the bench where Fay stood guard over the big collie. He had commandeered from other dog men a tin of water, a handful of dusty lumps of French chalk, a broken comb, and a bunch of soft rags. Fay recalled the elaborate kit of grooming appliances her father would take to shows, and her confidence began to flag. But it was restored when she saw the briskly workmanlike way Iry began to labor over the dog's coat.

Deftly he combed and cleaned and fluffed. Shamelessly he applied great quantities of French chalk to the spots where the grime refused to yield to gentler treatment and to the paws and the face-blaze. Under the clever grooming, Ronny began to look somewhat as he had before his disastrous walk with Fay. The swellings were disappearing fast. To increase the speed of their vanishing, Tevvis anointed the dog with witch hazel he begged from a neighboring exhibitor. A human would have carried those swellings for days. Ronald had gotten rid of them with incredible ease.

"Wasn't it perfectly gorgeous how he got himself all stung up and tortured, just to save *me?*" exclaimed Fay, lovingly stroking the shimmering coat of her chum. "Did you ever hear of a dog being so splendid? He—"

"I did," answered Iry, without pausing from his work. "I did, once. It was a collie of my own. He did just that very thing when my own kid bumped into a hornet nest when him and her was out for a stroll together. But he's dead this fifteen years. He was my pal. And he's dead. Like all dogs die, by the time they get to be a man's best chum and when he could spare fifty human folks out of his life easier than he could spare his chum dog. Just when they've got so close to the heart of you that you feel you can't get on without 'em, they up and die. Dogs die too soon, anyway. When I heard how this collie of yours done the same stunt, this morning, I made up my mind I'd do what I could for him here, kind of in memory of my own collie pal."

He laid down the cloth which he had been using as a sponge, and he went to work again with a lump of French chalk, applying it here and there with artistic touches.

"Collie judge isn't here yet," he continued. "It's pretty close to eleven o'clock. The judging will begin in a few minutes. If the collie judge don't get here soon, the four rings will all be taken by the other breeds. That'll mean the collies can't be judged till afternoon. So your pa will be here plenty early to fix up his dog and show him. I'm just getting him in shape in case the—"

Down the aisle hustled a white-coated show attendant, droning monotonously:

"Get your collies ready. Ring Number Three. Calling 'Male Puppy' Class. Numbers 225, 226, 227, 228, 229!"

Iry Tevvis stopped him as he scuttled past.

"I thought the collie judge wasn't here yet," said he. "How does—?"

"Just got here," replied the attendant, hustling on. "Told the superintendent he has to catch a train for the city at one o'clock, and he wants to do his judging job right off."

Down the aisle he continued, calling out his sing-song announcement. Instantly the collie section was abuzz with activity and nervous excitement. Iry glanced at the number tag on Ronald's collar, then at the catalogue he had borrowed from a momentarily vacant camp stool.

"Number 241," he mused. "Your pa has only entered him for the "American-bred" Class. That won't be called for another ten minutes. Maybe longer. "Novice" Class comes next to the "Puppy" Class. I'll have time to finish getting him in shape."

A vast wave of terror swept over Fay as she watched him. It was one thing to dream valorously beforehand of putting Ronald through his ring paces. It was quite another to contemplate at close quarters the prospect of responsibility for his victory or downfall. Her hands grew very wet and her mouth very dry. Then she braced herself all over.

"Ronny," she whispered, leaning over the dog as Tevvis fluffed out the plumed tail and hind end, "I got you into all that nasty mess. There's nobody but me that can make up to you for it. And I can't do it unless you help me a lot, Ronny. You'll just have to imagine it's daddy piloting you in the ring, and act the way he taught you to."

The collie wagged his tail (much to the annoyance of Iry, who was trying to comb it) and licked the scared little face so close to his own. Then, it seemed only a moment before the attendant was droning forth a new set of numbers at the end of the aisle and Iry was lifting the resplendent Coolharbor Ronald off his bench and handing her the leash. With numbed legs Fay made her way toward the million-mile distant show ring, in the wake of several other people who were leading collies thither for the "American-bred" Class—a class open to all dogs except champions.

Into the ring filed the six entrants for "American-bred" honors. In the center of the roped enclosure was the low judging block, or platform. In one corner of the ring was a table bearing an open judging book and a varicolored heap of ribbons. Beside the table stood a fat little man in tweeds. At the entrance to the ring another man checked off the numbers of the competing dogs.

"All in, sir," presently called this other man. The fat little judge came out of his studious apathy. Advancing from his corner, he surveyed the six collies as if he noticed their presence for the first time. Then he rasped:

"Walk your dogs, please!"

Around the ring plodded the six handlers, their dogs either pulling back on the leashes or else marching proudly alongside. Fay was familiar enough with the procedure. Presently the parade would be halted, and the judge would order one dog after another to be brought on to the block for his examination.

All this, unless some collie should be deemed unworthy of careful inspection. There had been such a collie at the Englewood show and another at Paterson. The judges then had ordered the outclassed dog taken away while the parade was still in progress.

As the procession started a second time around the ring, the judge stepped suddenly forward from his place near the block. Touching Fay on the shoulder, he said, none too gently:

"Take your dog out of the parade. Take him over in that corner, and keep him there."

Aghast, the child stared up at him, doubting her own ears. But with a peremptory twitch of his thumb toward the nearest corner of the ring, he turned away and called one of the other dogs to the block.

Into the corner Fay Denning piloted her loved and degraded chum. There she stood beside him, while the judging went on in the center. The ringside crowd seemed to eye the disheveled child and her discredited collie with amused scorn. She wished they would stop looking at her. Not that she minded it for herself, though she was increasingly aware of the shabby figure she cut. But she hated to have them grin so derisively at poor Ronny.

Ronny! And this was to have been his crowning day of triumph, the day when he should win canine immortality by winning his championship! He had been groomed and conditioned to the utmost by Denning. And it was she who had wrecked it all. Of course the judge must have seen at a glance the damage done to his massive coat by all that water and mud. The swellings on his classic head and his shapely lower legs must still be visible. And that well-meaning old Iry had only made him look worse, probably, by his clumsy efforts at grooming.

Thanks to her, the dog was stuck here in a corner—"gated," didn't they call it?—for everybody to snicker at. Why hadn't that snappy judge let her take him back to his bench, instead of sending him to this corner for people to make fun of? Furtively she began to edge toward the entrance of the ring. While the judge was busy over the five other dogs, she might be able to slip away with poor, beautiful, defeated Ronny, and get him out of sight.

But she was too late. Even as she sidled toward the gap the judge finished his inspection of the others and whirled around on her. Striding up to Ronny, he passed wondrous expert fingers lightly over the "gated" dog. Then he stood back and ran his eye over him with what seemed to Fay the most contemptuous sneer she had seen on a human face.

She sobbed under her breath, then steeled herself to glare back at her dear dog's tormentor. Low as was the sob, Ronny heard it. At once his ears went up, their tulip tips and the worriedly sympathetic glint in the eyes enlivening his whole expression. He whimpered softly.

The judge grunted and walked off without so much as another glance at him. He did not go back to the other dogs, but to the table where lay the judging book. Fay took this time to hurry to the entrance. But again she was too late.

"Stop!" ordered the judge.

She stopped, hesitant and rebellious. What new humiliation was the horrible man going to heap on Ronny? He came up to her, inspected the number on Ronny's tag, jotted a figure or two in the judging book, then thrust something into Fay's mud-grimed brown hand.

Some one clapped. A score of people clapped. The judge was bearing down on another dog and fingering his book. Fay looked dully at the thing he had handed her.

It was a dark-blue ribbon!

A dark-blue ribbon with gold lettering around the official gold seal of the American Kennel Club.

The blue ribbon! First prize in the class! It—why, it meant Ronny had —had *won!* It couldn't possibly be, after the way the judge had ignored him. Her dreamless dream about the bears had been more logical than this. But—

"*Good* little Miss Fay!" exulted Iry, meeting her at the ring entrance and shaking her hand in wild congratulation. "He done it! But then I knew he would as soon as I seen the judge send him into that corner. Ronny was so much better'n the rest of his class that he put him aside while he figgered out what dogs to give the second and third prizes to. Judges often do that. Now we'll take him back to his bench and groom him for the 'Winners' Class—the class for all the dogs that's won their own reg'lar classes—the class that gives the champ'nship points to the dog that wins it. Then'll come the 'specials,' after all the reg'lar classes is over you know. So it's up to us to put him at his best. Come along. Why —you look like you was asleep! Buck up! We just won the strongest class there's likely to be in this show."

It was a wrathful Malcolm Denning who hastened into the huge tent, with his indignant wife, an hour later. His first question, of a passing attendant, was whether or not the collies had yet been judged. When he was told their judging had been finished some minutes earlier, his wrath was not lessened. Stormily he made his way toward the collie section.

As he and his wife hurried along the aisle, a knot of people stopped their progress. The group was gathered around one bench in the long line. Denning peeped over the heads of those nearest him to see the cause of so much interest. His wife, through a gap in the shoulders of those in front of her, followed the direction of his gaze. Then they both stood spellbound, goggle-eyed.

On the bench reclined their lost dog, resplendent and majestic. Close beside him in the straw sat Fay, one arm around his shaggy neck, her eyes like stars in a murky lake. In her free hand she gripped proudly a gleaming silver cup half as large as herself. Above the bench, decorated by a blue ribbon and a purple rosette and several tricolored ribbons, Iry Tevvis had scrawled on a thumb-blackened sheet of wrapping paper the legend:

CHAMPION *Coolharbor Ronald; Winner and Best Collie Of Either Sex in Paignton Show.*

Iry himself, glowing like a sunset, stood beaming on all and sundry. At sight of the Dennings he lurched forward and caught them unceremoniously by the arms, drawing them back from the crowd. There, half-triumphantly, half-shamefacedly, he told them in dramatic fervor the tale of Fay's exploits.

Fay herself looked up from her admirers to see her father beckoning to her. Instantly, delirious happiness froze into terror. Yet, walking very straight, she came across to him through the clump of onlookers. Denning, without a word, piloted her to a deserted end of the tent. Then he spoke.

"Daughter," he said, in the rare judicial tone she always dreaded, "you disobeyed your mother and me this morning. You abused our trust in you. You betrayed us. Have you anything to say for yourself?"

Fay fought for words. Then, in a muffled little voice, she answered right bravely: "No, sir. I haven't got anything at all to say for myself. I did all those things."

Denning nodded, in what might almost have seemed approval, as she did not urge in her own defense the glorious fruits of her disobedience.

"That sort of thing has to be punished," went on the gravely judicial voice. "It has to be punished severely. Here is the punishment I am going to give you—a punishment you will remember all your life: I am going to condemn you to spoil your prettiest dress by rolling in a strawberry bed. Next, I am going to make you stand in a cold lake and wash a muddy dog. Next, I am going to make you get a bad hornet sting on the back of your hand and be more frightened and unhappy than you've ever been. There, daughter! You've heard your sentence."

Again he paused. She was blinking at him, uncomprehendingly. He resumed:

"Of course, if you have already suffered any or all of those punishments, I am not going to be so cruel as to make you go through them again. In that case, you've paid your bill and the slate is clean, which is a good deal more than *you* are just now."

"*Daddy!*"

"I—I think I heard your mother say something, a minute ago, about buying you that pink silk dress you were so crazy about the last time we were in the city," continued Malcolm Denning, gruffly. "As a handler fee, you know, for carrying Ronny to victory today. I never thought I should be so proud of anyone who is so dirty and so disobedient! Now stop crying and tell me about the show!"

The Feud

"What d'ye call him?" asked Bourke.

"A collie," answered Hurd.

"H'm!" sniffed Bourke, suspecting an attempt of the better educated farmer to patronize him by use of this unknown word. "Looks more to me like a shepherd dog."

"It's the same thing," patiently explained Hurd. "The old-timers used to call them shepherd dogs, but the Scotch called them collies. The name has crossed over to America. I found this one down at the Rumson dog pound a couple of months ago. I went there to look for that mongrel of Kernan's. The dog had disappeared and Kernan thought it might have gotten as far as Rumson and been raked in by the pound master. His dog wasn't there. In fact, it never has shown up, anywhere, since the day it vanished. But this young collie was at the pound. He had belonged to some folks that had to leave town one jump ahead of

131

the sheriff, and left their dog behind. The pound master had grabbed him. I bought him for ten dollars, and—"

"Ten dollars!" scoffed Bourke, with all a mountaineer's contempt for such useless waste of money. "Why, man, you could 'a' bought a trained coon dog for that! Ten dollars for a wuthless—"

"Not so worthless, maybe," contradicted Hurd. "I've only had him about two months, but in that time he has learned faster than we've been able to teach him. Look!"

He nodded toward his lower pasture lot. An uneasy heifer had been teasing a top rail of the makeshift fence with her half-grown horns until she had pried its rusty nails free and sent it toppling to the ground. Then she had attacked the second rail, with equal teasing persistence. As this rail tumbled she stepped through the gap, over the remaining rail, and headed gleefully for a nearby corn patch. The five other head of young cattle in the field came joyously through the gap, in her wake.

Bourke grinned. The day was sickeningly hot. The breached fence was a full two-hundred yards distant. That meant a fast run through the heat for Hurd, if he would head off the strays before they could begin to destroy the young corn. It would be amusing to stand there on the farmhouse porch and watch Hurd race around in the sun's glare after his absconding yearlings.

But Hurd showed no chagrin at the sight of his strays. Without moving a step, he snapped his fingers to the drowsing young collie at his feet. Instantly the dog was awake and up. Pointing to the straggling cattle, Hurd said:

"Turn 'em, Jock!"

Barking gaily, the collie dashed across the intervening ground like a fluffy and tawny thunderbolt. He caught up with the first heifer as she set forefoot in the corn.

Deftly he halted and wheeled her back. Then, getting her under way, he made for the others. In an incredibly brief space of time he had bunched the stragglers and had them in motion. He was here and there and everywhere, barking harrowingly, nipping where gentler persuasion failed.

Reluctantly the fugitives gave up their pleasant plan for a corn feast, and began to yield to his urge toward the fence gap through which they had found liberty. One by one Jock drove them through the gap, doubling back after two bolters; nor ceasing his task until every last one of the five was safe in the pasture. Then he stood panting in the gap, wagging his tail and looking to Hurd for further orders.

Hurd whistled. The collie came bounding back to the porch.

"You can stay here in the shade," Hurd told him, speaking as to a fellow human. "But watch 'em! *Watch* 'em!"

Turning to the interested Bourke, he added:

"He'll keep an eye on 'em, in case they try to get out again. I doubt if they'll try it more than once. Then, when it's cooler, along around sunset, I'll go down there and mend the fence. Handles cattle real pretty, don't he? Took to it from the first, like he had been doing it all his life. That's the collie of it. A lot of 'em pick up herding as easy as they pick up fleas. He's just the same with the sheep. No, Jock isn't worthless. Not by a mile. He's pretty near as useful as another hired man would be. That boy of mine thinks he's worth his weight in—"

"Shucks!" grunted Bourke, refusing to be impressed. "I'll bet he wouldn't be wuth a dern at cooning. I'd rather have a fust-class coon dog than all the shepherds that ever shepped. Rouser is wuth fifty of him."

He lifted his lanky frame from the chair into which he had lowered it on his arrival at the Hurd farm, ten minutes earlier.

"Well," he said, stretching, "I gotta trudge. I just dropped in, like I said, to see if maybe you might 'a' caught sight of Rouser anywheres. I'm asking everyone around here. He's too good to let go without giving a good look for him. He never strayed before in all the time I've had him. I can't understand it, nohow. He—"

A fourteen-year-old boy approached from the creek at the foot of the farm, a fishing pole over his shoulder and a string of six perch dangling from one hand. Hurd hailed him; then turning to Bourke, he explained:

"That son of mine is always traipsing around the woods, vacation-time, when his farm work's done. He'd have been more likely to see

Rouser than any of us grown folks would. Say, Ethan," he went on as the lad came up to the porch, "Mr. Bourke has lost that black coon hound of his. He—"

"Rouser?" asked the boy, in real interest. "That's funny!"

"Mebbe 'tis," rasped Bourke. "But I don't see the fun of it. That dog's wuth—"

"No, no," protested Ethan. "I didn't mean it that way. I meant it was queer that another dog has disappeared. That's the fourth in two months—four from just around here. And I don't ever remember hearing of any other dog being lost hereabouts till then. How long ago did you miss him?"

"Couple of days ago," answered Bourke. "I figured he had chased some fox so far he couldn't get back the same day. He did that once before, when he was a pup. But he'd never chase any fox so far that he couldn't get home again in *two* days. So this afternoon I been making inq'ries for him. You say he ain't the fust?"

"No, sir," replied Ethan excitedly. "He's the fourth. The fourth I've heard of. The first was Kernan's little crossbreed. Dad was looking for him when he found Jock at the pound. So that was one lucky lose for us. The second was Dan Foster's beagle. That was a month ago. Then, a couple of weeks back, the Landers' old coon dog strayed off and he hasn't ever been heard of again. And now it's Rouser. Funny, isn't it, Dad? All of them were dogs that had lived at their homes for years. Not a one of them was a runaway. They couldn't all four have been stolen. Nobody would have given a nickel for Kernan's mongrel. Nobody except Kernan."

Bourke was glowering at him and slowly chewing the big mouthful of tobacco he had just bitten from his plug. The mountaineer's small eyes puckered.

"Say, bub," he growled, "unless you're making this up, there's due to be an unholy lot of trouble over it. It ain't on the free list, in this region, to go around stealing folks' dogs. I've seen knives drawed quicker over a dog-stealing than over a bound'ry dispoot. If some one's trying to be funny or to settle some grudge by stealing our dogs, he might safer have bit into a hornet's nest. Soon or late he'll get nabbed. And when he does —well, I'm only speaking for myself, mind you. But if Rouser has been stole, the cuss that did it won't be fit to put in jail if I git to him before the const'ble does. So long."

He swung his lean body down onto the gravel walk and plodded out of the dooryard. Hurd looked after him worriedly.

"Say, Ethan," he rebuked, "you hadn't ought to have put that notion in Hi Bourke's mind. He's an old mountaineer. I know the breed. When he thinks some one's robbed him or done him some other harm, his first thought is that crooked old sheath knife of his, and his second thought is his bear rifle. He'll go sleuthing around now till he thinks he's found the man who stole his dog. Then there's li'ble to be work for a jury. Maybe the grand jury, at that. What makes you think Rouser was stolen?"

"I don't," returned Ethan. "I didn't say I did. I said the four dogs weren't likely to have been stolen. Two of 'em weren't worth stealing. I just said it was funny that all four of 'em should have disappeared in two months. I tell you I'm going to keep a mighty close eye on Jock and Eileen. Specially on Jock. Eileen's too old and wise to get lost anywhere."

At this second mention of her name a diminutive and ancient red setter came slowly out from her lair in the cool earth under the porch and approached Ethan, wagging a moth-eaten tail.

The runt of an illustrious litter, she had been bought by Hurd, for a mere trifle, eleven years earlier. Under his tutelage she had developed into one of the most renowned bird dogs in the county. Ludicrously small, she made up for dearth of size by her inspired scenting powers and field skill and by dauntless courage. Now age was silvering her red muzzle and stiffening her lithe muscles. But she was still adventurous and worthy of respect.

From the hour of his arrival at the farm Jock had worshiped the crotchety little old setter. And she had taken a pretty and motherly interest in him—she who usually would snap at other dogs. They were dear chums, the old setter and the young collie. Jock was even more deeply devoted to Eileen than to his human idols, Hurd and Ethan.

Now as she appeared from her dark lair under the porch Jock advanced to meet her, tail awag. The two touched noses and trotted off together toward the creek for a swim. But, halfway there, the collie seemed to remember his master's command to watch the cattle. He glanced sideways down the field toward the lower pasture.

The mischief-making heifer had become emboldened by his absence to make for the fence gap again. She was blundering through, toward the cornfield, the five other yearlings at her heels. This was no time for a swim. Barking, the collie raced after the strays.

Eileen watched him, as if wondering at his desertion. Then the heat of the day and the promise of coolness in the creek's fast waters made her trot on to her swim.

The cattle proved sulkier and more difficult than before. It was several minutes before Jock was able to get them all herded into the pasture. Then, as he was departing, one of them made another break for the gap. Impatiently he headed her back. To make certain she and the rest would not try to get out again the moment his back should be turned, he cleared the rail and chased the six in a huddled bunch to the far end of the pasture.

His work done, he saw Hurd coming down from the house with a hammer and nail box. The man, at this second attempt of the cattle to escape, had decided not to wait for a cooler hour, but to mend the broken fence at once. Jock realized his own vigil was at an end and that he was free to go for his coveted swim with Eileen.

"Hold on, Jockey!" called Ethan, as the collie loped past. "I left my other pole down there. I'll go with you."

Together the boy and the dog made their way across the meadow and to the rise of tree-fringed ground which marked the nearer bank of the creek. As they went, there came to them the sound of a distant bark. Both recognized it as Eileen's. Jock bounded forward, as at a summons. To him the timbre of the bark meant more than mere excitement. Ethan whistled him back.

"Your coat's too thick to go galloping after rabbits or coons or whatever she's put up, this sizzling weather," he said sternly to the collie. "Take your time. Dad says Eileen's only fault is that she *will* take out after coons and rabbits and such like when he's not gunning with her. In weather like this she's too old to go racing them. Don't encourage her by chasing along after her. Come back."

Unwillingly Jock obeyed. He was keen to rush off to Eileen at top speed. A dog's bark has a dozen shades of meaning which all other dogs and many dog men can read. In that one distant bark of Eileen's the collie read much. He craved mightily to join in the adventure, whatever it might be. But Ethan's word was his law. So, fidgeting, he came to heel.

Together, at leisurely pace, the lad and the collie reached the creek, arriving at its widest part, where Ethan's boat was moored. There was no sign of Eileen.

Fingers to lips, Ethan whistled piercingly. The shrill note split the hot silences of the summer afternoon. Twice he whistled. Then he strained his ears to catch the rustle and crack of undergrowth which should betoken the little old setter's return. But the silence hung dead in the torrid world.

"H'm!" said Ethan, aloud. "She must have run a big distance, not to hear that whistle of mine. She always comes on the jump when she hears it."

He frowned, perplexed. He knew that the stiffening legs of the aged setter could not have borne her so far in that brief time as to make his sharp whistle unheard. He knew, too, that such a call ordinarily would have brought her back to him at top speed.

Again he whistled, long and shrilly. Then he shouted. No answering bark or sound of tearing through the bushes. He turned to Jock. The collie seemed to have read the boy's thought before it was formed. He was casting about, in an irregular half-circle, nostrils close to the drought-parched grass.

"Good old Jockey!" approved Ethan. "Find her! Find Eileen. That's right."

Like many another well-trained collie, Jock knew well the meaning of the command, "Find!" Also he knew who was meant by Eileen. He was doing his best to obey. He had been doing so before the order was given. Perhaps he, too, wondered at the setter's non-response to the call.

In another second his sniffing nostrils ceased to quest. They had found the trail they sought.

Head down, he galloped along in a straight line, alongside the creek; Ethan following at top speed. After several yards he veered inland, quickly taking up a straight line again. Ethan understood. Eileen had detoured here to avoid a clump of brier and sumac and, having skirted it, had continued her course.

A hundred yards farther the dog swung at right angles to his former route. Here a noisy mountain brook spilled downward from the abruptly rising hillside and emptied into the creek. Up the hill, amid boulders and tree trunks, sped the collie, Ethan trying in vain to keep up with him.

Well did the boy know this abrupt slope of Raccoon Mountain, the southerly limit of Hurd's farm. The brook dropped, from a spring at the very summit, in a series of rapids and tiny cataracts, spreading out into large or small pools at various narrow plateaus amid the boulder-strewn slope.

At the first of these pools—a widish sheet of water, nowhere more than a foot deep—the collie had come to a halt. He was smelling around the rocky edges of the pool, and taking a hesitant step or two out into its stone-bottomed expanse.

Again Ethan understood. Even a dog's unerring sense of smell will not guide him through running water. There, all odor disperses. Eileen had come as far as this. Then she had run out into the pool.

Instantly Jock came back to land. He skirted the entire pool, nose to ground. But he could not pick up the scent again.

And now Ethan felt that he himself should have been as able as the dog to follow the trail. For the rocks on every side were dry and sun-baked. If a dog wades out into the water, and then comes back on such dry and grassless ground, there will be distinct wet footmarks visible for many minutes thereafter, as visible to the human eye as their scent is perceptible to a collie's nose.

But on no spot was there a single wet footprint. Eileen must have passed this way and splashed into the pool, not ten minutes earlier. Into the pool she had gone. Jock's unerring scent proved that. But she had not come out of it. There was not so much as a splash of water on the baked poolside rocks, except where Jock had tracked the moisture ashore on his own return from reconnoitering there.

The thing did not make sense.

Vexed at the mystery, Ethan took off his shoes and socks and waded out into the pool. The bottom was formed by a solid sheet of rock, slightly concave, perhaps twenty feet long by fifteen feet wide, and with its surface worn almost glass smooth by centuries of freshets hurtling down from the mountain above.

From end to end of the pool, and back and forth across it, waded Ethan, the water nowhere rising above his shins. No, there was no unseen crevice down which Eileen could have slipped. Nor was there a hidden patch of quicksand that could have sucked her in. The basin of rock was unbroken.

In midpool Ethan ceased his explorations. He felt queer in the stomach. This was like the magic he had read of in storybooks. Eileen had run up the hillside till she came to this pool. She had run out into the pool. There she had disappeared, though not even a lively cat could have drowned in it. The water was crystal clear against the bottom of pale gray rock. Ethan could see every inch of the shallow basin. There was nothing in it, not so much as a minnow.

Then his sense of awe departed and he grinned sheepishly at his own absurd fear. Why, the thing was simple enough!

At the pool's lower end the water filtered down in a thin cataract to the brook below. At its upper end it was fed by the brook from above. At this end the water tumbled down a steep slant, perhaps three feet wide, for a distance of some thirty yards, over boulders and gravel, to the lip of the next pool overhead.

Naturally, since Eileen had not come out of the pool at any of its sides, she had swarmed up that slant in the bubbling bed of the brook, pursuing whatever thing had chanced to be her prey.

Left to herself, she would have chosen the easier going, on the bank of the stream. But the creature she was chasing had apparently stuck to the brook bed—perhaps with an instinct of obliterating its own scent— and Eileen had not dared risk the loss of time involved in detouring by the longer and easier route.

The pool above was smaller, but much deeper, and with sharp juts of rock sticking out far below its surface. Ethan knew the place well. He had bathed there, sometimes, when August heat had made even the cold creek waters too warm for comfortable swimming. There, too, he had scraped his legs against the sharp shelves of rock and shale which jutted out at several places along the lower portions of the five-foot depths.

Still grinning at his momentary feeling of superstitious dread, he climbed the slope, close alongside the brook, till he came to this second pool. Jock ran beside him, still fruitlessly sniffing.

The pool lay black and peaceful, save where the falling waters from the steep slant above churned it to bubbles and froth.

No sign here of the missing Eileen. Summoning Jock, the boy made him circle the pool and then the brookside above it. Try as he would, the collie could pick up no scent.

Then, without warning, Jock shuddered violently all over, as if smitten with a convulsion. Sitting down, he lifted his classic muzzle to the sky, shattering the still afternoon air with a succession of eerie wolf howls so earsplitting and unearthly as to make the astounded Ethan shout angrily to him to be still.

The boy felt his own scalp crinkle at the horrible sound. Trying to shake off the unbidden terror of it, he said:

"Well, Eileen will hear that, anyhow, if she's in the same county with you. It'll bring her racing back to us, if anything will. But what in blue blazes ails you, Jockey? Have you gone crazy?"

The collie, still shivering convulsively, crouched with head adroop and tail between his legs, his eyes half shut. From his furry throat came sounds strangely like human sobs. To the startled boy this manifestation was more creepy than had been the deafening outburst. Ethan glanced nervously about him.

Aroused by the racket, a huge and elderly raccoon had thrust forth his comedy mask of a face from a cleft in the tumble of rocks above the pool. Now, at the sight of the boy and the dog, he drew back into his stony lair, like some ludicrous jack-in-the-box.

Ethan was not interested in the raccoon. Had the season been autumn or winter, he would have impressed Jock into service, then and there, as a coon dog, and would have tried to hustle the stones far enough aside to dislodge the beast. For raccoon pelts, in prime, were worth quite a bit, from any nearby dealer.

But at this stiflingly hot season raccoon fur was far off prime. The raccoons themselves were hog fat and of poor flavor for food. There was nothing to be gained in digging out this obese creature. So Ethan left it to its interrupted nap and shouted again for Eileen.

There was a quaver in his voice as he yelled the missing setter's name. He was beginning to be genuinely troubled as to her fate, the more so because of Jock's amazing behavior. The boy knew enough of collies not to discount the almost psychic phases that sometimes possess them. He did not like those eerie death howls, nor the subsequent shuddering and sobbing.

To quell his own disturbed fear, he called sharply to Jock and pursued his climb. Eileen had come part of the way along the wet course of the brook. It might be worthwhile to follow the brook upward and find at what point she had emerged from it. Damp footprints on the dry rocks would surely show him the exact spot where she had emerged. After that it would be simple for Jock to track her.

The collie needed a second sharp summons from his young master before consenting to follow. Then he crept along listlessly, constantly looking back and refusing to take any interest whatever in the hunt.

At last, after a hot and breathtaking climb, Ethan reached the summit and the bubbling big spring which was the mountain brook's source.

Nowhere had he seen trace of Eileen. He looked around. Jock was no longer at his heels. The collie had turned and started downhill.

Ethan called him peremptorily. With much reluctance, the collie trotted uphill toward him. For another half-hour the boy searched the mountain, Jock following sullenly, at his repeated orders, but taking no part in the hunt, nor so much as sniffing. Instead, he kept turning back toward the second pool.

It was sunset when Ethan and the dog reached home. There the boy called once more to Eileen, half hoping to see the silver-muzzled little red body come wriggling out from under the porch to greet him.

"Listen, Jock," he said to the collie, as they tramped up the walk, "she isn't here. She isn't ever coming back. She's gone. Just as those four other dogs went. You knew that before I did. It don't make sense, but it's true. She disappeared somewhere on the side of the mountain. There's Something up yonder that isn't good for dogs. You've been trying to get back there every time I looked the other way. You're not going back there. Understand? I'm going to put you in the old calf paddock for the night. It's wired, and you can't get out of it. Tomorrow I'm going to keep an eye on you till my chores are done. Then we're going back there together. With the rifle, maybe. There's no bears or panthers or even wild cats around here. So there's nothing that could have killed those dogs or hidden them too close for them to get loose and come home. Just the same, they didn't come home. Yes, we'll take the rifle."

As ever, he talked to the wise young dog as he would have talked to a human. Jock as a rule was highly flattered at such conversation. Tonight he gave it no heed. Nor would he eat his supper. Twice, before he was shut into the disused calf paddock for the night, Ethan found him trying to creep away in the direction of Raccoon Mountain. The gay collie had undergone a grim change that the boy could not understand.

Hurd and the rest of the family sought at first to make light of Ethan's fantastic theories as to the vanishing of Eileen. But when day dawned and the setter had not returned, Hurd himself took the morning off to look for her.

Old as she was, Hurd felt she could not have been done away with by any wild animal. In the first place, there was no wild thing within miles that was as large as she or that could have conquered her in a stand-up fight. And even had she been set upon and overcome by a bear, the sound of battle would surely have reached Ethan at the creek, and he and Jock would have seen unmistakable signs of such conflict when they followed her trail. No, she had disappeared in a way wholly beyond her woodsman master's experience or conjecture.

On his way back from the fruitless search, Hurd chanced to meet Bourke, who also had been wandering the hills and farms for sign of his beloved coonhound, Rouser.

Hurd told him of his own loss. The mountaineer's thick brows folded down over his small eyes.

"That boy of your'n has got sense," he declared. "It ain't in reason that five dogs would all stray off from the homes where they'd always lived, and fergit to come back. There's been foul play, I'm telling you. Eth was right. Somebody's a-tryin' to be funny or else to pay off some grudge. Nobody that wanted to steal a dog for profit would 'a' stole Kernan's mutt; nor yet that no-count beagle of Dan Forster's. That dog was a plumb fool. Nope. A smart Alec or else some grudge-toter is doin' this. Likewise I aim to find out who he is. When I do, I'm—well, I'm a-hopin' there'll be enough dog owners on my jury to let me off easy."

"More feuds have started in these mountains over dogs than over everything else put together," said Hurd. "Think careful a couple of times, before you start another, Hi. Don't go off half cocked. Like as not, you and my boy are both clean wrong in your notions. Keep your head."

"Keep my head!" mocked Bourke. "Easy enough for you to say that. Eileen was past her day. You told me you wa'n't going to hunt her ag'in. But how about Rouser? That coon dog was in his prime. He was the best in the county, bar none. Why, he was ready money to me! I don't git robbed of spot cash without gitting arter the skunk that robbed me."

Hurd could realize what the loss of Rouser must mean to the impoverished mountaineer. Bourke was a renowned coon hunter. He paid his taxes and paid for such repairs as his farm was lucky enough to get and for many a square meal, out of the raccoons and red foxes he was able to shoot or to trap in wintertime.

From at least one firm of furriers in the ten-mile-distant city of Rumson there was a ready market and fair price for all the raccoon and fox pelts Bourke could get hold of. By a trick well known to the trade, but known neither to Bourke nor to the public, a strange and profitable blend was made of these two dissimilar types of fur.

Cleverly were the red fox pelts dyed a lustrous black, except for the white tail tips and an occasional single white hind foot. Then the long silvery "guard hairs" of the raccoon were inserted deftly, here and there, into the dyed pelt, with an electric needle. The result was a pelt so closely akin to that of the rare "silver fox" that none but an expert could tell the two apart, and then only by sense of touch.

Undeterred by his father's failure, Ethan prepared to set off on his own account that afternoon as soon as his farm work was done. All morning he had kept Jock close to him. Sulky, half rebellious, Jock had accompanied the boy here and there. Always his wrathful eyes kept turning toward Raccoon Mountain. More than once he growled under his breath.

Jock had worshiped the little old setter that had mothered him so prettily. Her disappearance had changed him to a sullenly wrathful brute whose only desire was to get back to the scene of her vanishing. Not even Hi Bourke was so ridden by the sense of feud and revenge as was this sunny-tempered collie.

Moreover, Jock's nostrils had told him more than could be gleaned by the mere woodcraft of any human. It had not given him a positive clue to his setter chum's fate, but it had given him something to connect it with. Nor was this in any way akin to the odd canine sixth sense which suddenly had apprised him that the loved setter was dead.

All afternoon, boy and dog ranged the mountain, following the pools and the brook that linked them. The dog had been frantically eager to get to the mountain. Yet when he reached the second pool, he merely sniffed its banks, snarling under his breath, and was persuaded to continue the search from there only by Ethan's imperative command.

Tired and discouraged, Ethan brought Jock home at nightfall. They had drawn a blank.

Weary as he was, Ethan slept badly. The night was stickily warm and breathless. He awoke at first gray tinge of dawn. Not for another hour was he due to get up. Yet he was restless and hot and unhappy. It occurred to him that a swim before breakfast would brace him for the day's work.

Silently he put on trousers and shirt. Then he crept downstairs and out into the dew-soaked dooryard. On the porch stood the squirrel rifle, where he had left it when he came home. Perhaps there might be a gray squirrel or so, at this early hour, in the creekside trees. The boy picked up the rifle, loaded it, and slipped a few spare cartridges into his pocket. Then, letting Jock out of the paddock, he started for the creek.

The collie did not bound forth at him, as usual, in eager greeting, but trotted out, head down, paying no heed to Ethan, and heading at once toward the base of Raccoon Mountain.

Ethan caught him by the scruff of the neck and scolded him into walking alongside, instead of deserting him for a silly return to the pool. Together they made their way down the meadow and to the rise of ground which marked the edge of the creek.

Ethan stuck an exploratory bare toe into the water. The hot days and nights had made the usually chilly creek warm to the touch. The boy recalled the icily limpid second pool where sometimes he bathed. The added coolness would be worth the climb. He set forth to the spot where the brook ran into the creek, and began to follow it up the hill.

At the second step of his ascent something fat and grayish and shapeless scuttled out of sight, up a turn of the brook bed, a few yards in front of him. The listless Jock at once gave furious chase. Ethan's lips parted to call him back. Then he decided to let the dog go ahead.

His own fleeting glimpse of the gray creature had been enough to tell him it was a large raccoon that had been hunting for crayfish and minnows in the shallows of the brook. Probably it was the same raccoon whose comic face had peered out from the rock cleft above the second pool two days earlier. The collie might tree him or might more likely lose him among the scores of rock holes along the way. In either event the excitement of the chase might lift Jock from the glum misery that had been his since the loss of Eileen.

So he allowed the dog to continue the race, quickening his own steps up the rough incline and letting the rifle hang idle in his hand. There was no sense in shooting the coon. Far better let him alone till the beast's fur should be prime and his flesh more palatable.

The noisy scramble of the dog's feet amid the loose stones came clearly to the climbing boy. Then all at once the scrambling sounds ceased. There was an angry growl, followed by a gurgling noise, then a splash, and dead silence. Ethan broke into a run.

Up the brook bed the raccoon had fled. Close behind had dashed the collie. The raccoon, like its big cousin the bear, is an unwieldy-looking creature. But at a pinch it is capable of brief spurts of really creditable speed. The nature of the ground aided this fugitive's slithering gallop, while it impeded the rush of the dog.

No raccoon can maintain a lead over a collie for any distance. This the pursued coon, with the wisdom of the wild, must have known. For raccoons have brains—queer, wily, half-human brains—when they care to use them. Clown-like in aspect and in superficial mental processes, yet they are capable of uncanny processes of mind and of action.

The coon did not take advantage of any of the several rock-crannies or overhanging trees to escape from his foe. He stuck to the brook bed, flowing, rather than running, up its stony center. The collie splashed after him, gaining at every leap.

Thus they came to the first pool and tore through its shallows. Up the brook toward the second and far deeper pool raced the coon, the dog's snapping jaws now at his ringed fat tail.

At the edge of the second pool the raccoon whizzed about, shifting sidewise to avoid the snap of Jock's teeth at his back.

As the collie lunged forward in his averted assault, the raccoon slipped, eel-like, under the charging bulk. Both his arms went about the

At once his ears went up, their tulip tips
enlivening his whole expression.
Runaway, page 128

A huge raccoon had thrust forth
his comedy mask of a face.
The Feud, page 141

collie's furry throat in a constrictor grip, the agile black hands meeting. The razor teeth dug deep into Jock's neck. The braced hind legs heaved.

It was all done in the fraction of a second. The unbelievably tight grasp of the arms cut off Jock's breath. One fierce snarl alone escaped him—even as a single bark of angry surprise had come from Eileen's squeezed throat, two days earlier. Then he was wrestling and thrashing about on the pool's slippery brink, striving in vain to close his jaws on his elusive enemy.

The raccoon would have made a fortune, as a human, on the wrestling mat. Every secret of leverage and of balance was known to his crafty brain. Now, with hindlegs iron-braced, he seized the opportunity to enforce Jock's first forward pitch by throwing all his own twenty-six-pound weight and supple strength in the same direction. Under the double urge, the collie staggered across the slimy verge and into the pool.

With a mighty splash he fell in, the raccoon with him. As he went, one curved eyetooth succeeded in slashing deep into the coon's back. But the point penetrated little beyond the tremendous rolls of fat which upholstered the other's body.

The raccoon was similarly impeded. When he had gotten his strangle hold on the four other dogs, it had been no great feat for him to nuzzle his sharp nose through the fur and to send his teeth to the jugular. But a collie's throat is armored with a mattress of nearly impenetrable hair— outer and undercoat combined. The jugular is not easy to pierce. The murderous rodent teeth toiled busily. But they made scant progress.

Moreover, this collie was far larger and stronger and faster and more aggressively vigorous than had been any of the coon's four other victims —even the brave little Rouser. More by luck than by maneuvering he had gotten Jock into the water. The throat-cutting promised to be impossible.

Yet this did not greatly disturb the murderer. By instinct and by experience he knew he could stay alive under water much longer than could any dog. Therefore he devoted his weight and strength and skill to preventing Jock from rising to the surface.

The collie fought like mad for a moment or so. Then he realized that the water was strangling him far more quickly and effectively than were the coon's tense arms. He battled wildly to rise to the surface. But the coon had gripped the lowest of the several outjuts of underwater rock with his nimble hind feet and was clinging to them viciously. In vain did the collie fight to tear free. The hind feet held the rock ledge. The arms encircled the dog's neck. The teeth held their chewed mouthful of throat fur and skin.

Jock gave over his struggles to escape. Turning on the coon, the strangling collie fought insanely to wound him.

It was this scene which met Ethan Hurd's staring eyes as he came swarming up the brook bed in the gray dawn. The pool was lashed to foam and whirlpool. But as it was bottomed and lined with dirtless rock, no roiling of the waters hid from the boy's unbelieving sight the warfare a foot or so beneath the surface. Into his memory flashed long-forgotten and disbelieved tales of trappers concerning raccoons which lure pursuing hounds into the water and drown them.

Dropping his rifle, he flung himself on his face at the poolside. Down he thrust his right arm and clutched the half-drowned collie by the nape of the neck. With one mighty heave he pulled the battling Jock and the raccoon upward. The latter, looking up through the water, saw the boy. At once he loosed his stranglehold and teeth grip and sank to the bottom of the pool.

Ethan dragged Jock out of the water and onto the rocky bank. There the dog sprawled, sneezing and gulping, the water pouring from mouth and nose.

Ethan got to his feet, picking up the spattered rifle and standing at ease, looking down into the depths. On the boy's face were grimness and quiet determination. He could see the coon, five feet below him, its black hands holding fast to an irregularity of rock, to keep from rising to the top.

"Take your time," Ethan addressed the creature staring up at him. "You've drowned better animals than you are, in that pool. Let's see how long you can stand it down there. If—"

His words broke off in a choke. The fight of the dog and the coon had turned the placid basin into a furious whirlpool, whose clawing fingers had whipped every side of the basin to foam. These eddies had done more. They had swept the two or three wide underwater ledges as compellingly as a groping arm.

Now, from under the broadest ledge, forced outward by the swirling eddies, slid into view a half-shapeless little mass of reddish fur. Behind this came floating out what was left of a long-dead beagle.

"You—you devil!" panted Ethan. "You drowned 'em, and then you shoved 'em under those ledges, so they couldn't ever come to the top! It's Eileen! And it's—"

More ghastly canine remains were slipping into view drawn out by the whirlpool. But Ethan did not stop to note them. For, slowly, unwillingly, the raccoon was coming to the surface. His supply of breath at last was giving out. Rather than drown, he was coming up, to take his chances with the human and with the collie.

With deadly calm Ethan cocked and raised the rifle. The raccoon stuck the black tip of his nose a half inch above the water and took a long breath. Then with bewildering speed he swarmed up over the lip of the pool and sped for the rock-cleft from which Ethan had seen his face emerge two days before.

The boy did not hurry. He was not minded to risk a bad shot even at that range. Indeed, the raccoon's nose was in the cleft before Ethan pulled the trigger.

At the report the coon's body doubled and jumped high in air. Then it slumped lifeless at the entrance to the cleft.

"Your feud is off before it's on, Hi," explained Hurd, an hour later, lifting the dead raccoon by the tail for the benefit of his before-breakfast guest. "Take a good look at this critter. The second biggest I ever saw. Forty-two and a half inches from tip to tip. Twenty-six pounds, three ounces. And the brains of a cunning human."

"Huh!" growled Bourke. "My Rouser would 'a' made one mouthful of him! He—" He broke off with a grunt, as of physical pain, as he remembered the story Ethan had just told him. "Mebbe I'll git me a collie next time," he ruminated sadly. "They seem to be luckier. What price do you put on that big collie of your'n?"

"Eight million dollars and nine cents!" spoke up Ethan, before his father could answer. "And, now this coon's death has cured him of grieving so for Eileen, he's dirt cheap at that. Hey, Jock?"

THE DESTROYER FROM NOWHERE

His sire was Champion Greyfield Giant. His dam was Imported Lassie of Lothian. His brothers and sisters were destined to make collie history at a hundred bench shows. He himself was worthless.

He was worthless because he had no chance of fulfilling the purpose for which he and his immediate ancestors had been born. He was a one-hundred-percent liability in a kennel which was run for assets only and in which sentiment had no place.

His nose was snubby, his eyes were round and pale topaz in color and large, his golden coat was kinky, his tail was short and bushy like a wolf's. His head was domed like Daniel Webster's. Moreover, he was the smallest of the litter—a litter whose other members gave promise of classically chiseled wedge-shaped heads and slanting small dark eyes and long tails and wavy, harsh outer coats.

There are such "throwbacks" in many a highborn litter. They are useless to professional breeders. Sometimes they are sold for pets.

151

Sometimes, when they are atrociously bad-looking from a technical viewpoint, they are destroyed, lest their presence on earth give a bad name to the registered kennel which bred them.

Such a pup was this. One circumstance, and one alone, kept him from immersion in a water pail before his eyes were open. His mother and another famous female collie had puppies within a day of each other. The second mother's babies were but three in number. They died before they were twenty-four hours old—on the mystic plan which makes a collie the easiest or the hardest dog on earth to raise.

The worthless pup of the other litter was put into the brood nest of the bereft mother, to console her for the loss of her own young. Thus, up to six weeks, he was allowed to live. Thus, up to six weeks, he got all the nourishment that ordinarily would have been divided among several puppies. He grew strong and large and fat under these extra rations.

But at six weeks he was homelier and more faulty of physique than at birth. And so the kennel owner bade one of his men to take the miserable specimen to the river, tie a stone around his neck, and toss him in.

The kennel man obeyed. He was in a hurry to get home at the end of his day's work. A delivery car had called at the kennels with supplies and was just starting for the village, two miles away, where the man lived. By availing himself of a proffered ride he could save a hot two-mile trudge at the end of a hard day. He was not about to lose the chance just because he had a useless puppy to drown.

Snatching up a stone and a cord in one hand and the unsuspecting puppy in the other, he clambered aboard the delivery car. A mile away, the road crossed the bridge that spanned the river. By the time the fast-driven car had come to this bridge the kennel man had one end of the cord tied around the puppy's furry throat and the other end around the stone.

As the car sped swiftly over the bridge he threw the puppy and the stone and the cord far out over the coping and into the water. Then, his work done, he settled back to full enjoyment of the homeward ride.

* * *

Brant Millar had had a hard day, too. He had been haying under a grilling sun in his south pasture, which sloped down to the river edge. He was tired and he was soaked with sweat. His thin clothes stuck to him. He felt as if he was smeared with glue.

It is a pretty picture—to ride past in a covered car or to sit on a shaded porch and watch a sunlit field where haying is in progress. But the pleasure is all in the watching. There is scant bliss in tossing hay into a wagon, hour after hour, when the thermometer is in the nineties, and then to stand in a suffocating loft, catching and distributing the forkfuls that are flung up from the wagon. Heat and hayseed and heavy labor, and dust in the throat and nostrils: these are some of the less poetic and more real experiences of haymaking.

These were the things in which Brant Millar had been wallowing since as soon after sunrise as the hay was dry enough to pitch.

At six o'clock the last load was in the barn. Brant sent home his hired man. Then, while the horses were cooling down enough to be fed and watered for the night, Millar headed for the south meadow again and across it to the cool river at its foot. In one hand he carried a torn towel, in the other a pair of shabby swimming trunks.

It was good past words to strip off his sticky, damp clothes and to dive into the cold water. It was good to stretch out on his back and float drowsily downstream with the current, looking upward at the flaring blue sky and the setting copper sun from between half-shut eyes as the water gurgled and rippled in cool caress around him.

Under the bridge he let his tired body float. For a moment the glare of light was cut off by the dim gray under vault of the stone span. Then he floated out into the sunset light again.

As he did so he fancied that two large fish broke water, one on either side of him, with a great splash that deluged his face. At the same time something thin pressed sharply across his upturned throat, cutting almost through the tanned flesh.

Instantly, and with a snort of amaze, Brant Millar ceased to float languidly downstream. His feet groped for the rocky bottom of the river and found it. He stood up, shoulder deep in the fast-flowing water.

From one of his broad shoulders hung a stone. From the other wriggled a wet and indignant baby collie. Binding the two was the stout cord which had pressed against his throat.

The kennel man might have made that same cast fifty times without lassoing the unseen swimmer below the bridge. The car had chugged on and had rounded the turn beyond the bridge. The kennel man had not bothered to look back. He had seen the puppy and the stone go hurtling over the railing into the stream. That was enough for him. He had obeyed orders.

Had he looked, as the car rounded the turn, he would have seen a dumfounded young farmer standing shoulder deep in the drought-shallowed river, and festooned grotesquely with that same stone and puppy.

Brant Millar's momentary astonishment faded. He understood what had happened. He had heard the rumble of a car above the bridge while he was floating under it. The puppy and the stone, tied together, told their own story.

Millar looked down at the helplessly but gallantly struggling pup hanging across his arm on the end of the deep-cutting cord. The little fellow did not whimper. Baby as he was, he made no outcry at the pain and shock of it all. He fought mutely, with all his pudgy baby force, to get free from the strangling cord.

"Plucky little cuss!" approved Brant, half aloud. "Must be good blood back of him somewhere. Most pups would be squalling bloody murder."

While he talked he tucked the stone under his arm, easing its pull from around the collie's neck. Then, deftly, he untied the cord's clumsy knot from the fluffy throat. The stone glugged noisily down into the river, the cord hanging to it, but no tortured little dog was dragged down by the soggy weight.

Holding the puppy against his chest and out of reach of the hungrily lapping water, Brant waded upstream with him to where he had left his clothes. There he deposited the collie on the bank and began to dress.

"I don't rightly know what I'm going to do with you, youngster," he addressed the pup. "I've gotten on pretty well without a dog since old Bruno died. When he went, the wife and I both said we'd never be able to find another like him, so we'd go without. But I can't leave you here for some weasel or fox or mink to get. That'd be worse than leaving you to drown. And I can't give you away, I suppose. If you had been worth having, your folks wouldn't have chucked you into the creek. Well— come on home, anyhow, for tonight. I'll give you some bread and milk and you can sleep in the shed. Maybe the wife can figure out what to do about you, after then."

He finished his rudimentary dressing and picked up the puppy once more. Then he started across the meadow for his house, a half-mile distant. The pup did not resent being caught up and carried. He was still at the age when all the world is a friendly and delightful place, populated by friendly and delightful folk who are wonderful playmates.

His brief experience with the river had not shaken this faith. Wherefore he licked Brant's lean face ecstatically, and sought to chew his fingers and otherwise to lure the man into a romp. Millar petted him absent mindedly, and continued his homeward way.

On the narrow front porch of the farmhouse sat a sweet-faced young woman, a basket of mending in her lap. This was the wife whom Brant had married two years earlier.

Her day's work was done. Supper was on the table, a green mosquito net guarding it from the flies. She had come out here in the sunset to watch for her husband's return from his swim.

Rising to meet him as he plodded up the path, she noticed for the first time the queer little burden he carried. Brant halted and set the puppy on the ground. The pup took one interested glance at everything around him. Then his topaz eyes fell on Helen Millar coming down the steps.

Pricking up his lopped ears, he cantered eagerly toward her with the gait of a fat rocking horse.

"Oh, Brant!" Helen was expostulating. "We decided we would never have another dog, after Bruno! Why did you bring home this crazy-looking—"

She got no further. The puppy's clumsy run had brought him to her. His fat forepaws on her apron, he was peering up into her face with adoring friendliness. For some strange reason, the confidingly loving look and action of the absurd youngster made the woman's throat contract.

On impulse, she stooped and gathered him into her arms. There the pup cuddled, crooning and clucking in great contentment, softly licking the hand that held him.

"I'll try to find some sucker who'll be fool enough to take him off our hands, tomorrow," promised Brant, sheepishly. "If I can't, I'll put him out of the way as painlessly as I can. I—"

"You won't do anything of the sort!" she declared, with fleet shift of mind. "This is *my* dog. He's elected me as his owner. We're going to keep him. Where did he come from, anyhow? He's all soaking wet."

Brant blinked at her, wondering at her abrupt change of feeling toward the newcomer. Then he said:

"The little cuss came out of the sky. Anyhow, when I was floating on my back, over yonder in the creek, he dropped down on me like a ton of brick. That's true. Honest, it is."

He did not think it was necessary to add the details of the cord and stone and the hurrying delivery car. He saw the puppy had caught his wife's fancy, even as he had caught Brant's own. He thought that a spice of mystery might add to the woman's new interest in the collie and make her the more willing to keep him.

"What in the world are you talking about?" demanded Helen. "'Came out of the sky'? What—"

"Well," compromised Millar. "Maybe he didn't come from quite so far up as that. It isn't the kind of weather, anyhow, when it rains cats and dogs. I wish it was, now that the hay is in. But he dropped down on me, just as I told you, while I was floating there. I didn't see anyone on the bank. There wasn't any airplane overhead—At least, come to think of it, I never even looked up to see if there was. Maybe he tumbled out of an airplane. Anyhow, he landed, *plop!* right onto me. So I brought him home."

"Out of the sky!" mused Helen, her imagination struck by the oddity of the idea. "Probably he was being carried somewhere in an airplane and fell out. How lucky you were there! The poor baby might have been drowned! What kind of dog do you suppose he is?"

"Well," ruminated Brant, "considering the direction he came from, I'd say he's most likely a Skye terrier. What'll we call him?"

"Let's feed him first," suggested Helen. "He'd rather be fed than named. I'm sure he would. Wouldn't you, baby? Come along in here."

She set him down and led the way into the kitchen. The puppy followed at a wavering canter, trying at every step to seize the hem of her alluringly elusive skirt.

Helen poured out a saucer of fresh milk and crumbled into it a handful of stale bread. The puppy fell upon this feast ravenously. At the kennels one of the men had taught him to lap milk, off and on, during the past two weeks—not as an accomplishment, but to wean him earlier, so that he might sooner be drowned.

"I've got it!" cried Helen, as she and Brant stood watching amusedly the greedy feasting of their new pet. "I mean I've got the name for him. I've been trying to remember it ever since you told me about his dropping down out of the air."

"Fire away!" exhorted Millar, as she hesitated with puckered brows.

"It—it was in a poem we had to learn in high school," she said, slowly. "A line of it was—was—was— There! I can't remember the poem, after all. But now I remember the man's name—the man who was tossed down from the skies in mythology times. His name was Vulcan. That was it. Vulcan. And that's what I'm going to call our puppy here. Isn't it a pretty name? And queer, too."

"It's queer, all right," admitted Brant. "But if you're looking for a pretty name, what's the matter with Ponto or Rover or Shep or Tige or—"

"His name," said Helen, sweetly, but with calm finality, "is *Vulcan*."

The puppy had finished his supper. Feeling that he could eat much more, he turned suddenly from his empty dish and ran over to Helen, who had given him the bread and milk. By sheer coincidence he chanced to gallop across to her just as she had uttered the word "Vulcan."

"Oh, Brant!" exclaimed the woman, in delighted astonishment. "He answers to his name the very first time he hears it. I never saw anything so clever in my life. That settles it. Vulcan he is. That's his name."

Thus it was that the worthless runt of a royal collie litter became the pet and chum of two people who understood dog nature well enough to bring out the best in him. Thus did his training and life work begin.

A clever collie pup—well and wisely and kindly raised by people who can give much time to his education—is capable of unbelievable mental development. Vulcan's brain expanded nearly as fast as his well-fed and well-exercised body.

At six months he could handle sheep and cattle like a veteran. At a year he was a giant in body and in strength and was the loved and honored housemate of his owners. Brant used to brag that the collie could do the work of a hired man with sheep and cows, and that he was a better guard for the house than a company of militiamen.

An artist, stopping at the farm for a drink of milk, first told them Vulcan's breed. Before this they had been in doubt as to whether he were shepherd dog or retriever or mongrel.

"He's a collie," said the artist. "I've bred them all my life. He's a collie. Purebred, at that."

Noting Helen's pride in her canine chum, the artist added the information that Vulcan was the worst specimen of collie, from a bench-show point of view, that he had had the bad luck to behold. Gravely he listened to Helen's narrative of the dog's dropping from the heavens upon her swimming husband's shoulder.

"If they raise good collies up there," he said to himself, "I don't blame them for throwing this one out."

It was at the end of Vulcan's third year that the Valley was scourged from end to end by a pest which threatened to offset the prosperity of a bumper crop by demolishing the livestock of the entire community.

Nobody knew what the creature might be that was causing all this devastation. A thrill of superstition possessed the Valley at mention of it. None had seen it. None had been able to find track of it.

Clem Robard, a sheepman who lived two miles up the Valley from

Brant's homestead, went into his upper sheep pasture one morning to find thirty of his yearling ewes and sheep lying dead, their throats torn out. Three more were missing. The remainder were huddled in fence corners, quivering with mortal terror. In midfield lay Clem's aged sheepdog, his neck broken as if by giant pincers.

Up and down the Valley sped the black tidings that a killer dog was loose upon the world. The farmers hastened to view the carnage. They trooped into Robard's upper pasture in scores, scanning the dry hardpan of earth for tracks, examining the torn sheep, making Sherlock Holmes investigations—and learning nothing.

News of an epidemic of some mortal disease carries no more terror with it in a crowded city than does the report among grazers that a killer dog is at large. The term "killer" does not apply merely to some mischievous cur that chances to chase and kill a sheep or two.

It is the phrase used to describe such rare dogs as chance to go insane on the subject of slaughter. Once in a while a trained sheepdog will do so. Incredible cunning goes with this form of canine mania. A killer will wreak awesome havoc in a field, for the pure love of murder, and will vanish, leaving no clue to his identity. The next night he will harry a flock or a herd twenty miles away. Sometimes he returns to his own home, living there, unsuspected, in intervals between depredations.

There could be no doubt that Clem Robard's sheep had fallen victim to such a killer. Three of his victims he had lugged away—nobody could find where. But the remaining thirty he had killed from pure lust of slaughter and had left them where they lay.

All summer, in the hitherto immune Valley, the flocks and herds had wandered at will through pastures and woodlands. Chickens had roosted at large or in unguarded hen coops. House dogs had been deemed sufficient protection to barn and fold and hen roost.

Now, in a breath, all this changed. From morning till late dusk that day farmers and their men tightened and strengthened enclosures into which their livestock were to be driven at night. Volunteers made ready to patrol the Valley all night and every night. Innocent dogs were eyed askance.

Brant Millar alone made no such panic preparations for the safety of his flock. Beyond driving the sheep into the home pasture for the night, he did nothing to insure them against the killer.

"Vulcan sleeps on the porch these summer nights," he told his nearest neighbor, Harvey Blane, who remonstrated with him against such carelessness. "And he sleeps with both ears and one eye open. Why, a lamb can't bleat or a hen can't flutter off a roost in the night or a horse can't cast himself in his stall or a heifer can't get to stamping, but what Vulcan's on his feet in a second and off to see what's wrong. He patrols the whole home tract a couple of times or more every night, too. He's a born watchdog. My critters are as safe, with him on guard, as if they were in one of those steel vaults they've put in over at the Paignton bank."

"H'm!" grunted Blane, who had come across from his adjoining farm to borrow nails for the extra palings he was putting on one of his paddocks. "H'm! Maybe so. Maybe not. Every fellow blows about his own cur. I'm not taking chances. I got my forty head of registered-stock Guernsey calves to look out for. I'm not trusting to any dog to keep them from the killer, either. Know my calf paddock? Well, into that they go tonight, the whole forty of them. What's more, I'm running an extra line of planks around it, on top of the reg'lar fence. I'm putting a line of barbed wire on top of that. I aim to have a stockade seven foot high and topped with barbed wire, all around my calf paddock, by nightfall. If any dog—killer or no—can shinny up that seven-foot wall and over the wire—well, he'll do more'n any dog I ever seen or heard of."

Brant watched his neighbor depart on his stockade-building expedition. Then he noted that Vulcan was standing close beside him. Millar stooped and patted the dog's broad head.

"The killer that tackles you, old boy," said he, affectionately, "will think he's bit into a couple of hornets' nests and a rattlesnake. I'll take my chance on your guarding anything Helen and I have got. Anything from Baby to my best bunch of Merino lambs."

He passed his hand appraisingly along the collie's head to the mighty-muscled shoulders and the deep chest and slender loins. Vulcan was built with the powerful grace of a timber wolf. In more than one fight with marauding curs he had shown himself as terrible at warfare as he was gentle to the defenseless animals he guarded.

Out from the house toddled a little gold-and-white bunch of fluff which, as it came into the sunlight, resolved itself into a three-year-old baby girl—the Millars' only child and Vulcan's worshiped deity. As strong as was the collie's love for Brant and Helen, he idolized baby May above all the world.

Now, at sight of May, he trotted forward in wriggling joy to greet her. The baby squealed with pleasure at seeing her dear playmate. She seized him by both sensitive ears and hugged his shaggy head to her tiny chest. The dog suffered the rough handling with utter delight, and pressed close to her side as she moved forward.

But as May reached the edge of the porch on her outward progress, Vulcan slipped quickly and unobtrusively between her and the two-foot abyss toward which she was toddling. Very gently he pushed her away from the edge and toward the more negotiable flight of shallow steps.

Brant nodded approvingly.

"As good as a machine gun company, for guarding," he said to himself, "and ten times better'n a hired nurse for keeping baby out of danger, and better'n any one hired man at handling stock. Gee! That was one lucky swim I took, three years back!"

Yet next morning, at sunrise, Millar made the rounds of his farm with greater care than usual and with some slight anxiety. Despite his assurance of security, in his talk with Harvey Blane, the thought of the killer had made his night's sleep fitful.

He might well have spared the worry. His livestock were intact. No harm had come to them in the sinister hours between dusk and dawn. Again Millar's hand rested approvingly on the wide head of the dog which paced majestically at his side during his rounds of inspection.

As Brant and Vulcan were returning to the house for breakfast, someone came running in from the roadway and up the path toward them. At sight of the furiously running man Vulcan growled. He stepped menacingly forward, as if to protect his master from possible harm. Then he dropped back to Millar's side again. For he had recognized the excited intruder as Harvey Blane.

Blane's face was purple. His eyes were goggling and bloodshot. He was all but blubbering. Millar stared in amusement at his wontedly calm neighbor.

"What in blue blazes—?" began Brant.

"Twenty-two of them!" blithered Harvey, deliriously. "Twenty-two! And not a one of them worth a cent under—"

"Twenty-two *what?*" demanded Brant, perplexed at the outburst. "What are you talking about?"

"Twenty-two of my registered-stock Guernsey calves!" roared Blane. "They—"

"I thought you were going to put them all in a seven-foot stockade, with barbed wire on it," said Millar. "You don't mean to say the killer—?"

"I mean to say the killer climbed the stockade or else he flew down into it!" stormed Blane. "Wire and all, he got in, and he killed twenty-two of my calves. Killed them without their making enough noise to wake me or any of us. Then he got out again, the way he came. Got away *clean!* Never left a trace. Dropped down from the sky, looks like, and then flew back again. No critter without wings could jump a seven-foot fence with barbed wire on top of it. Come along with me, Brant. I haven't touched a one of them. I left them as they was when I found them, ten minutes ago. I came over here to fetch you, as a 'disint'rested witness' that the law calls for, so as you can testify for me when I ask the county for dam'ges."

Without a word, Brant fell into step with his neighbor, and started with him toward the nearby Blane farm. Well did Millar know the state law regarding the slaying of livestock by an unknown animal. If such killing can be established, the county must pay the owner a fair value on the slain animal or animals. A disinterested witness's testimony is required to avert fraud.

Vulcan bounded along in front of the two until they reached the gate. Collie-like, he welcomed this chance to go for a walk with his master.

But the opening of a door behind them made the dog glance back. Baby May had toddled out on to the porch. As usual, she was making straight for its edge. With a rush the collie regained the porch and was interposing his shaggy body between the child and a fall.

As Helen did not come out to relieve him of his nursemaid responsibilities, Vulcan stayed where he was, instead of following Millar.

Brant found trouble in keeping pace with his hurrying and sputtering neighbor. Panting, they reached Blane's home and went past the house and barns and back to the reinforced calf paddock. At the open door of the enclosure was standing a little group of horrified people—Blane's wife and his two sons and his hired man—all gazing into the yard.

Brant noted the awkward but highly efficient way in which the four-foot paddock fence had been transformed into a seven-foot stockade. As he approached he studied the wooden wall carefully. It offered no slope or foothold whereby a dog could take a preliminary run and then scramble up the sides of it. Here was a perpendicular wall, seven feet in height, and with a strand of barbed wire running some six inches above it.

"The door was shut and locked when I got here this morning," Blane was assuring him. "I can take oath to that. So can my man. He was with me. I had the key to the padlock in my pants. Nobody nor nothing could have got in. You c'n see that yourself, Brant."

They came to the doorway. The group divided and Millar entered the paddock. The place was a shambles.

Some eighteen beautiful red-and-white Guernsey calves were milling and lowing in a tightly packed jam in its far corner, leaving the rest of the enclosure bare. This open space was heaped with the carcasses of twenty-two dead calves. One and all, their throats had been torn out and mangled. No attempt had been made to devour any of them.

Millar examined carefully the hideous damage done to his neighbor's livestock and fortune. He scanned the hoof-scored ground for print of a padded paw. But the myriad pattering and stamping feet of the frenzied calves had obliterated any trace of alien presence.

Next, Brant walked about the stockade from the outside, seeking claw marks on the boards or bloodstains on the line of barbed wire. He found nothing.

"Dropped down from the sky, he did, I tell you!" raged Blane. "He couldn't have got in any other way. *Say!*" He broke off, abruptly, wheeling on Brant. "What was that rigmarole your wife told mine, a couple or three years back, about your collie dog 'dropping down from the sky'? How about it? If he could drop down from the sky once, why couldn't he—?"

"Oh, that was just a joke!" said Millar, astonished at the frantic man's credulity. "I explained it all to her afterward. Vulcan was thrown off the bridge with a stone tied to his neck. Some one tried to drown him. I was swimming underneath and he fell on me. That was all there was to it."

"H'm!" grunted Blane, scowling at the dead calves. "Maybe so. Maybe not. Anyhow, you'll testify to what you've seen here?"

"I sure will," promised Millar. "No fraud about this thing. I'll swear to that. And no explanation about it, either, worse luck!"

Again up and down the Valley surged the hideous tidings. Again farmers made stout their fences and cleaned their guns and appointed guards. The county farmers' association offered a reward of $300 for the killer.

Yet that night—within a hundred feet of a patrolling guard—the henhouse of Abner Cobban was entered and sixty of his best fowls were killed. They were killed without a sound of the wholesale slaying reaching the patrolling man outside. Five of them were eaten. Many strewn feathers and a few chewed bones attested to that. The other fifty-five had been killed in wanton murder lust. The heads of most of them had been bitten off. The killer had burst the flimsy lock of the henhouse, presumably by the simple expedient of pressing his heavy body against it. The rotting wood around the lock had given away with too slight a sound to be heard by the guard.

For the next three nights nothing happened anywhere along the Valley. But the tense waiting began to get on the men's nerves more acutely than had the actual killings.

On the fourth morning baby May elected to go for a walk. Her mother saw her trudge sturdily across the dooryard toward the meadow. Helen was about to call her back, when she saw Vulcan get up from his mat on the porch and trot after the child, ranging alongside her and accommodating his pace to hers. With one chubby hand clenched deep in the fur of the collie's ruff to steady her, May struck out at a better gait.

Helen did not interfere. She knew the baby would be safer with the great dog than with any human, and that when Vulcan should decide May had gone far enough he would herd her gently back. He had done so a score of times.

The morning was cool and bracing. A ramble across the meadow and to the shade of the woods beyond would be pleasant exercise for the little girl.

Helen herself had been planning to go to the wood edge for ferns for the rock garden she was making. Putting on her sunhat now, and taking her trowel and a basket, she prepared to set out after the baby and the dog. A telephone call detained her. When at last she started, May and her escort were at the end of the meadow and almost in the shade of the woodland.

Brant looked up from a log he was chopping in the dooryard as his wife passed by him.

"I'm going after those ferns I told you about," she said. "Baby and Vulcan have gone on ahead."

It was a few seconds later that Brant looked up again. This time his ears had caught the clump of several pairs of approaching feet. Around the corner of the house came Harvey Blane and his two sons. The faces of all three were grim. Blane carried a shotgun in the crook of his left arm. Without a word of greeting the trio advanced on Millar.

Harvey held out his right hand. Brant, wondering, held out his own. Then he saw Blane did not intend to shake hands. In his flattened palm he exhibited a tuft of tawny hair.

"Well?" queried Millar, puzzled. "What's the idea?"

"The idea," answered Blane, speaking slowly, "is that my boys and me were taking down that length of barbed wire, just now, from the stockade, to put up an extra line of stakes. On one of the barbs, over behind the corner stake, we found this."

He nodded at the hair tuft in his palm.

"Well?" queried Brant, still mystified.

"This here is a bunch of hair," expounded Blane. "Hair off'n the critter that jumped my stockade and killed my calves. Nothing else could have put it up there, seven foot above ground. The killer hopped the fence. As he was going over the wire, a jag of it tore off this bunch of his hair."

Brant whistled.

"I see!" he said. "Behind one of the corner stakes, hey? That's why we didn't notice it when we looked, I suppose. But—"

"There's just one critter here or hereabouts," went on Harvey, "that has longish and yellow hair that color. That critter is a dog. That critter," he said, his voice slower and deeper, "that critter is your collie dog!"

"Nonsense!" scoffed Brant, contemptuously. "Why, Vulcan is—!"

"Vulcan is the killer," finished Blane. "Likewise, we're here to kill him, or to force you to kill him, like the law says."

"The law says nothing of the kind!" blazed Millar. "And if it did, you'd have to kill me before you got through to my dog! It's the craziest foolishness I ever heard. Because you find a tuft of brownish yellow hair on your fence and because my dog happens to be brownish yellow—"

"That's the idee," said Blane, curtly. "Where's your dog?"

"It's none of your business where he is!" shouted Brant, in sudden rage. "If you lift that gun against him, you'll find yourself on your back with a broken gun barrel hammering your skull. You and your two hulking sons as well. That dog of mine would no sooner kill—"

The wrathful words died in his throat. All four men whirled about. From the direction of the woods echoed a distant sound of strife—wild, confused, hideously discordant.

It was followed by a woman's scream of mortal horror.

Without a word the men broke into a run, Brant still unconsciously gripping his ax and Blane swinging his forgotten gun.

Across the meadow they ran at top speed, toward the fringe of woodland. But Brant Millar was far in the lead. He raced along like a madman, his eyes glassy, his brain sick with dread, for he had recognized Helen's voice in that terrified shriek.

May and Vulcan had made their leisurely way across the meadow, the child clinging to the collie's coat and using him as a support for her none-too-certain feet. Presently they reached the woods and passed into the cathedral-like shade of the lofty pines. There, just ahead, the child caught sight of a glowing patch of cardinal flowers clustering about a tiny spring at the base of a high mass of rocks.

She ran forward to play with the glowing flowers. Vulcan did not join her at once. He had come to a sudden halt. Stockstill he stood, his sensitive nostrils sniffing the still woodland air with growing aversion. The stiff hairs between his shoulder blades began to bristle. A white tusk showed from under an up-curling lip. His nearsighted topaz eyes glanced in every direction to locate the odor which had assailed him.

Far too faint to have been registered by human nose nerves, yet this scent was strong and increasingly distinct to the dog. Far back in the ages-old memory of his subconscious brain it awoke a strange hostility. At last his suspiciously wandering gaze focused among the higher reaches of the rocks, above and directly in front of him.

There, as by a giant sword, the rock had been cleft and cleft again into fissures and crannies and caverns. It was on one of these caverns that Vulcan's eyes riveted themselves—but only for the briefest instant.

Then with a wild-beast roar he hurled himself forward at Baby May.

The child was knee deep in the patch of cardinal flowers, pulling them up by the handful and chuckling happily to herself. Vulcan rushed at her and seized her by the shoulder of her gingham dress.

His mighty jaws did not so much as bruise her flesh as he spun her about and thrust her far behind him. She lost her footing and rolled over and over among the crushed red flowers.

It was this insane attack upon the child Vulcan loved that Helen

Millar first saw as she entered the woodland. She stood thunderstruck at the incredible sight.

But as May fell, a yellow-tawny thunderbolt launched itself from the rocks above. With a thud it landed on the spot where the baby had been standing when the collie tossed her out of the way of the impending leap. Helen stared, aghast.

Scarcely had the creature landed among the flowers when Vulcan was upon it. Before the momentum of the futile bound gave the intruder a chance to recover balance the dog was at its throat.

There was a multiple roaring and screeching as the two tawny bodies crashed to earth together, struggling murderously. Helen screamed in fear as she recognized the brute that had tried to pounce upon her baby.

Never outside of a circus tent had she seen such an animal. But now, at a glance, she knew it for a panther.

(Ten miles away, at Paignton, the owner of an itinerant one-ring circus had sworn in loud fury at the careless attendant who, a week earlier, had left the Rocky Mountain puma's cage door insecurely latched after the evening performance. The exhibit was neither rare nor expensive. Yet its loss meant much to so poor a menagerie.)

As though Helen's scream frightened it, the puma broke loose from the battling collie and sprang back to the base of the rocks. Bleeding, torn, bruised, the dog gathered himself together for a fresh assault.

Never before had Vulcan seen a puma. Yet his wolf ancestors, for thousands of years, had been the foes to this and all other members of the cat tribe. Now, into Vulcan's wise collie brain, seeped a glint of hereditary knowledge as to those ancestors' tactics in fighting the mountain lion.

Instead of rushing blindly into battle as before, he sprang at the snarling puma, which bounded forward to demolish him. But midway in his charge the collie veered sharply to the left with the speed of light. The puma's crushingly raking claws missed him in their double stroke, one of them whizzing within a hair'sbreadth of his head.

Then, in what seemed to Helen to be the same motion, the dog spun in, to the right, just behind the smiting paws, and drove his terrible teeth into the base of the puma's neck. Here and here alone could he or any other dog hope to compete on anything like equal terms with a mountain lion.

By that skull-base grip had countless wolves averted death from the rending claws of such great cats; and sometimes they had been able to grind their own tusk-like eyeteeth into the spinal cord of their enemy.

This, now, Vulcan was attempting to do. But the puma was one swirl of dynamic fury. Around and around it spun, in mad effort to break the grip and to rake the dog with its saber claws. Twice the claws found a glancing mark on Vulcan's shaggy sides, tearing through to the rib bones. But the collie's jaws had gained their one possible hold, a hold that the furious cat could not yet dislodge.

Then into the woods stormed the four panting men. Up went Harvey Blane's gun, after its owner had given one unbelieving look at the battle in front of him. But he hesitated. To shoot one of the gyrating combatants, without risk of killing the other was impossible.

Brant Millar did not hesitate. In he ran, ax aloft. As he ran he struck. With all the force and skill of a veteran woodsman he struck.

The panther's skull was split in half. It gave one last convulsive heave that hurled Vulcan against the rocks in a breathtaking impact and then the giant cat lay kicking and trembling.

Slowly the wounded dog relinquished his grip. Slowly he got to his feet, lurching over to where baby May sat weeping unheeded. Gently Vulcan licked the wet little face and whimpered in loving reassurance. Then with a long sigh he lay down and closed his friendly eyes.

Not until a veterinarian had toiled over him for nearly two weeks was the collie able to stand up again and to resume the burden of life.

"The—the creature dropped down from that cave up there in one leap!" exclaimed Helen, shuddering.

"H'm!" mused Harvey Blane. "And he must have got up there, first off, in one leap, too. No other way for him to do it. That cave's a good eighteen inches higher'n my stockade. Neighbor Millar, I figger I've played the fool. If I'd shot that dog of yours, and then found out, I'd have used the second barrel on myself. The killer is kilt. And—the man who ever speaks bad of Vulcan where I am—well, there's still two ca'tridges left in this gun! Lemme help you carry him home. He c'n have my best spare-room bed to lay on, if he's a mind to."

FOSTER BROTHERS

Bobby Theron called Thor his twin. For the big gray collie had been born on Bobby's twelfth birthday. Thor's mother, Lassie, had six other pups born that day: pups for which Lassie's master, Colonel Theron, envisioned bright futures as farmworkers.

But six of the seven pups died—for no special reason—within twenty-four hours after they were born. A collie pup is the easiest or the hardest of all dogs to rear. Nobody knows why. A knowledge of the secret would cut down the price and quadruple the number of collies in no time.

It was no fault of Lassie's that six-sevenths of this litter died. She was a born mother. Once she had even carried a squalling baby kitten to her brood nest and insisted on bringing it up with some newborn pups. Now, she grieved pitifully over the six dead infants and she concentrated all her care on the seventh.

Colonel Theron had promised Bobby one of the pups. When six of them died, the colonel stuck to his word. He gave his son the only surviving puppy—the fuzzy gray youngster that was a throwback to his merle grandsire.

The day was Thursday. Bobby had just begun the study of mythology at school. His teacher had told him that "Thursday" was derived from "Thor's day" and was named in honor of the Norse god of thunder. There was a terrific thunderstorm that morning. So Bobby accepted the omen and called his puppy Thor.

Among other devastating things wrought by that thunderstorm was the smashing of a giant oak in the forest, a mile behind the Theron farm. This oak had ever reared its crest high above the neighboring trees. Bobby and his father were standing at an upper window of the farmhouse, watching the storm, when they saw it struck.

As soon as the sky cleared they walked out to get a closer view of the scene.

The oak had crashed down across the lesser denizens of the forest with the force of a falling tower, leaving a swath of shattered limbs. It had done more. Its trunk had smitten squarely against an overslanting outcrop of granite, smashing it and driving part of it into the earth.

From beneath this mass of broken stones issued a trickle of blood and the stifled moaning of some stricken thing. On the instant Colonel Theron and Bobby were feverishly at work hauling aside such of the rock particles as were not too much for their combined strength. With bare hands, and then using saplings as levers, they toiled. Presently they came upon what they sought and upon a sight that told its own story.

A huge black bear—one of the very few still left in that recently cleared region—had chosen the leafy hole beneath the granite slant as her brood nest. Here she lay crushed and dying. Under her side lay a killed cub. At sight of the man and the boy the mother bear sought to rear her bloody head and shoulders in defense of her young. The effort was too much for her. She slumped back, dead.

But her futile motion had shown the onlookers a second newborn bear cub, hitherto hidden by his mother's head. This baby had somehow been wedged under a spur of slanting stone which did not crumble with the rest. He was unhurt—a puny and naked and blind and tiny morsel of life.

Bobby felt a lump in his own throat at the mother bear's instinctive attempt to shield her young, even in the moment of death. With this twinge of pity still stirring him, he stooped and picked up the one surviving cub and cuddled it gently under his coat.

"What are you doing that for?" asked his father, looking up from his calculations on the value of the dead bear's off-prime pelt and flesh. "It would be more merciful to knock him in the head. He'll starve without his mother."

"If Lassie would adopt a baby kitten, there's no reason she won't adopt a baby bear," answered Bobby. "She's so unhappy over her six puppies dying, that she'll maybe like to have this new baby to bring up."

Colonel Theron was on the point of forbidding such an absurd project. Then he remembered it was his boy's birthday and that Bobby's impulse of kindness was more or less commendable.

"All right," he assented. "Only, don't feel bad if Lassie eats him or if he starves. One of those two things is due to happen. I never heard of a dog nursing a bear."

"I did," said Bobby, eagerly. "I read it in one of those old trapping books in the school library. If one dog did it, another one can."

He was right. After a doubtful preliminary sniff at the hairless little creature that reeked of the wilderness, Lassie's all-encompassing mother instinct asserted itself. She forbore to thrust away the hungry little thing which Bobby had laid close to her udder.

Thus it was that a black bear and a gray collie came to be foster brothers. Both thrived quickly under the nourishment that had been planned for seven ravenous pups. After the first few hours, Lassie did not seem to remember which of the two was her own baby and which was the wildling. She lavished on both alike her solicitous mother care.

If Lassie did not realize increasingly the difference between her nestlings, she must have been blinded by affection. During the first few days there was no vast divergence between the helpless little fellows, except that one looked like a blind and grayish rat, while the other looked like a rat that was not only blind, but also hairless. Then, day by day, the change grew stronger.

At the end of eleven days, Thor could see. (In spite of common wisdom, a collie pup's eyes open more often on the eleventh day than on the ninth.) At the end of three weeks he was stumbling clumsily around the brood nest on wavering feet. Also he was learning to lap milk and he was beginning to look less like a rat than like a dog.

But up to the fifth week the bear remained sightless and nude and utterly dependent on Lassie for everything. By that time Thor was weaned and was fully equipped in a fuzzy coat of silver-and-snow. Patiently Lassie cared for the helpless bear, long after Thor had no further use for her except as a teacher and a playfellow.

Yet to Bobby Theron it seemed almost no time at all before the cub had taken Lassie's place as playfellow to the collie pup. Though the bear was slow to start growing, once he had begun he made mighty progress.

Bobby named him Ursus. His teacher told him it was the Latin for "bear." The boy was at the exciting point of education when he made use of every interesting name or word he picked up at school.

Ursus and Thor were adoring pals to each other, never happy unless they were together. They romped and played by the hour, none too gently, getting into hot little gusts of temper when a pinch or a scratch or a tumble was over-vehement; battling doughtily for a moment or so, then forgetting their wrath in some new twist of the game.

It was pretty to see them roll over and over in a scrambling embrace or chase each other around the kennel yard. Neighbors used to drop in to watch the oddly matched playmates. The first time, presumably, that Thor realized his chum was not like himself was the day Ursus first tried to climb a tree.

The bear paused in a race around the yard and began gravely to shin up an oak sapling which grew there. Slowly and hesitatingly and awkwardly he ascended the slender trunk. Thor watched with eyes of dumb amazement. Then he, too, rushed at the tree and tried to run up its side. A fall on his furry back rewarded the effort.

Breathless and bruised, he burst into falsetto barks of wrath and

leaped upward again, this time for the bear. His milk teeth seized Ursus
by the stumpy tail and hung on. Ursus struggled to maintain his new-
found grip on the trunk. Then the twenty-pound weight was too much
for him. Down he fell, on top of Thor. A fierce combat waged for several
seconds, until both warriors chanced to see a cat mincing along just
outside the yard's wire fence. With tacit agreement they abandoned
their scrimmage and dashed at her.

But that first climb was the forerunner of many such an ascent. Worriedly, Thor would lie at the foot of the tree and watch the clumsy but
sure progress of his chum toward the upper branches. Thus he would lie,
in patient sorrow, till Ursus came slowly down to earth again, hindquarters first, with much loud scratching of the tender bark.

In their rough-and-tumble play, bit by bit Ursus's increasing strength
and size gave him an ever greater advantage over his collie friend. Also,
he had a quite bewildering way of using all four feet as weapons as well
as his teeth, while Thor—like other dogs—could rely only on his jaws for
offensive work. At close quarters Thor was no match for the bear. But at
footwork, and at flashing in and out, Ursus was his hopeless inferior.
Thor discovered this. Nine times in ten he would dance around his
gawky opponent, flashing in to nip the fat Ursus and then slipping safely
back out of range of the bear's short arm swipes and futile bites.

The tenth time, it was another story. Let Ursus get a grip on the collie
or land a swinging blow on him, and Thor had not the remotest chance
against the bear. But all their mock fighting and rare flashes of temper
were governed by mutual good-fellowship that astonished the human
onlookers. The two youngsters had a deep and genuine love for each
other.

For months the young bear lived happily enough in his kennel yard.
Meanwhile his education and Thor's had begun. While Ursus spent all
his time in the fenced enclosure, Thor spent more and more hours
outside of it.

Bobby Theron had not only made a house dog of his big gray collie,
but he and his father were teaching Thor to herd sheep and cattle. Not
until he was a year old, and as fleet and wiry as a wolf, did they trust him

to drive hogs. Not that he could not have mastered that duty as readily as sheep-and-cattle herding, but because of its peril to himself.

A hog is neither a safe nor an easy animal for a dog to manage. A drove of pigs, such as Colonel Theron kept in his east orchard and low bog-lot, cannot be turned and controlled as can even the most recalcitrant cattle. A collie can learn with ease to avoid the flying heels or tossing horns of a cow, and to nip or bark her into line. A hog is different.

There is something latently murderous about an unpenned hog, especially a hog that is accustomed to root for a living and to roam at will. The tough hide is hard to hurt by even the sharpest nip. The teeth are tearing and terrible. There is a vicious devil lurking behind the red-rimmed pale little eyes.

Yet, when he was a little over a year old, Thor was taught hog-driving. He made a gay and gallant job of it, though in the bottom of his stout heart he loathed the task. Instinctively he seemed to realize its stark danger, and the fate that would be his if he should slip or lose his balance on the slimy bog footing, when a hog or a group of hogs chanced to turn on him, as often happened during a single drive from marsh to pen.

The life of a farm collie in those days, on a big farm in the new-cleared region, was no flowery bed of ease. But Thor reveled in it all—except in the hog-driving.

Bobby was busy, in his own few spare hours, educating Ursus. But the bear's education was purely ornamental. Bobby had a gift with animals. He had the knack of making them understand what he wanted them to do, and then, as a rule, of being able to make them do it. This with no cruelty or flare of anger, but by dint of gently firm patience.

For instance, he taught Ursus to stand up and beg, to turn around, at command, on his hind-legs; to roll over, to wrestle, to do a score of other simple tricks. It was a pretty sight to watch the boy put the huge brute through his paces, with Thor standing at one side, his head cocked critically, and with the bear enjoying the performance as much as did either of the others.

So things went on for the first eighteen months of Ursus's life. In all that time it had never once occurred to the captive bear that he was not free. But one day, in trying to slap a bumblebee that had alighted on the wire of his yard, Ursus made a rent in the netting that a man could have walked through.

He crawled out through the ragged and jagged aperture and made his way to the road. There he encountered a passing farmer, whose horses promptly ran away.

The farmer was thrown out and hurt. He threatened suit and he made a complaint to the selectmen of the township. True, Ursus had been caught and returned to his yard within five minutes of his escape. But the mischief was done. Colonel Theron was notified officially that he was maintaining a dangerous wild animal and he was instructed either to shoot the bear or to place him in safe confinement.

Accordingly, Bobby and his father rigged up an empty box stall as a cage for Ursus, knocking out enough of the barn wall at one side of the cage to make a barrier of heavy stakes. These stakes were less than a foot apart. The bear could not possibly slip through them, though Thor could and did wriggle his own lithe bulk in and out of the cage at will.

In this cramped space Ursus discovered for the first time that he was a prisoner. His collie chum could come and go at will. The bear could not. This knowledge and the lack of exercise and advancing maturity combined to sour the captive's temper.

It is always so with a tame bear. Let him be brought up with the wisest and most friendly care, the time will come when the wilderness will reclaim her own—when he will forget he is a pet and become a menace. It is so with every wild animal. He is man's servant only on sufferance and for a limited time. Sooner or later he will escape or he will attack.

Luckily for Bobby Theron, the bear escaped before he could so far forget his fondness for his master as to attack him.

For perhaps two months Ursus sulked in that miserable stall-cage, with only Thor's companionship and Bobby's occasional visits to amuse him. As the spring farm work was at its height, Bobby was able to spend little time with him. Thor, too, was always at Bobby's heels. The lonely Ursus moped; then, by degrees, he grew savage.

One night he tried to break or bite the tough hickory bars of his cage in two. Failing that, another idea came to him. He shambled across to the stall door. Unable to push it down, he stooped, hooked his claws under it, and lifted it bodily from the hinges. One thrust of the shaggy black shoulders and he was loose in the barn. A second mighty shove burst the rotting lock on the barn's outer door.

Ursus ambled through to freedom. The night was moonlit. The nearby forest was full of alluring smells and softly whispering invitation. Head down and big body swaying, Ursus lurched across the acres of cleared ground toward the woodland where he had been born.

Never had he been forced to find one mouthful of food for himself. Yet before he had advanced even two hundred yards into the forest, some instinct made him halt and turn over a rotting log. From beneath it he scooped a handful of fat white grubs and ate them with a delight he had never felt for his farm food.

Thus it was that Ursus returned to the wild, mysteriously able, as have been hundreds of other forest-born creatures in like situation, to forage richly for himself and to keep out of the way of humans.

Next morning Bobby was keenly unhappy at his pet's departure. He had grown fond of the clown-like animal whose puny life he had saved nearly two years earlier. Colonel Theron did not share his son's unhappiness. He was relieved that Ursus had solved his own problem by escaping.

The bear had been a useless and expensive luxury at the thrifty homestead. There was always danger, too, of his getting his owners into trouble with the law. Bobby was so attached to him that the colonel had not liked to suggest the bear be killed for his rather valuable pelt.

A century earlier the colonel's grandfather had founded a tidy little fortune by purchasing black bear skins from Indian trappers and selling them to exporters. In those days there was an insatiable demand for such fur. No fewer than twenty-five thousand black-bear pelts had been sent yearly, from America, to England alone.

A yellow-tawny thunderbolt launched itself
from the rocks above.
The Destroyer from Nowhere, page 168

Ursus came slowly down to earth again,
hindquarters first.
Foster Brothers, page 175

Well, Ursus was gone. That was all there was to it. Presently Bobby reconciled himself to his loss. He and Thor were the only two who had cared for the bear. Bobby had other things to think of. Yet it puzzled him that Thor showed no greater sorrow over his beloved chum's vanishing. The collie did not seem to miss Ursus at all, though, on the farm, they had been inseparable.

The reason Thor did not grieve for losing his pal was that he had not lost him. He knew perfectly well where Ursus was. Before daybreak on the morning after the bear's escape, the collie, in his patrolling of the farm, had come upon his scent.

He had followed it and had caught up with his friend as Ursus was completing the robbery of a bee tree. He and Thor feasted happily, side by side, there in the gray dawn, on giant hunks of sticky honeycomb, undeterred by the assaults of such few bees as followed their treasure from its broken hollow limb to the ground below.

Scarcely a day passed when Thor did not find time for a romp or a hunt with Ursus in the forest. Always it was ridiculously easy to pick up the bear's trail and to find him. Ursus was delighted to be found. Often he lurked for hours at the very edge of the woods, hoping his scent might attract Thor to him—as usually it did.

To Ursus, the humans at the farm and the life he himself had led there were growing vague in memory. He felt the natural distaste for them that is the heritage of woodland creatures. Existence in the food-rich forest was an endless joy. He had no mind to jeopardize it by letting any human catch sight of him or by revisiting his old home.

But Thor was different. Ursus loved the collie that had been his foster brother and his daily playmate. Perhaps it was the far-back strain of the wild, hidden in every collie, that made the bear continue to hanker for the companionship of the dog. In any event, the chumship increased rather than diminished.

True, there were things about this new Ursus which puzzled Thor; as when, in late autumn, he found the bear one day chewing and swallowing great mouthfuls of pine needles and hemlock twigs.

Ursus was soggy with fat at this season—the fat which was to carry him through the long cold season of hibernating. Now he was gorging the evergreen food which was to stuff his stomach throughout the hungry months—the stuffing which he would eject disgustedly from his mouth on the first warm day of very early spring.

On another daybreak Thor trotted to the woodland and caught Ursus's trail, as usual. It led him through the bitter cold and driving snow to a shale hillock against whose southerly base lay a big windfall.

Daintily the collie made his way over the fallen trunk to a low-apertured little cave behind it, completely hidden from casual view. In the back of the cave lay Ursus, huddled in a corner and as motionless as the dead. In vain did Thor sniff at him and even paw his fat sides to awaken him.

His chum was asleep and would not or could not be roused. But he was alive. Thor was not worried. Only he felt strangely lonesome as he trotted back to the farm and to his day's work.

Again and again during the long icy winter Thor made his way to the cave behind the windfall. Something seemed to tell him that his comrade would come to life again.

One muggy dawn in early April, when the forest was adrip and misty with unseasonable heat, Thor neared the windfall in time to see Ursus crawl atop it. The bear was nauseated, bone thin, weak as a sick cat. Together the chums ranged the woods for food that morning, but at a snail's pace. And so recommenced their forest friendship.

One day when Ursus had been gone for perhaps two years, Colonel Theron rode into the village courthouse as witness in a land-boundary case. The hired man was busy in the south mowing, nearly a mile from the house. Bobby—now nearly sixteen—set off, across lots, to join the man, Thor, as ever, at his heels.

The boy's course took him alongside the tight-fenced bog meadow where at this season some twenty of the Theron hogs rooted. Bobby paused to note with surprise that not a hog was in sight. Closer inspection showed him the reason.

At the forest side of the meadow some uneasy pig had rooted away at the bottom rail of the ancient fence until the wormy wood had split asunder. The pig had tried to wiggle through the opening. The leverage of his tough back had broken the rail above. That was enough. He had blazed a path that any hog might follow.

Indeed, every hog had followed it. All twenty had rioted through the gap and into the lush forest beyond. Not one was in sight, though a blind puppy might have followed the drove's devastating trail into the heart of the woodland.

Had Colonel Theron been at home he would have let the hogs root there in the acorns and beechnuts and the mold all day, and then would have had Thor round them up and drive them back to their pen in late afternoon when they should be tired and full of food.

But Bobby had all the conscientious energy of his father, without the latter's long experience. The hogs had gotten away. Perhaps, like Ursus, they might never return or be found. At the very least, there was strong chance they might double back, and emerge in the field of young corn just to northward. They must be gotten back into their meadow and into the pen.

Bobby whistled to Thor, who was sniffing interestedly at a woodchuck hole. Pointing to the trampled swath through the undergrowth, the boy commanded:

"Get 'em, Thor! Round 'em up!"

With no outward sign of reluctance, the collie bounded forward on his unpleasant duty. Bobby ran close behind him. The two entered the woods and plunged deeper and deeper into them, following the unmistakable trail of the runaway hogs.

Thor soon left Bobby behind in the chase. The running boy put on a new burst of speed as he heard the dog begin to bark. He could read the meanings of his collie's various barks as well as he could read print. This was the harrowing nagging bark, with which Thor was wont to start cattle or hogs from their grazing as he began to round them up.

Out through the trampled undergrowth ran Bobby, hot and panting. He was at the edge of an oak glade on whose every side arose the bushes and saplings in an almost impenetrable wall. The glade's moldering fallen leaves were wet and greasy from last night's rain.

Scattered through the cleared space were the twenty strayed hogs. Glumly greedy, they had been munching the half-decayed acorns. At Thor's clamorous summons they lifted sullen heads, in no way minded to be interrupted at their feast.

The dog was not interested in their likes and dislikes. His job was to cluster them and start them homeward. This he prepared to do in true businesslike fashion. His flying feet sent up swirls of sodden leaves behind him as he darted among the hogs.

Crankily, most of them obeyed his threatening summons. A half-dozen of the largest and oldest paid no overt attention to him, but grouped themselves a little closer together and pretended to go on eating.

Too excited to realize that this was not a promising sign, Bobby ran at the six, while Thor was herding the less recalcitrant majority of the bunch toward the path they had blazed when they entered the glade. Straight at the sulking brutes the boy ran, shouting. Closer the six pressed to one another.

As Bobby was almost upon the nearest of the half-dozen—a lean old tusker whose furrowed sides told of many battles and victories—the hog wheeled about and charged him.

In astonishment at such an unlooked-for move, Bobby slid to a standstill. His heels slipped on the greasy mold in his effort to halt. Up went his feet and down went the rest of him, full in the path of the charging hog.

At sight of the lad's fall the other five members of the group joined ferociously in their leader's onslaught upon the helpless human. Bobby, by instinct, rolled quickly aside, in time to miss the gouging tusks and razor hoofs of the first assailant by little more than a hair's breadth.

But before he could get to his feet the six were at him.

As he had fallen he had cried out in dismay. That involuntary cry saved his life. Thor, herding the rest of the drove, had whirled at sound of it.

Now, as the six rushed in, a silver-and-snow catapult landed among them from nowhere in particular, snarling, snapping, slashing.

No longer had Thor any use for the finesse which had been taught him as part of his education as a herder. His master was down. These grunting devils were pressing in avidly, to rip him to pieces. It was a moment for stark action.

With a wild-beast roar, the collie threw his furry bulk between the struggling boy and the hogs.

As he sprang, he slashed clean through the forward-thrusting pink snout of the nearest tusker, and in the same motion he flung his sixty pounds of weight across the head of the second. He was stabbed to the rib bone for his daring. Giving no heed to the deep flesh wound, he hurled himself forward and back and sidewise among the galloping hogs, to fend their charge from Bobby.

Not all Thor's fierce war prowess nor all his generalship could have stayed that porcine avalanche for more than a fraction of a second. But a fraction of a second was long enough for the nimble boy to get his own legs under him and leap up.

With his back to a tree whose trunk was far too thick for shinnying, he braced himself for the oncoming murder wave. As he had risen he had snatched a heavy stick that lay within reach of his clawing hand. With this he laid a mighty blow across the eyes of the tusker that was all but upon him.

The blow numbed Bobby's arm to the elbow. It jarred the hog to a brief halt. It broke the cudgel in three pieces.

And now down upon the vainly battling boy and dog swept the six hogs. Bobby, with back braced against the tree, kicked with all his football prowess at the lowered heads. The collie rent and tore and slashed as he was forced backward against his master by the sheer weight of the forward-jostling hogs.

Thor knew well that he could take to his heels and leave this crew of murderers a mile behind him. But he would not run and leave Bobby there.

The lad, at his own first step, realized that his ankle had turned under him as he fell, and that it was either sprained or broken. Flight was out of the question. The best he could do was to keep his back to the tree and kick his hardest, for such few seconds as might remain before the blood-mad hogs should pull him down.

Then all at once appeared a giant figure infinitely taller than himself, that ranged close beside the boy. It had advanced from the nearby wall of undergrowth at unbelievable speed. Out of the corner of his eye Bobby could glimpse it in blurred fashion. Someone had come to reinforce or rescue him. His heart throbbed at the relief.

But Bobby Theron was wholly wrong. The newcomer had not arrived thus opportunely for the sake of rescuing him. The newcomer had no interest whatever in rescuing him. So far as the newcomer was concerned, the hogs might have torn the boy to fragments and eaten him.

No, it was Thor the rescuer was seeking to aid. It was Thor and Thor alone.

Rooting for grubs near the edge of the glade, Ursus had caught the scent of his chum. But with it was a faintly remembered human scent, as well. Therefore the bear did not shamble forth as usual to greet his pal. Then, a second or so later, Ursus had heard the collie's stark battle roar. He had smelled spilled blood, too—his chum's blood. That was all the incentive Ursus needed.

The hog leader's rush banged Thor up against Bobby's knees before the collie could elude it. As the tusker gouged for the pinioned dog's throat, a vast black paw descended from just above, falling with the speed of light and the force of a piledriver. Its five curved claws stood out distinct from one another, like a quintet of saber blades.

Down slumped the hog leader, with a skull crushed as if by a sledge hammer. But already the second hog was tearing for Thor's throat. With a swiftness that had an oddly leisurely look Ursus gathered the pig in his short arms, lifting him aloft and cuddling him for an instant to his hairy breast. Then he let his victim slither to the ground, with four broken ribs and a snapped foreleg.

Without waiting for further preliminaries, Ursus waded luxuriously into the fray. His first two encounters had not consumed two seconds of time between them. The four other hogs were still trying to push past one another's impeding bodies to the slaughter of the trapped boy and the dog. Just as they succeeded in doing so Ursus strolled among them with his clownlike gait and solemnly swaying black head.

He made no attempt at self-defense, but received unheedingly the impact of one hog's body against his middle and the crunch of another's overshot jaws on his haunch.

At the same time he aimed a gravely careful blow with each uplifted forepaw. A hog crumpled into the slime with a broken back. Another rolled over with a crushed shoulder blade.

Then for the first time Ursus seemed to note that he was assailed amidships by the two remaining pigs of the stricken sextet. With true comedic effect he swung aloft the hog that was tearing at his haunch, and he flailed the squirming body down, with much precision and with supernatural strength, upon its colleague.

It was all over before Bobby Theron could get his breath or realize fully what miracle had befallen him. Panting, the boy stared down at the dead and crippled hogs in front of him. Then he stared up at the towering form of his onetime pet. He tried to speak or to move. But he could not.

Ursus was paying no attention to him. After sniffing at each of the motionless or spasmodically twitching hogs on the ground, he dropped on all fours and waddled over to Thor.

Lovingly he touched noses with the bleeding and breathless collie. The contact seemed to assure Ursus, somehow, that his chum was not dangerously hurt. His comical little eyes roved to the remaining fourteen hogs, bunched in terror at the far end of the glade.

Rearing his mighty frame once more onto his hind legs, Ursus walked majestically toward them. But he did not go far.

At the bear's second forward step each and every one of the fourteen spun about, with a deafening chorus of squeals, and tore homeward through the undergrowth. Nor did they check their panic flight until they reached their own meadow and crowded one another noisily for precedence under the broken fence into the only sanctuary they knew.

Bobby could have sworn there was a glint of happy mischief in the bear's eyes as he watched that headlong stampede.

Again Ursus and Thor touched noses; the collie's plumed tail wagging happily. Then the bear waddled slowly back into the undergrowth.

Thor made as though to follow him, but presently checked himself and came back to Bobby's side, looking wistfully up at his human god for whose sake he had just deserted the four-footed chum to whom he owed his life.

Bobby stooped and petted the collie's classic head. Then he stared blankly at the shambles in front of him. Then his eyes roved toward the swaying underbrush which marked the leisurely passage of the departing Ursus. Half aloud, the bewildered lad babbled:

"Yet—yet they say the—the *Jungle Book* isn't true! I guess India hasn't got much on the U.S.A. when it comes to—to Mowgli stuff!"

COLLIE!

Glamis found the cabin, with no difficulty at all, though twelve years had passed since his last visit to it or to the virgin wilderness in whose center it stood.

He found it and he made it habitable and stocked it with emergency provisions. Then he settled down to a mode of life once very familiar to him.

From boyhood, he had known the outdoors and every detail of camping and of living off the wilderness, all this as a diversion, and as a change from the city life whose activities claimed him for ten months of the year. But now, when the results of those same activities made him a fugitive from the law, he turned to forest life as a refuge, and not as a diversion.

The oil-lands swindle, which he had fathered, was exposed. It was a matter for federal prison, not for mere state penitentiary. And Uncle

Sam has a bothersome way of sticking to the trail of federal criminals. So Glamis had hit on the one hiding place likely to outwit his trailers.

The ports were watched. He knew that. Moreover, his crime was extraditable. Hence, Canada was closed to him. All his known haunts were shadowed. But—well, along the semi-trackless wilderness from eastern Maine to western New York, close to the Canadian line, there were thousands of square miles of wild forest-and-lake country. Scattered through it, in those days, were hundreds of woodsmen—hunters, trappers, petty farmsteaders, guides, and the like. They minded their own business. The outer world meddled with them not at all, except when the season for moose or for salmon lured well-to-do tourists to the fringe of the wilderness hinterland.

Were a "city chap" to invade this region and restore a tumbledown cabin and set up housekeeping there and become a permanent inhabitant, the news would spread among the back-country folk. In time it would seep all the way from Bangor to Buffalo and presently to the authorities.

But nothing of the sort happened.

A bronzed and unshaven fellow, who spoke English with a strong French accent when his glum taciturnity could be broken through at all, slouched into White Timber one day, from the direction of the border. He bought a wisely chosen supply of provisions and utensils from the White Timber storekeeper, to whom he gave a smudgily penciled note of introduction from Jean Baptiste Louvremont, a former guide. That was all—except that the Canadian newcomer had taken squatter occupancy of the decrepit Louvremont cabin, six miles back from White Timber, and that he paid cash and kept to himself and very evidently was a lifelong woodsman.

There was nothing about such an arrival to rouse talk or even a passing interest. The tidings did not travel. Nobody was interested in the hermit-like man who picked up a fair living by his traps and his rifle, and who discouraged intimacy. There were many such in the backwoods fastnesses. The hermit called himself "Grau," and a weekly paper, printed in French, came to him by that name, from Quebec.

If any of the neighbors recalled that a spruce New Yorker had saved Jean Baptiste Louvremont from drowning in No Bottom Lake some years earlier, assuredly none of them connected this frowsy trapper with the tourist. Indeed, few of them recalled the long-departed guide at all. Louvremont had left the White Timber country for his birthplace near Quebec on coming into a little legacy, and neither his backwoods cabin nor his backwoods friends had seen him since.

His tracks covered, Hugh Glamis was leading the free life he had always craved. Even though it was a bare and rugged life at times, and starkly lonesome all day and every day, it was a million times better than a federal prison. In another five or six years, the government might give him up for dead or as hopelessly lost, and then, with the secretly invested bundle of cash he had saved from the wreck of his hopes, he might be able to start his financial life afresh, in Montreal or Buenos Aires or Mexico City.

In the meanwhile he was as secure from arrest as though he were on the planet Mars. Not for naught had he planned every move of this sort, from the very first days when a crash had begun to seem possible. Each step was cleverly safeguarded.

This story begins on a day when a ferocious spell of heat had gripped the late spring wilderness. The air hung pulsing, stifling, burning, over the suffering world. The sun rode like a copper ball in the sky. The moon was red and bleary. The clouds had forgotten how to water the thirsty earth. Nature panted in an agony of heat and drought. All this, at a season when, usually, the woodlands were fresh and dewy and when all the universe smiled.

Blackflies made life a horror for every breathing thing. So did mosquitoes and "no-see-'ems" and the like. The insect tribe alone rejoiced in this period of hot misery.

Word went forth from the forest wardens, bidding folk use every precaution against the red terror of fire. Men went about their duties dourly. The wilderness animals were as worn of temper and as frayed of nerves as were their human superiors.

At four o'clock one morning, at the latter part of this heat spell, three denizens of the hinterland set forth to find food. Of the trio, one was a cow moose, shaggy, black, hideous. Leaving her shapeless calf in a dense thicket where the June flies would be less likely to torture it than in the open, she plodded lakeward for a dawn feast of watergrass and for a wallow in the ice-cool shallows before the rising sun should turn these shallows lukewarm and wilt the brief freshness from the lakeside herbage.

At about the same time Hugh Glamis turned out of his tumbled cot, sleepless and mosquito-bitten. Rod in hand, he sought the lake edge for enough fish to vary his usual ham-and-flapjack breakfast. On a muggy morning like this, the thought of a fresh-broiled lake trout was more appetizing than that of a soggy meal of salt meat and sourdough.

The third member of the food-seeking trio was a gray and gaunt and wild-cat-tempered she-wolf, whose late-born litter of three had been abiding under a windfall at the edge of an inshelving ledge of rock. The heat and the comparative lateness of their birthtime and the hordes of winged pests—these had not been aids to health for the trio of newborn wolves.

Two of them had sickened and died before they were a week old. The third, now at the age of four weeks, was husky enough, though too lean. But the deaths of his two brethren had done queer things to the dam's always overstrung nerves, and had made her savage beyond even what was normal for wolf mothers.

Also, it had made her unduly anxious to get enough food to suckle properly this last and only cub of hers. Hence, of late, she had been taking chances which normal lupine wiliness would have forbidden. Morbidly courageous, she ranged everywhere and anywhere for meat.

Otherwise—even after drawing blank in her night's food-hunt—she would have had too much caution to start from her lair by dawn light, in quest of the baby moose whose scent came so fresh to her from the nearby thicket. For baby moose do not roam alone through the forest at dawn. They are attended by mothers who are as formidable to child-stealers as they are repulsive to look upon.

The wolf slunk noiselessly along—a silent shadow scarcely denser than that of the departing night. Straight to the thicket she made her way. So deftly did she enter the copse that scarcely a leaf stirred. Yet rounding a corner of the trail, twenty yards below, Hugh Glamis had the merest fleeting glimpse of her brush tip, as it vanished among the lower branches.

At the distance and by such faint light, the man could not be certain what he had seen. Quickening his pace, his moccasined feet as noiseless on the soft trail as the she-wolf's, he walked toward the spot where he had seen the fleeting flicker of white-gray fur.

A tiny breath of breeze shook the dead stillness of the air. There was just enough of it to send warning to the nostrils of the moose that a wolf was nearing the copse where her gangling baby lay hidden. Almost at the brink of the lake she wheeled, and plunged with ungainly speed toward the thicket. At the fourth or fifth bound, her canter changed to a charge. For from the underbrush came to her flapping ears the sound of a terrified and pain-wrung bleat.

The she-wolf had sprung on the gawky calf.

Before the gray thief could fairly sink her curved tusks into the shambling little victim's throat, a brown-black thunderbolt burst through the tough copse stems and down upon the marauder.

The wolf dropped her prey and flashed to one side with the bewildering speed of a cat, in her instinctive effort to avoid the furious charge. But it is easier for a galloping moose to tear through a thicket hedge of stout bush-stems than for a sideways-jumping wolf. The intruder caromed against a bunch of stiff boughs that threw her backward and out of her stride. Before she could recover herself the moose's spear-like forefoot struck her glancingly.

Beneath that fearful blow, her right shoulder blade and the leg beneath it were broken like rotten wood. To the earth tumbled the wolf mother, screaming once with torment as she fell. But, wolf-like, as she went down she rolled to one side. Thus the pair of battering forefeet missed her, clean. And on the instant she was up and away, scurrying through the impeding thicket stems on three legs, the fourth leg trailing like a dead thing. The moose thundered along in vengeful chase.

Now, with anything like an even chance, there is no wolf that cannot escape at will from a moose. But here these chances were anything but even. In the first place the thicket hindered the wolf's every step. Yet its toughest branches were as gossamer to the giant pursuer. In the second place, one cannot run as fast or dodge as well on three legs as on four.

At the copse edge the moose's forefoot caught the wolf on the hip. There was a snapping sound. Over and over on the ground the broken-backed creature rolled, shrieking. The moose, in midcharge, caught sight and scent of the man standing not thirty feet away.

She halted, irresolute, too angry to retreat at once, but too wary by nature to continue the chase. With splayfeet pawing up great clods of forest loam, and with ugly head lunging, she hesitated.

The wolf, ceasing to roll and howl, also caught sight of the man. And she did a most amazing thing. Getting her legs under her as best she might—half rolling, half crawling—she made off at right angles to her former course, her snakelike wrigglings getting the broken-backed sufferer over the ground at an astonishing rate of speed.

Twice she peered over her crumpled shoulder at the horrendous black foe behind her. At the second of these terrified glances her bloodshot eye fell on Glamis, standing spellbound within ten feet of her. The moose took a plunging step forward. The wolf gave one final agonized scramble and vanished under the nearby windfall.

The moose's incipient charge halted a second time, as sight and scent of the man counterbalanced her insane maternal rage against the wolf. And—old-time hunter and forest dweller as he was—Hugh Glamis stood motionless staring at this closeup of raw woodland passions. But only for an instant did the queer stage-wait endure.

Then, from under the windfall the stricken wolf reappeared. Feebler now, and scarcely able to make her tortured muscles obey her dying commands, she emerged from her refuge. Again she eyed the pawing and snorting moose.

Then, unfalteringly, she writhed across the short stretch of clearing, straight toward the man. She seemed to realize that Glamis's presence held her murderous enemy in check, Also, goaded by her infinitely greater dread, she seemed to have lost entirely her race's innate fear of man.

As he gaped, open-mouthed, Hugh saw the wolf was carrying something between her slavering jaws. The "something" was a fuzzy, yellow-gray creature, perhaps twice the size of a rat. It twisted and whimpered in the unsteady grip of the dying mother. Focusing his eyes in the dim dawn light, Glamis saw that the morsel was a baby wolf.

The anguished mother wolf, feeling death close upon her, had wriggled her painful way to her lair, and had taken from there her whelp. Perhaps she reasoned that a moose has as keen scenting powers as has a wolf and that the moose mother might smell out and kill the helpless baby once its dam was dead.

Perhaps, too, she was merely moving the whelp to some safer hiding place, and chose to pass close to the man in doing so, that his presence might protect her and her offspring from attack by the furious moose. It is not for humans to try to fathom the deeper instincts of the wild, especially when those instincts are made unnaturally sharp by the approach of death. One can only relate the facts as they stand.

Up to the gaping man crawled the broken and crushed mother wolf. To within a yard of his motionless form she came. Then her jaws relaxed. Out of their cavernous grasp rolled the shapeless wolf pup. It rolled to Glamis's feet and lay there, whimpering and twisting in baby impotence.

The mother, as her mouth opened, cried out and lay flat on her stomach. Glamis saw at a glance that she was dead. The moose saw it, too, and her own red rage departed, leaving only the ancestral terror of humans. With a bellow of fright the huge creature whirled about and disappeared, crashing through the undergrowth.

Glamis stood blinking after her. Then he looked at the mangled gray body of the mother wolf. Last of all, his blank stare fell upon the whimpering infant at his feet. And he began to mutter dazedly to himself.

"Brought the pup straight up to me—to—to protect!" he mused, incredulously. "Trusted me to save it from that filthy cow moose! Trusted *me*—a—a *man!* Lord! It doesn't make sense!"

To Glamis there was but one solution to what had happened. He believed that the wolf, dying, and in fear lest the whelp also be slain, had cast aside her hatred for his race and had brought her adored baby to him for protection. To the death, she had trusted him—had trusted Hugh Glamis, whose financial record showed him worthy of nobody's trust.

At the fantastic thought a mist swam for an instant before the man's shrewd eyes. Then, frowning, he shook himself back to sanity.

This dead wolf and her miserable cub represented bounty money back at White Timber. This, apart from such slight sum as the mother's trampled pelt might bring. Appraisingly, Hugh ran his eye over the dead mother. Then, lifting one moccasined foot, he prepared to drive his heel into the shapeless head of the orphaned wolfling. Money was money there in the hinterland. And he had won it without a lick of work. He had won it, in addition to seeing a mighty entertaining forest drama enacted.

Then down came his heel. But it came softly to earth, instead of smashing down upon the baby wolf's skull. Something was at work on the over-lonely man's imagination and perhaps on his heart as well.

No one likes to know the whole world distrusts him. This had not been a pleasant thought to Glamis, in the long months of solitude. And now, he had been trusted—"to the death," he told himself again. And by a wolf. He had heard that animals' instinct is a surer guide than human logic.

His own world—the world of men and of finance—had branded him as an outcast. Wasn't it possible, perhaps, that this creature of the wilds had had clearer vision into his character? And now, was he going to treat that trust as he had treated the trust of his business associates? Was he going to prove unworthy even of this?

(Yes, solitude and nerve-strain had done odd things to Glamis's power of reasoning, as to those of many another solitary and hunted man!)

Long he stood there, glowering down at the ground and sometimes mumbling disjointedly to himself. The dawn smiled into red sunrise and the forest around him took on a myriad wondrous dancing lights and shadows. The bird songs were in full chorus. The pulsing of heat could be seen in the open spaces ahead. And at his feet whined and whimpered and wriggled the helpless baby wolf.

At last, as though half ashamed of himself, he stooped down and ran his calloused hand gently along the fuzzy back of the tiny woodland orphan. Instantly the baby's whimper merged into a really creditable snarl. A double set of needle-like little milk teeth were driven into Glamis's thumb.

The man jerked back his pricked hand. Again his heel was raised to end the foolish scene. But, as before, he set his foot softly to the ground again. A grin crept over his sullen face. This ridiculous wisp of life had not feared him. Powerless against his strength, it had not cringed, but had fought back, valorously, at the supposed assailant. That was true pluck. The outcast's heart warmed still further toward the wolf baby.

Presently, Glamis had made up his mind. It was characteristic of the man that his decisions, once formed, were changeless. Lifting the dead mother wolf in his arms, he carried her to the windfall and shoved her stiffening body in through the opening of the lair. Then, taking off his cotton shirt, he threw it over the snarling, battling youngster. He picked up the squirming bundle and set forth for his cabin.

Ten minutes later, his hands encased in tough leather gloves, he was offering a saucer of condensed milk and heated water to the rebellious cub.

Naturally, the whelp had no idea what to do with the food, and its angry kicking upset the saucer all over the cabin's fairly clean floor. In no impatience at all Glamis heated and mixed a new dish of milk and water.

As he did so, he recalled a boyhood memory of a litter of motherless collie pups he had brought up by hand, and he began to review the various stages of such feeding.

All his life, Hugh Glamis had been a dog man. It had not been the least of his griefs that the flight into exile had forced him to give up his kennel of thoroughbred collies. He had heard of the strange resemblance between collie and wolf, and he resolved to bring into play his collie-training experiences in the rearing of this wolf whelp he had adopted.

First of all, taking the growling baby by the nape of the neck, he stuck its nose gently into the warm milk, then let go of the captive head. Disgustedly, the cub pulled back from the contact. But a few drops of milk had adhered to nose and lips. By instinct the youngster began to lick these off, and, finding they were food, it made somewhat less resistance at the second immersion of mouth and muzzle into the saucer. The third time, the cub approached the saucer, unbidden, and nuzzled at its contents. Within a half hour the pink little tongue was lapping vigorously and happily at the warm milk.

"That's so much gained," commented Glamis, proud of the lesson's success. "Now after this you'll know how to lap it up. You'll do it pretty sloppily for a day or two, till you get the full hang of it. But if I feed you often enough you'll get all you really need to keep you alive. And now you and I are going to have a chat, Wolfie. If I left you to your own devices or kept you in a pen, you'd grow up, all right. But you'd grow up a wolf. And a wolf is one of the meanest things Nature ever created.

"So I'm going to keep you here in the cabin and try to humanize you. In the first place, you're going to forget you started out as a wolf. You're going to be a collie. And you're going to be my chum. Lord knows I need one! As a first step, we're going to call you Collie. That's going to be your name. In another month, I expect you to know it and to come when I call you 'Collie.' Understand?"

This was quite the longest speech Glamis had made in a year, and he felt a vague satisfaction in being able to talk again, as freely as of old and without the carefully acquired French-Canadian accent.

He set about, diligently, converting an old dry-goods box into a roomy and comfortable bed for his new pet. Then, when Collie had eaten much and showed signs of drowsiness, the man picked him up, carefully, and held him on his lap. The whelp snarled and snapped, but not with the former zest. Warm food had done its work. The shock of first contact with mankind was gone. And there was something namelessly comforting in being cuddled and talked to and rubbed behind the ears. There was a charm about the human voice, as ever to puppies.

"That's better!" approved Glamis as, after less and less snarling, the baby consented at last to lie sleepily supine under the caressing hand. "Now, Collie, before I put you to bed I'm going to tell you something more about your education. If you'd been left to yourself, out yonder, and if your mother had lived—do you know what you'd have grown into?

"You'd have grown into a wolf. That means you'd have had a tucked-in stomach and that your tail would have spent all its time between your hind legs, tucked in as tightly as your stomach itself; and your coat would have been mostly burrs and scratches; and your eyes would have been shallow and yellowish and furtive.

"You'd have been a skulker and an outlaw—like—like—well, never mind who—and you'd have been as mean as dirt. Now, you aren't going to be any of those things. You're going to be a collie dog. And if there's anything finer and more of a chum than the right kind of collie dog— well, I've never seen it.

"A collie is the cleverest dog alive. Where does he get his brains? He gets them from his wolf ancestors. Well, if that's true, then a wolf must have about all the brains there are. And *this* wolf is going to be trained to use his brains, to make himself a collie and not a varmint. I— There! You've gone to sleep. Right at the best part of my lecture. Now for bed."

He laid the baby on a tangle of soft blanket at the bottom of the box, and left him there for a snooze.

Oddly happy and amused, Glamis went about his own morning chores. The devil of lonesomeness seemed to have departed from the shack. Life had a new interest. It was almost good to be alive.

So began a period of genuine pleasure for the fugitive. With all the zest of an unemployed active man, and with all the skill of long years as a canine trainer, Hugh threw himself into the task of making Collie forget to be a wolf and learn to be a dog. This was the easier, of course, by reason of the pupil's youth and lack of anything but instinct to bind him to the wolf family. He had no memories to warn him, nothing but the ingrained feelings of his forbears to tell him that man and wolf are foes, and under human friendliness this was wearing away.

From the age of one month to two months a well-nourished wolf pup more than doubles in weight and increases still more rapidly in intelligence. At nine weeks, Collie was another creature from the paunchy but thin morsel of fuzz and bone and savage temper which had come to the cabin in Hugh Glamis's shirt.

Thanks to such non-lupine dainties as condensed milk and broth-soaked biscuit and the like, he was as round as he was long, and he had grown most amazingly. Thanks to daily and hourly association with a wise master, he had lost practically all his furtive ways and his sullenness and distrust. He would roll and romp by the half-hour with Hugh. Head on one side, he would sit at Glamis's feet for an endless time, listening to the companionable voice droning at him.

More as a game than as a task, Collie had begun to learn the meanings of certain simple words and simpler tricks. Glamis had not been wrong in attributing brains to wolves. But not even Glamis had realized the uncanny swiftness wherewith a rightly taught young wolf can pick up an education. Not the cleverest of Hugh's long line of collies had learned with such ease and eager intelligence as did this foundling. It was a joy to teach him. At five months old he was better educated and wiser than is the average yearling dog.

Hugh Glamis was not given to deeds of unselfish kindliness. Nor had he spent all this time on Collie's training from mere altruism. The wolf's bewildering wisdom and ease of learning had delighted the man. It was no duty, but a positive joy, for an animal man to train such a pet. And in the course of the training there stole into Hugh's bitter heart a depth of affection for Collie, such as never had he been able to feel for even his favorite dogs. Man and wolf grew to be staunch comrades. And by reason of this the wolfling learned the faster and became daily the more humanized.

It was not until Collie was six months old that he saw a man other than Hugh. Then, one sourly cold gray morning in late autumn, a trapper named Brace chanced to round the trail leading to the cabin. The wind was in his face and did not send forth his scent or light footsteps as a herald of his coming. Thus he arrived in view of the dooryard unnoted. There he stopped in stupid astonishment at sight of the hermit-like "Grau" sitting on a chopping block, in seeming conversation with an overgrown young wolf. As Brace still gazed, unbelieving, he saw Hugh fumble in his pocket for something, and then heard him say in a conversational tone to his weird companion:

"I left my tobacco pouch on the table, inside, Collie. Go get it for me."

The wolf turned, scampered indoors, and came back instantly, carrying between his teeth a dirty leather bag. Up to Hugh he trotted, and was about to drop the pouch into the lazily outstretched hand when, from a corner of his eye, he beheld the trapper.

On the instant Collie dropped the bag and spun about, head lowered, fangs bared, hackles abristle, to face the intruder.

Thanks to Hugh's training, he had lost the inherent lupine fear of man, but he had not had a chance to lose his race's hatred for humans in general. To this stranger he offered deadly challenge.

Before Brace had chance to whip his rifle to his shoulder or even to take a snap shot from the hip, Collie had flown at him. Noiseless, terrible, lightning swift, the wolf charged. Glamis's sharp cry of *"Collie! Back!"* reached him just as he was launching himself for a throat spring; yet, obedient as ever to his god, Collie dropped to earth and sulkily retraced his steps to Hugh's side. Yet, always, as he went, he looked obliquely over his shoulder at Brace, and he snarled hideously at him.

"I catch 'im, a bebby," explained Hugh, in his best French-Canadian accent. "I make 'im—wot you call it?—pet. He gentle. Vair good. See, he mind. *T'accouche-toi*, Collie!"

Never before had Collie been addressed in French. Never before had he heard his master speak so mincingly. Yet well did he understand the simple gesture of the forefinger that went with the words, and he dropped to the ground, obedient, at Hugh's side. Not once, however, did he take his distrustful eyes from Brace, nor did he abate that snarl of utter hatred.

And thus passed off Collie's first meeting with any man other than his master. But that meeting was to have far-reaching results.

The fact that an obscure backwoodsman had made a pet of a wolf was not of any tremendous interest in that wild region, where raccoons and foxes and even skunks had been pressed into a like service. True, one or two neighbors dropped in at the cabin during the next few months, to verify Brace's report and to see for themselves the wolf that behaved like a dog. But as the taciturn Glamis did not encourage the visits or offer the slightest hospitality to his unbidden guests, the curiosity-seekers were not many, nor did they come often.

Collie showed a lessening of surprise as he saw man after man, but no slackening of hostility. Even as there are many one-man dogs, so, in greater measure, this was a one-man wolf. He had learned Glamis was not the only man in the wilderness, but he could not learn to tolerate the others. Nor did Hugh want him to.

Once, when Glamis was off on a round of his traps—having left Collie at home on account of a cut foot—he returned to the cabin in bare time to save the life of a forest ne'er-do-well who had come snooping around the supposedly deserted shack and whom Collie had hurled to the floor. As Glamis ran up, shouting, the wolf had just gained a death grip on the tramp's throat, and with difficulty was made to relinquish it. That story spread, too, and from then on Glamis's cabin was as safe from petty thieves as though it had been a police station.

For two years thereafter, man and wolf lived contentedly together in the silences of the wilderness. The cabin was off the beaten trail and seldom were its occupants molested.

Sometimes, in the endless winter evenings, when the dry snow, gale-blown, scratched hungrily at the windows, and the world lay white and dead under the horrible chill of the north, other voices would add themselves to the screech of the wind. These were the voices of the wolf pack, swirling past, in search of hard-hunted food.

At such times Collie would jump up from the scrap of rag rug where he sprawled dozing at Glamis's feet. He would tremble all over, while strange yellow glints showed from his wistful eyes.

Again, in late March, while the forest lay black and dripping and the days waxed longer and the nights less deathly cold, there would be scurryings of light feet on the trail beyond, and the whisk of running bodies through the sodden undergrowth. Then Collie's wistfulness would brim from his eyes and he would whimper softly, looking alternately from Glamis to the door. For this was the mating season for the wolf folk, the season when the pack split up into pairs at first breath of far-off spring.

On one such eager night Hugh walked to the door and flung it wide. Then he stood aside and watched. Across the threshold and out on to the clearing sped Collie. The eerie low mate howl quavered from his shaggy throat. For perhaps a hundred yards he flew onward, like a gray shadow.

The man spoke no word, made no motion. Yet the deep lines at his mouth corners set themselves in a cast of grim unhappiness. At the end of the hundred yards Collie's sweeping stride broke and slackened. The wolf came to a hesitant standstill. Then, with something like a human sob in his throat, he trotted back to his master and lay down, quivering all over, at Glamis's feet.

Across the man's face came the first smile that had brightened it in many a long month. He had thrown down the gauntlet of battle to the wilderness, for the love and loyalty of this wilderness comrade of his. And he had won.

Stooping, he flung both arms about the great wolf, and hugged him. Then, ashamed of the unaccustomed caress, he went back indoors, Collie at his heels.

Next week a sheep was killed at a White Timber farm, ten miles distant. It was unquestionably the work of a wolf, and an irate farmer trudged ten miles to Glamis's cabin to demand satisfaction. Nor would he credit Hugh's solemn assurance that Collie had not been out of his master's sight at any time for a single hour. Another farmer, a few miles farther away, suffered similar loss during April and made like complaint. And again Hugh had much difficulty eluding dire punishment for his chum.

"It's the beginning of the end, Collie!" he told his four-footed worshiper when they were alone again. "Those sheep were killed by a wolf. You're a wolf. So they figure you must have done it. They forget these woods are full of wolves—wolves that killed sheep, hereabouts, years before you were ever born. If it keeps up, they'll make trouble for us. That means we'll have to move. I don't care to show up in a backwoods court and have a hundred people staring at me. Some of them might remember that my picture was scattered pretty freely through the police stations and village courtrooms, from Canada to Miami, a couple of years ago. We must be ready to light out, anytime now. If Brace hadn't blundered in here on us, that time, and blabbed about it, nobody'd need know anything about you."

But Brace did more to bother the two. Varying his trade of trapper by acting as guide for tourists, he chanced to mention, one night at a campfire, that a Frenchie about five miles north had a tame wolf that minded as well as any collie pup. Two bored members of the party wanted to see the queer pet. One of them especially, a professional photographer, foresaw a salable picture, and begged Brace to take him to the cabin. Brace consented, though none too willingly, and he insisted that the camera be kept in the background. Grau, he said, was a cranky cuss and mightn't like to be snapped.

Next day the tourists, under the convoy of Brace, dropped in at the cabin just as Glamis was about to start for the lake. Hugh received them glumly enough and he strove by sheer ungraciousness to shorten their visit. He succeeded. They did not stay staring at him and at the snarling wolf more than five minutes. So great was his annoyed effort to freeze them off, Glamis took no special note of one of the party who hung around modestly in the background, with something that looked as if it might be a fish-creel all but covered by the mackinaw he carried over his arm.

Four weeks later a news syndicate carried in all its fifteen Sunday papers a photograph of Hugh Glamis as he stood scowling in front of a wilderness cabin, with an equally inhospitable giant wolf sitting beside him.

On the day after this picture was printed a government agent called on the photographer for what scant information he could give. On the following day a trio of federal officers set out for the region in which their quarry had hidden himself so successfully for nearly three years.

Now the wilderness does strange things to the minds and instincts of those who live long enough and wisely enough in its borders. At three o'clock on an early summer morning Hugh Glamis woke. He woke wide. He woke breathlessly tense. Through every atom of him pulsed a sensation of warning. He could not account for it. It was pure instinct. For nothing tangible or visible or audible had awakened him. Of this he was sure.

The night hush was still on the forest. As Hugh lay there, ears astrain, nerves taut, he could hear the first cockcrow from the far-off farm of his nearest neighbor. Then through the hush came the first triple flute-notes of a thrush. A robin's "laugh" took up the call. Minute by minute, the rest of the bird folk awakened, to pour forth their gloriously joyous thanksgiving hymn for having been kept safe throughout the forest night. The blue-black oblong of the cabin doorway softened to ashy gray. Dawn was at hand.

Angry at himself for his queer nervousness, Hugh lay still, listening for he knew not what and striving for calm. Then he stirred restlessly. At once Collie was on his feet. Leaving his mat in the doorway, the wolf trotted eagerly across to his master's bunk, placed his two forefeet on its edge, and thrust his cold nose lovingly into Hugh's face. His bushy tail was awag. His round eyes were glowing with loving welcome. So, daily, it was his custom to greet Glamis's awakening. Ever he would lie still until a stir from the bunk told him Hugh was awake.

Today the greeting found but absent-minded response from Glamis. Carelessly he stroked the great head and shoulders of his pet. Then, getting up, he started for the spring, for his morning wash. Collie gamboled along gleefully at his side. Together they traversed the hundred yards from cabin to spring. Then, as he reached the water, Hugh looked ruefully down at his own empty hands.

"I'm so rattled—all about nothing at all—that I clean forgot my towel," he told Collie, speaking to the wolf, as always, in the way he would have spoken to a fellow-human. "Run back and get it for me. Towel, Collie. *Towel.*"

Understanding perfectly—for this was by no means the first time he had been sent by his absent-minded master on the same errand—the wolf galloped to the house. Once, halfway, he paused, and sniffed doubtfully at the air. But the light dawn wind was running at right angles between spring and cabin, and, beyond an impalpable suspicion, it told him nothing. Glamis, seeing him pause, called out to him to hurry on. Collie obeyed.

Into the cabin he ran, and on into the shed at the back where hung the grimy towel. Standing on his hind legs, he proceeded to pull it down from its nail. At the same instant Hugh Glamis lifted his face, dripping and gasping, from its deep plunge into the ice-cold water of the overflow tub beside the spring. He had heard something—or sensed something—that set his nerves athrob once more. Gouging the water from his eyes, he peered about him.

He looked into the pistol muzzles of three men who had crept soundlessly from out of the dusky undergrowth directly in front of him.

For a long second Hugh stood there, unmoving and aghast. The three men were as motionless, as wordless as he. He knew who and what they were. And he was unarmed—cut off, weaponless and helpless. This, then, was the end of his long trail.

A faint snarl—wolves do not bark—broke the spell of silence. Collie had come out of the doorway. At sight of the men he had dropped the towel from between his teeth and stood gazing. But his involuntary snarl had carried a message to Glamis. Impulsively, wholly without conscious volition, Hugh shouted:

"*Collie!*"

There was more than the mere calling of the name. Hugh's cry fairly vibrated with fear and with stark despair. And its message went straight to Collie's brain. Even as a dog knows every inflection of his master's tone, so, tenfold, did this creature of the wilderness recognize the awful need behind Glamis's summons. He flew into action.

These men were threatening his god! Collie forgot all at once to be a dog and reverted back to the wolf. He did not speed across the clearing a frontal charge, giving tongue to mortal defiance as he went. Instead, his stomach tucked itself high under his loins; his tail whipped in between his legs and plastered itself to the uptucked stomach; he dropped close to earth and made for the nearest cover, like a gray wraith.

"One more squawk for help," decreed the nearest of the three federal officers, breaking the trio's menacing silence, "and we'll take you in, dead instead of alive. Our orders leave us full discretion which we're to do. Now suppose you just put these wet hands of yours high above your head—*high*, I told you. That's better. Keep 'em there. Dawson, go through him for artillery. He—"

The speaker's crisply efficient words ended in a strangled scream. Seventy pounds of noiseless gray demon had launched itself from the undergrowth directly behind him and had landed full on his back. A double set of teeth had torn away the officer's whole left cheek in a single rending slash, and those same ravening jaws were now seeking the throat as the man plunged forward under the impact of Collie's leap.

By the time the victim had fairly touched ground the jaws had found a mark. Not in the throat, but in the left shoulder blade, which they cracked as readily as though it were a nut. And Collie, all caution now flung aside, was raging at the other two strangers.

A slash, aimed with the devilish craft of his breed, cut a tendon in one officer's leg and let him down to earth in a yelling heap, just as the third of the visitors found coolness and time to level his automatic at the ramping creature and to pull the trigger.

The high-powered bullet, at point-blank range, drilled Collie clean through, coming out at the far side. With a yelp which held more of wrath than pain, the giant wolf rolled over twice on the ground, then gathered his feet under him again and sprang foaming at his assailant's face. Once more the officer fired, point-blank, at the on-flying gray devil. This time his bullet shore a cleft along Collie's side, a mere flesh wound that had no power to stop his charge.

Down went the man, dropping his pistol and clawing frantically at the frightful creature which ravened above him.

The wolf's yelp, as the first pistol shot bowled him over, had brought Glamis out of his trance of amazed horror. The sight of his adored pet, wounded, yet fighting so gallantly for him, restored him to his usual quickness of thought and action. One of his enemies was thrashing about, nursing a mangled cheek and a broken collarbone. The second sprawled, hamstrung, on the ground. The third was reeling back under the frenzied weight of the wolf that had just struck him in the chest. Taking advantage of all this, Glamis made a bolt for the nearby cover. Once in its shelter, he knew himself a good enough woodsman to elude these men of cities. As he ran he shouted:

"Collie!"

As ever, on the call, the mighty wolf responded. Leaping over his falling victim, Collie made after his master. The two reached the high bushes side by side, just as the third officer caught up his pistol and fired a futile shot after them.

There was a momentary crashing in the undergrowth, then a dead silence. Man and beast were well skilled in the forest runner's art of traveling rapidly through the woods without making a sound.

And so, in maze-like convolutions, at top speed, they fled through the familiar tangle of thickets. This until they reached a glade a mile beyond. There Hugh stopped for breath and to plan his course. Collie came very close to his side and pressed his head lovingly against the panting man's knee. Glamis let one hand drop gratefully on the wolf's broad head.

"If it hadn't been for you, old friend," he murmured, "I'd have been—"

He broke off, surprised, in his idle words of praise, for the great head was no longer under his hand. Quietly, without cry or other manifestation, Collie had sunk to the ground at his master's feet. Glamis looked down wonderingly. The wolf lifted his head in an effort to lick the hand that was just beyond his reach. He wagged his tail once, then shivered and lay over on his side, with a tired sigh as of one who has come to the end of a long journey. It is not every hero that can fight like a wild cat and then travel for a mile—with a bullet wound through his body. Now that the gripping need of battle and of escape seemed to be over, Collie allowed himself the luxury of dying.

Ten minutes later the third federal officer made his way to the glade, following easily the track of blood drops. There he found that he, too, had come to the end of his quest, for Hugh Glamis, arch-swindler and fugitive from federal law, was sitting on the ground, crying like a heart-broken baby. In his lap he held tenderly the head of a huge dead wolf. At sound of the officer's feet at the glade edge Hugh looked up, list-lessly, into the muzzle of the menacing pistol.

"All right," he said, his voice as dead as the chum whose furry head he was clasping. "All right. I'll come along. There's nothing to stay here for—not anymore."